MURDER MOST
ROYAL

SJ Bennett was born in Yorkshire and travelled the world as an army child. She had a varied career including lobbyist and strategy consultant, before her first novel was published when she was 42. Since then her books have won the RNA Romance Novel of the Year, been optioned for TV, and have been translated into over 20 languages.

She was once asked to interview for the role of Assistant Private Secretary to the Queen and still considers it the job that got away. A curious royal watcher for many years, she lives in London where she can often be found haunting its palaces, museums, galleries and libraries.

You can find her at SJBennettBooks.com for all things crime and royal, on Instagram @sophiabennett_writer and on Twitter @sophiabennett.

To receive Royal Correspondence about the Her Majesty The Queen Investigates series – including royal family trivia and more – sign up at bit.ly/SJBennett

Also by S. J. Bennett

The Windsor Knot
A Three Dog Problem

Her Majesty The Queen
Investigates

MURDER
MOST
ROYAL

S. J. Bennett

ZAFFRE

First published in the UK in 2022
This edition published in 2023 by
ZAFFRE
An imprint of Bonnier Books UK
4th Floor, Victoria House, Bloomsbury Square, London, WC1B 4DA
Owned by Bonnier Books
Sveavägen 56, Stockholm, Sweden

A CIP catalogue record for this book is
available from the British Library.

ISBN: 978–1–83877–620–6

Also available as an ebook and an audiobook

1 3 5 7 9 10 8 6 4 2

Typeset by IDSUK (Data Connection) Ltd
Printed and bound in Great Britain by Clays Ltd, Elcograf S.p.A.

Zaffre is an imprint of Bonnier Books UK
www.bonnierbooks.co.uk

Elizabeth II, 1926–2022

This book is dedicated to the Queen, with love and gratitude

Character List

Royal family (2016)

The Queen
Prince Philip (the Duke of Edinburgh)
Prince Charles (the Prince of Wales)
Camilla, Charles's wife
Anne (the Princess Royal), the Queen's daughter
Andrew, the Queen's second son
William, the Queen's grandson
Harry, the Queen's grandson
Zara, the Queen's granddaughter
Peter Philips, the Queen's grandson
Beatrice, the Queen's granddaughter
Eugenie, the Queen's granddaughter
Edward (Earl of Wessex), Queen's third son
Sophie (Countess of Wessex), Edward's wife

Royal household

Mrs Maddox – housekeeper at Sandringham
Sir Simon Holcroft – the Queen's Private Secretary
Rozie Oshodi – the Queen's Assistant Private Secretary
Lady Caroline Cadwallader – the Queen's lady in waiting
Captain Henry Marshal-Ward – the Queen's temporary equerry
Chief Inspector Jackson – personal protection officer (PPO)
Chief Inspector Tony Depiscopo – personal protection officer (PPO)

Friends, neighbours and estate staff

Edward St Cyr (Ned) – grandson of the tenth Baron Mundy, owner of the Abbottswood estate

Georgina St Cyr – Ned's late mother

Jack Lions – Ned's estranged son

Astrid Westover – Ned's fiancée

Moira Westover – Astrid's mother

Hugh St Cyr, twelfth Baron Mundy, owner of the Ladybridge estate

Lee St Cyr, Baroness Mundy – Hugh's late wife

Valentine St Cyr – Hugh's son

Flora Osborne – Hugh's daughter

Emerald, Elinor and Eden (Figgy) Osborne – Flora's daughters

Roland Peng – Valentine's business partner

Matt and Helena Fisher – owners of the nearby Muncaster estate

Julian Cassidy (the 'bean counter') – agronomist at Sandringham, who used to work for Matt Fisher

Judy Raspberry – Dersingham resident and treasurer of the West Newton Women's Institute

Ivy Raspberry – Judy's niece

Arthur Raspberry – Judy's nephew

Simon Day – the Queen's pigeon loft manager

Katie Briggs – the Queen's previous Assistant Private Secretary, Rozie's predecessor

Other

Nigel Bloomfield – Chief Constable of Norfolk

Ollie Knight – freelance journalist for *The Recorder*

Chris and Laura Wallace – tenants of the Ladybridge estate

Mary Collathorn – wild swimmer and tenant of the Ladybridge estate

Mrs Capelton – tenant of the Ladybridge estate

PART 1

THE HAND OF FATE

We do not inherit the earth from our ancestors;
we borrow it from our children.

Native American proverb

DECEMBER 2016

The girl on the beach emerged into the light and stared out across the mudflats at the horizon. She had been checking the hides at the end of the path to the wild-life reserve at Snettisham, on the Norfolk coast, to see how they had weathered the night's heavy storm. By day, the huts were home to birdwatchers who came from miles around to observe the geese and gulls and waders. By night, they were an occasional refuge from the cold sea breeze for beers and . . . more intimate activities. The last big storm surge had smashed up some of the hides and carried them into the lagoons beyond. This time, she was glad to see, the little piggies at the Royal Society for the Protection of Birds had built their home out of more solid wood.

Back outside, the girl studied the skyline. One of the things she loved about this place was that here, at the edge of East Anglia, on the eastern most coast of the United King-dom, the beach stubbornly faced due west. It looked out on to the Wash, a bay formed like a rectangular bite out of the coastline between Norfolk and Lincolnshire, where a clutch of rivers ran into the North Sea. No pale pink sunrise here; instead, the sun had risen above the lagoons at her back. Ahead, a bank of cloud sat low and heavy, but the watery light gave it a pale gold glow that was mirrored in the mud-flats, so that it was hard to tell where the earth ended and the air began.

Not far from the lagoons, a little further along the shore to her left, lay the marshy fringes of the Sandringham Estate. Normally, the Queen was there by now, with Christmas so close, but the girl hadn't heard of her arrival yet, which was strange. The Queen, like the sunrise and the tides, was generally a reliable way of marking time.

She glanced upwards, where a trailing skein of pink-footed geese flew in arrowhead formation, home from the sea. Higher still, and closer, a hen harrier circled in the air. There was a brutal, brooding quality to Snettisham Beach. The concrete pathway at her feet, and the skeletal wooden structures jutting out into the mudflats beyond the shingle, were relics of her great-grandfather's war. Shingle mining for airbase runways had helped create the lagoons, where ducks and geese and waders now gathered in their thousands, filling the air with their hoots and honks and quacks. The gulls had deserted the land for decades, her father said, after the constant bombardment of artillery practice into the sea. Their return was a triumph of nature. And goodness knew, Nature needed her little triumphs. She was up against so much.

Most of the birds themselves were out of sight, but they'd been busy. The expansive mudflats ahead were the scene of a recent massacre, pitted with thousands upon thousands of footprints of all sizes, where goldeneyes and sandpipers had landed once the tide receded, to feast on the creatures who lived in the sand.

Suddenly, a black-and-white bundle of fur caught the girl's eye as it raced from right to left across the mud. She recognised it: a collie-cocker cross from a litter in the village last year who belonged to someone she didn't consider a friend. With no sign of its owner, the puppy sped towards the nearest wooden structure, its attention caught by something bobbing in the sky-coloured seawater that eddied around the nearest rotten post.

The storm had littered the beach with all sorts of detritus, natural and man-made. Dead fish were dumped with plastic bottles and dense, bright tangles of fraying fishing nets. She thought of jellyfish. They washed up here, too. The stupid young dog could easily try to eat one and get stung and poisoned in the process.

'Hey!' she shouted. The puppy ignored her. 'Come here!'

She began to run. Arms pumping, she hurtled across the scrubby band of lichen and samphire that led down to the shingle. Now she was on the mudflats, too, the subterranean water seeping into each footprint left by her Doc Martens in the sand.

'Stop that, you idiot!'

The puppy was worrying at an amorphous, soggy shape. He turned to look at her just as she grabbed at his collar. She yanked him away.

The floating object was a plastic bag: an old supermarket one, stretched and torn, its handles knotted, with two pale tentacles poking through. Grabbing a stick that floated nearby, she used the tip to lift it out of the puppy's reach and looked nervously inside. Not a jellyfish, no: some other sea creature, pale and bloated, wrapped in seaweed. She intended to take the bag back with her for disposal later, but as she walked back towards the beach, the puppy straining against his collar at her feet, the contents slithered through a rip and plopped onto the damp, dark sand.

The girl assumed at first that it was a mutant, pale-coloured starfish, but on closer inspection, moving the seaweed aside with her stick, she realised it was something different. She marvelled for a moment at how almost-human it looked, with those tentacles like fingers at one end. Then she saw a glint of gold. Somehow one of the tentacles had got caught up in something metal, round and shiny. She peered closer and counted the baggy, waxy 'tentacles': one, two, three, four, five. The golden glint came from a ring on the little finger. The 'tentacles' had peeling human fingernails.

She dropped the broken bag and screamed fit to fill the sky.

Chapter 1

The Queen felt absolutely dreadful in body and spirit. She regarded Sir Simon Holcroft's retreating back with a mixture of regret and hopeless fury, then retrieved a fresh handkerchief from the open handbag beside her study desk to wipe her streaming nose.

The doctor is adamant . . . A train journey is out of the question . . . The duke should not be travelling at all . . .

If her headache hadn't been pounding quite so forcefully, she would have found the right words to persuade her private secretary of the simple fact that one always took the train to Sandringham. The journey from London to King's Lynn had been in the diary for months. The station master and his team would be expecting her in four and a half hours, and would have polished every bit of brass, swept every square inch of platform and no doubt had their uniforms dry-cleaned to look their best for the occasion. One didn't throw all one's plans in the air over a sniffle. If no bones were broken, if no close family had recently died, one soldiered on.

But her headache *had* pounded. Her little speech had been marred by a severe bout of coughing. Philip had not been there to back her up because he was tucked up in bed, as he had been all yesterday. He had no doubt caught the infernal bug from one of the great-grandchildren at the pre-Christmas party they had thrown at Buckingham Palace for the wider family. 'Little Petri dishes', he called them. It wasn't their fault, of course, but they inevitably caught everything going at nursery school and prep school, and passed it around like pudgy-cheeked biological weapons. Which young family should she blame? They had all seemed perfectly healthy at the time.

She picked up the telephone on her study desk and asked the switchboard to put her through to the duke.

He was awake, but groggy.

'What? Speak up, woman! You sound as though you're at the bottom of a lake.'

'I *said* . . .' she paused to blow her nose '. . . that Simon says we must fly to Sandringham tomorrow instead of taking the train today.' She left out the bit where Sir Simon had suggested Philip should remain at the palace full stop.

'In the helicopter?' he barked.

'We can hardly use a 747.' Her head hurt and she was feeling tetchy.

'In the navy we were banned . . .' wheeze '. . . from flying with a cold. Bloody dangerous.'

'You won't be piloting the flight.'

'If it bursts my eardrums you can personally blame Simon from me. Bloody fool. Doesn't know what he's talking about.'

The Queen refrained from pointing out that Sir Simon was an ex-naval helicopter pilot and the GP who had advised him was thoroughly sound. He had his reasons for counselling in favour of a quick journey by air instead of a long one by rail. Philip was ninety-five – hard to believe, but true. He shouldn't really be out of bed at all, with his raging temperature. Oh, what a year this had been, and what a fitting end to it. Despite her delightful birthday celebrations in the spring, she would be glad to see the back of 2016.

'The decision is made, I'm afraid. We'll fly tomorrow.'

She pretended she didn't hear Philip's wheezy in-breath before what would no doubt be a catalogue of complaints, and put the phone down. Christmas was fast approaching and she just wanted to be quietly tucked up in the familiar rural comfort of Sandringham, and to be able to focus on her paperwork without it swimming in front of her eyes.

The autumn and early winter had been fraught with uncertainty. The Brexit referendum and the US elections had revealed deep divisions in Whitehall and Washington that it would take a very steady hand to repair. Through it all, the Queen had played host to presidents and politicians, she had been a greeter of ambassadors, a pinner-on of medals and a host for charity events – mostly at Buckingham Palace, the place she thought of as the gilded office block on the roundabout. Now Norfolk drew her with its wide-open spaces and enfolding pines, its teeming marshes, vast English skies and freewheeling birds.

She had been dreaming of it for days. Sandringham *was* Christmas. Her father had spent it there, and his father before him, and his father before *him*. When the children were small, it had been easier to celebrate at Windsor for a while, but her own childhood Christmases were Norfolk ones.

The following day the helicopter whisked the royal couple, blankets on their knees, dogs at their feet, past Cambridge, past the magnificent medieval towers of Ely Cathedral, the 'ship of the fens', and on, north-eastwards towards King's Lynn. Soon, wetlands gave way to farmland that was patched with pine woods, with paddocks and flint cottages. Below them, briefly, was the shell-pink Regency villa at Abbottswood, where she was surprised to see a herd of deer ambling slowly across the lawn. Next came the stubbly, immaculate fields and scattered copses of the Muncaster Estate, whose furthest reaches bordered one of the royal farms, and then at last the fields, dykes and villages of the Sandringham Estate itself. As the helicopter made its turn, the Queen saw a glint of seawater in the distant Wash and a minute later Sandringham House appeared behind a ridge of pines, with its formal and informal gardens, its lakes and its sweeping lawns amply big enough for them to land.

The house, built for Edward VII when he was Prince of Wales, was a Victorian architect's red-brick, beturreted idea of what a Jacobean house should be, and people who cared a lot about architecture were generally appalled by it. The Queen, like her father before her, was enormously fond of its idiosyncratic nooks and crannies. Philip, who had strong views about architecture, had once unsuccessfully proposed to have it knocked down. However, what really mattered were the twenty thousand acres of bog, marsh, woodland, arable land and orchards that made up the surrounding estate. The Queen was a natural countrywoman and here she and Philip could quietly be farmers. Not the kind who mended fences in the lashing rain and were on lambing at dawn, true, but together, they looked after and loved it because it was a small part of the planet that was *theirs*. Here, in north Norfolk, they could actively participate in trying to make the world a better place: for wildlife, for the consumers of their crops, for the people who worked the land, for the future. It was a quiet legacy – one they didn't talk about in public (Charles's experience on that front illustrated why) – but one they cared about very much.

In her office at the 'working' end of the house, Rozie Oshodi looked up from her laptop screen in time to see the helicopter skirt the edge of the treeline before coming in to land. As the Queen's assistant private secretary, Rozie had arrived by train earlier that morning. For now, the suite of staff rooms, with its functional Edwardian furniture – and to an extent the whole house, and in a way, the nation – was her domain. According to Rozie's mother it was, anyway. Sir Simon, who ran the Private Office with the combined skills of the admiral and ambassador he might have been, had gone to the Highlands for the first part of the holiday. He and his wife Sarah had been given the use of a cottage at Balmoral for the Christmas break in recognition of his sterling work over the autumn, and as a result, for two precious weeks, Rozie was in charge. '*It's all down to you,*' her mother had said.

'*No pressure. But think, you're like the first black Thomas Cromwell. You're the right-hand woman. The eyes and ears. Don't mess it up.*' She'd never had her mother down as a big fan of Tudor history. Hilary Mantel had a lot to answer for.

This close to Christmas, Rozie didn't expect to have much to do. With no monasteries to dissolve or royal marriages to broker, the main job of the Private Office was to liaise with the Government, manage communications and organise the Queen's public schedule. But Whitehall and Downing Street had effectively shut down for the holidays; the media were fixated on holiday stories; the Queen's next public event was in three weeks, and even that was only a tea party in the village. Thomas Cromwell would have found it all very tame. Rozie had mostly been catching up with the residue of emails that had somehow never made the 'urgent' list in her inbox. However, an hour ago a new one had come in. Perhaps this break wasn't going to be as quiet as she'd anticipated, after all.

Lined up outside the entrance hall, Mrs Maddox, the immaculate housekeeper, and her team were waiting to welcome the royal couple back. Today, the interior smelled deliciously of woodsmoke from the fire that popped and crackled in the saloon behind them, where the family would gather later for drinks and games. The dogs happily padded inside, keen to be back, while Philip took himself straight off to bed.

The Queen had just enough energy to do justice to a couple of freshly made mince pies and a pot of Darjeeling in the light and airy drawing room at the back of the house, whose large bay windows overlooked the lawn. In one of the bays a Christmas tree was already in place, its branches partly decorated on a red and gold theme, ready to be completed when the rest of the family arrived tomorrow. Normally, she chose the tree herself, but this year there hadn't been time. A small price to pay for a cosy afternoon indoors, which she very much needed.

She had just finished talking to Mrs Maddox about the next few days' arrangements when Rozie appeared at the drawing room door. As her efficient APS curtsied, the Queen noticed that, rather ominously, she held a closed laptop under her arm. 'Your Majesty, do you have a moment?'

'Is there a problem?' the Queen asked, hoping there wasn't.

'Not exactly, but there's something you ought to know about.'

'Oh, dear.' They caught each other's eye, and the Queen sighed. 'The small drawing room, I think.'

She led the way to the room next door, whose floral, silk-lined walls gave it a gentle, feminine air, somewhat in contrast to the lively bird sculptures that Prince Philip chose to keep there: reminders of one of his chief pleasures of the estate.

Rozie closed the door behind them. The Queen looked up at her. Rozie, a striking young woman of thirty, was over six feet tall in her signature heels. At her age, and at a shrinking five foot two, the Queen was used to looking up at almost everybody . . . figuratively speaking. She didn't find it problematic, except when she had to shout up at tall, deaf dukes and ministers. Fortunately, her APS's hearing was excellent.

'All right. What is it? Nothing to do with the new president?'

'No, ma'am. The police have been in touch. I'm afraid there's been a discovery.'

'Oh?'

'A hand was found yesterday morning, in the mudflats at Snettisham Beach.'

The Queen was startled. 'A human hand?'

'Yes, ma'am. It was washed up by a storm, wrapped in a plastic bag.'

'My goodness. No sense of where it came from?'

'Ocado, ma'am, since you ask. They deliver food from Waitrose.'

'I meant the hand.'

The APS frowned. 'Not yet. They hope to identify the victim soon. One of the fingers was wearing an unusual ring, which may help.'

'So, a *woman's* hand?'

Rozie shook her head. 'A man's. It's a signet ring.'

At last, the Queen understood the presence of the laptop. Sir Simon would have come without it, but fortunately – in the circumstances – he wasn't here. Her private secretary liked to spare her any 'unpleasantness'. But after ninety years, an abdication, a world war, the early loss of her father and a rich selection of family scandals, she was more capable of dealing with unpleasantness than most. Rozie was more realistic. Women understood each other, the Queen found. They knew each other's strengths and weaknesses, and didn't underestimate the strengths.

'May I see?' she asked.

Rozie placed the laptop on a little writing desk in front of the window. When she opened it, the screen came to life, revealing four grisly images. The Queen put on her bifocals to examine them more closely. They had been taken in a forensic laboratory and showed what was unmistakably a male left hand and wrist with a pattern of fair hairs below the knuckles, the skin deadly white, bloated, but largely intact. It looked, absolutely, like a gruesome theatre prop, or a model for a practical joke. Her eyes rested on the final image showing the little finger in close-up. Set tight into the ghostly flesh was the gold ring Rozie had mentioned. It was indeed unusual: large for its type, featuring a reddish-black oval stone carved with a crest.

Rozie explained the situation. 'The hand was found by a local girl, ma'am. She was out dog-walking from what I understand. They're working on the identification now. It shouldn't take longer than a few days, even with the Christmas holiday. They think it may belong to a drug dealer because a holdall containing drugs washed up further down the beach. There's a theory the victim may have been kidnapped and the hand cut off as some sort of message, or possibly for ransom. It was done with some violence, but there's no proof the owner is actually dead. They're casting the net widely. They—'

'I can save them the trouble,' the Queen said, looking up.

Rozie frowned. 'Ma'am?'

'Of casting the net widely. This is the hand of Edward St Cyr.'

The Queen briefly closed her eyes. *Ned*, she thought to herself. *Dear God. Ned.*

Rozie looked astonished. 'You *know* him? From this?'

In answer, the Queen pointed to the top left-hand photograph. 'Do you see that flat-topped middle finger? He cut off the tip doing some carpentry when he was a teenager. But it's the signet ring, of course . . . Bloodstone. Quite distinctive. And that carving is of a swan from the family crest.' She peered again at the final picture. The ring was a garish thing; she had never liked it. All the men in the St Cyr family wore one like it, but none of the others had lost the tip of their middle finger. Ned must have been about sixteen when he did it, such an eager, inventive boy. That was over half a century ago.

'I take it he wasn't a local drug baron, ma'am,' Rozie ventured.

'No,' the Queen agreed, looking up at her. 'He was the grandson of an *actual* baron. Not that that means he was necessarily a stranger to drugs of course. Or *is*,' she corrected herself. It was troubling, this idea, as Rozie suggested, that he might not be dead – but he probably was, surely? And God knew what state he must be in if he wasn't. 'I hope they get to the bottom of it soon.'

'This will certainly speed them up, ma'am.'

The Queen's blue eyes met Rozie's brown ones. 'We needn't say exactly who recognised the ring.'

'Of course.' After a year in her service, Rozie knew the drill: the Queen categorically did *not* solve, or even help solve crimes. She was merely an interested observer. However, as

Rozie had learned, her interest sometimes went deeper than most people knew. 'Is there anything else you'd like me to do?' she asked.

'Not this time.' The Queen was firm. 'I think that will be enough.'

Terrible though the news was, she reflected with relief that Snettisham, though close, was a nature reserve run by the RSPB. This was not, to put it bluntly, her problem. And just before Christmas, after a devil of a year, nor did she want it to be.

'Certainly, ma'am.' Rozie closed the laptop and left the Boss to get on with her day.

Chapter 2

The Queen accompanied Mrs Maddox on a quick tour of the house to check that everything had been set up to her satisfaction, which as always, under this housekeeper's care, it had been. Afterwards, she was drawn back to the saloon, with its inviting smell of woodsmoke. Most of Sandringham's rooms were quite small and intimate by royal standards, but the saloon was designed to impress. It was double height, with a plasterwork ceiling, a minstrels' gallery and a grand piano. The tapestries and royal portraits on the walls might have made it look like a museum, which it effectively was when she wasn't here, but modern sofas, cream walls and soft lamplight gave it a cosy, welcoming air. The crackling fire in the hearth – the only one in the house these days – was a Christmas highlight.

Among plentiful photographs of family, the ornaments were mainly horse bronzes and silver statuettes. If it was possible to be surrounded by too many representations of the horse, the Queen hadn't yet discovered how. Beyond the windows she caught a glimpse of the splendid new life-size statue of one of her favourite racehorses, the magnificent Estimate, which had recently been installed at the far end of the courtyard opposite the front porch and rounded out her collection rather nicely. For now, though, she approached a baize-covered table next to the piano, where a wooden jigsaw had been set out. Jigsaws were a feature of her six-week stay at Sandringham and she studied this one carefully. It was a Constable painting, she noted – lots of open sky and feathery trees. Tomorrow it would be disassembled, ready to be made again. There was no additional picture, which added a certain piquancy to the challenge. One had to rely on memory and patience – something not all members of the family possessed in equal measure.

She had hoped to distract herself with the picture, but her mind inevitably drifted back to Ned St Cyr. He was two years older than Charles, which would make him seventy now. Three-score years and ten, she thought. A biblical lifetime, although now one could easily live to a hundred, as witnessed by her own mother and all the centenary birthday telegrams one sent these days.

Poor, dear Ned. In her mind, he was still a schoolboy. He had been a regular visitor here in the fifties, in the company of his glamorous mother and her family, with his shock of strawberry blond hair and always a winning smile, usually in apology for something he had just done, or was about to do. He had once persuaded a youthful Charles that it would be a good idea to hide a few of the jigsaw pieces for a joke. Philip's expression when Charles admitted to it after a fortnight had been something to behold.

Ned, when he visited the next time, took his scolding with good grace. He had arrived with a home-made bird

19

table, she seemed to remember, to be given as penance, and a couple of jokes from school that had made Philip hoot with laughter.

Ned usually got away with his naughtiness. Like his mother and his beloved uncle Patrick, his charm and charisma made him 'one of those special people', as her own mother always put it, and she should know, because the Queen Mother had been the very definition of 'one of those special people' herself.

Perhaps it was an accident. Perhaps Ned had died at sea and a boat propeller had somehow caused the hand to become detached. Except, no – there was the bag. Somebody must have . . .

She prayed that at least they would find the body soon, otherwise intact. She really must not indulge her worst imaginings. The Queen brought her mind back to the jigsaw and tried to lose herself, unsuccessfully, in Constable's feathery trees.

Back at her desk, Rozie stared in frustration at her computer screen. After a stint as a captain in the Royal Horse Artillery and a couple of years on a fast-track role in the City, she could strip and reassemble a rifle blindfold, disarm an attacker, tack up a horse and break down a P & L statement – but the kind of estate she grew up on in West London did not feature farms and country houses, and there was still a lot the royal family took for granted that she had yet to learn.

In this case, she had googled 'Edward Sincere' and looked him up in every directory she could think of, starting with *Debrett's*, but there was no aristocrat with that name. She couldn't ask the house staff, because they were all rushing around like blue-arsed flies, as Prince Philip would say, getting ready for the arrival of multi-generational royals tomorrow. But there was one person who would certainly be able to help, if she could bear to ask for it.

Sir Simon Holcroft hadn't risen to the heights of private secretary without being a bit of a control freak. He had exhorted her to call him in Scotland 'at any time, day or night' if she had any questions or concerns of any kind. For her part, Rozie hadn't survived several years as a black female officer in the British Army without developing a strong sense of self-sufficiency, so she had equally vowed to herself that she wouldn't. Yet the Queen had been here for less than two hours, and already Rozie's finger was hovering over Sir Simon's number in her phone. She could hardly call the police to identify the victim if she didn't know who he was. And one didn't ask Her Majesty for the same information twice.

Damn.

Sir Simon was all charm. There was the clinking of glasses and the hum of congenial chatter in the background. He sounded as if he was in a bar or social club of some sort, having a good time.

'Rozie, Rozie. Edward Sincere, d'you say? How did you spell it?'

Rozie frowned. How many ways could you spell Sin—? *Damn.*

He voiced the thought as it entered her brain. 'Don't tell me it was "S-i-n-c-e—"

'Yes it was,' she said crossly, tapping a nail on the leather-topped desk in front of her.

'Have I taught you nothing about the British upper classes? Think "Chumley".'

Rozie did. It was spelled Cholmondeley. He had taught her how to sidestep the pitfalls that were the '*Bee*vors' (Belvoir), '*Orl*trups' (Althorp), 'Book*loos*' (Buccleuch) and '*Sin*jons' (St John). She should have known.

'Is it "Saint" Something?'

'Exactly. S-t C-y-r.' He spelled it out for her. 'It's the family name of Baron Mundy. They're based at Ladybridge Hall. It's a lovely place with a moat, not very large, about a forty-minute drive from you. The Mundys are ancient Norfolk aristocracy. They were first ennobled by King John in the thirteenth century,' he went on. Of course, Sir Simon, the amateur historian, would know. 'He was the king who famously lost the Crown Jewels in the Wash. Why?'

'Why what?' Rozie asked. She was still thinking about the Crown Jewels, lost at sea, a bit like the hand with the signet ring.

'Why d'you need to know?'

'Nothing to worry about,' she said firmly. It was true: the recent discovery was hardly the Private Office's business. Now she had the name right, the police could take care of it.

'Nothing is ever nothing to worry about,' Sir Simon countered, unhelpfully. Rozie couldn't hear the clinking glasses in the background anymore. He had gone somewhere quiet to concentrate. She reluctantly explained about the hand and the ring.

'Oh, Lord,' he said. 'How grotesque.' He was silent for a minute, contemplating the news. 'Was it literally just the hand? No sign of any other body parts?'

'Not yet.'

'Be very careful, Rozie.' He was suddenly deadly serious. 'Keep the Boss out of it, whatever it takes.'

'Absolutely,' she agreed, crossing her fingers. Rozie knew that keeping the Boss out of anything the Boss wanted to be into was very unlikely, regardless of what she did or didn't do. Sir Simon didn't know Her Majesty in quite the way she did. 'She mentioned that the victim was a baron's grandson.'

'Not this baron,' Sir Simon said. 'Distant cousin, I think. However, we should probably call Ladybridge Hall; let Lord Mundy know.'

'Why?' Rozie asked. 'If he's a distant cousin?'

'He's a friend of the Boss. And family's family. He won't want to hear this on the news and then find out the identification came from someone at Sandringham and we didn't tell him first.'

After a brief call to her contact at the Norfolk constabulary HQ to update them on the identity, Rozie called Ladybridge Hall. She had half hoped to speak to an underling such as herself who could pass on the grisly details, but it was the Right Honourable the Lord Mundy himself (she had looked it up to make sure of his title) who answered the phone. He was silent for a long time, pondering the news. Having said her piece as gently as she could, Rozie wondered if he was still on the line.

'Are you all right, My Lord?'

'Goodness me.' He sounded breathless. 'I need to sit down. Oh, my goodness.'

'I'm sorry to be the one to—'

'Oh, no, my dear, don't apologise. And do call me Hugh. Thank you for calling. Very considerate of you.' He had the cut-glass accent and almost exaggerated good manners of his class, reminding Rozie of the many earls and dukes she had encountered in this job. But they usually sounded formal and composed, whereas he seemed all at sea. 'So you've informed the police?'

'Yes, just now.'

'Oh, dear me.' His voice fluttered up and down. 'Oh my goodness. A *hand*, you say? I saw him only recently . . . We hadn't spoken for years, as you probably know.'

'No, I didn't,' Rozie admitted. Sir Simon probably did.

'But after my wife's funeral in the summer . . . He was very *decent* about it. I sensed that he wanted to extend an olive branch. Do they have any idea how . . .?'

'It's early days,' Rozie explained. 'The police don't really know anything yet.'

'Well, you're very kind to inform me. I . . . Excuse me. I don't know what to . . . How did Her Majesty find out about it?'

'The hand was found near Sandringham. The police told us as a courtesy.'

'Near *Sandringham* . . . How ghastly. Her Majesty must be . . . Do give her my sympathies. We're supposed to be seeing her after Christmas, but if this makes things difficult,

I quite understand. How did they know it was Edward, by the way?'

Rozie took a breath. 'It was the ring, My Lord.' She couldn't call him Hugh. She hadn't yet developed Sir Simon's ease at hobnobbing with the aristocracy.

'My goodness ... The ring ... I have one myself, just like it ...'

He tailed off again and Rozie pictured him staring at his own left hand.

'I'm sorry.'

'Don't be. There's nothing you ... Oh, my goodness. Thank you for calling, my dear. Please wish Her Majesty a happy Christmas on our behalf. I hope she feels better soon.'

Rozie was a bit startled by this last remark. How did he know the Queen was unwell? Then she remembered that it had been reported in *The Times* because of the cancelled train trip.

'I'll tell her,' she assured him, but she wouldn't. The last thing the Boss would want was people outside the family circle remarking on her ill health.

Afterwards, she went back to her laptop and typed in 'Edward St Cyr'.

Wikipedia informed her that he was born in 1946, the only grandson of the tenth Baron Mundy. After growing up at the St Cyr family seat and brief sojourns in Greece, London and California in the 1970s, where he had managed two failed rock bands, he had joined his mother at a small estate called Abbottswood, south of King's Lynn, where he hosted a couple of controversial rock concerts and, later, what was briefly the second-most popular literary festival in Norfolk. He had been married and divorced three times, his second wife being the nanny to the children with his first. There were links here to various newspaper articles about the scandal, which Rozie ignored. He was on the boards of various charities, two of which were anti-addiction and one that supported the welfare of refugees in Greece.

While she was at it, she looked up the current Lord Mundy. Hugh was the son of Ralph, the eleventh baron, who in turn was the nephew of Edward's grandfather, the tenth baron, who had died without a living male heir. That made Hugh and Edward St Cyr second cousins. Sir Simon was right again. Rozie thought about the equivalent in her own family. She had a raft of second and third cousins, some in Nigeria, some in Texas and New York, and some in Peckham, South London. Thanks to social media, and the endless family chats set up by her mum and her aunties, she couldn't avoid hearing what most of them were up to: the 'good students' (Rozie was one of these), the 'bad boys', the pastors, the finance whizz-kids, the Gen Z tech gurus, the ones who were settling down with kids ('*See, Rozie?*' as her mother would say), and the ones who, to her mother's gentle despair, were trying to get their own lives under control before they created more Oshodis. It wasn't quite the same thing as being 'an ancient Norfolk family', but a big family – yeah, she got that. And yes, if something happened to one of them, her mum would absolutely want to know.

A subsequent search on Google Images brought up pictures of a tall, rangy man with skin the colour of milky tea, a sharp nose, ruddy cheeks and straight, bushy eyebrows over eyes as blue and piercing as the Queen's.

In earlier pictures, Edward lounged moodily as a young man against bougainvillea-clad white walls, barefoot in bell-bottom jeans and faded T-shirts, accompanied by women in minidresses with Brigitte Bardot hair. Later, alongside a variety of slim, blonde companions in tight-fitting dresses, he seemed to favour pink and purple jackets that were just this side of fancy dress.

By the most recent photographs, he seemed to have adopted the more relaxed country style of a waxed jacket over a denim shirt, a battered trilby hat and a fringed cotton scarf that brought out the colour of his eyes. His face could look forbidding, accentuated by those eyebrows and prominent nose, but when he smiled, showing bright, white, un-British dentistry, he had a charisma that drew you instantly to him, even in the images where his hair had faded from burnished copper to spun gold.

In the latest photograph she could find, he was standing at the rear of an old Land Rover Defender, painted pink, with three dogs sitting in the back. He was resting his arm against the open door and the signet ring was clearly visible on the little finger of his left hand. It made her shiver.

Chapter 3

After supper, which the Queen ate in the dining room with her lady-in-waiting, Philip called down from his bed.

'I hear Ned St Cyr has been chopped into pieces. What on God's earth?'

He sounded utterly appalled, and slightly better.

'Not exactly. They found one piece.' The Queen was enjoying a post-prandial whisky in the saloon with her lady-in-waiting before going up to bed herself. Who had told him? Gossip spread among the staff like wildfire and tended to mutate like Chinese whispers. Goodness knew what they were saying in the servants' hall.

'D'you remember that white ball he and Patrick did here for your mother?'

The Queen did. It was in the early sixties, when they still saw him on a regular basis. Ned must have been in his late teens, no more, but he and his uncle Patrick were already in partnership as party organisers to the gentry in about five counties. The idea for the ball at Sandringham had come in part from Truman Capote's Black and White Ball in New York, and in part from portraits of royal princesses by Franz

28

Winterhalter, who romantically depicted them in off-the-shoulder white dresses with generous crinolines. There was one such picture of the young Queen Victoria opposite the chair where the Queen was sitting now. Her own mother had dazzled like a film star that night in several tiers of ivory tulle. Ned had gone to enormous lengths to decorate the house with flowers from the famous white garden at Ladybridge, along with elaborate paper decorations he had made himself and hung in every room. The night had been magical . . . until an over-oiled guest had managed to throw up in one of the pianos, but that was hardly Ned's fault.

'It was months before that piano was right again,' Philip muttered. 'Years. There was always something with Ned. He *is* dead, I take it?'

'I'll come up,' the Queen said. This was not a conversation to have over the phone, with her lady-in-waiting listening intently and a footman standing at the door.

On the way upstairs, an image came to her of Ned's glamorous mother, Georgina – Patrick's oldest sister – descending this very staircase in velvet Dior that night. Georgina had been a frequent guest at Sandringham in the fifties and sixties. She was about the Queen's age, a star of her starry generation. She rode, she farmed, she gardened to an international standard, she collected modern art (she was one of the first people to spot the potential of a young artist called David Hockney), she looked equally fashionable in Parisian couture or tweeds and a cardigan with pockets for her secateurs. She had once famously combined several of her passions by sitting for a portrait in a ball gown astride her favourite hunter in the drawing room at Ladybridge. Ned, an only child, adored her, and Georgina was a very indulgent mother. The Queen, who had tried to be one too, but with many absences and less opportunity to do so, had sometimes been a little jealous of their relationship.

Philip was sitting up against the pillows looking much less grey than he had this morning. The country air was already having its effect.

'Ah, hello, Cabbage. So. As I said, we assume he's dead?'

'It's hard to imagine otherwise,' she agreed.

'Astonishing. Ned was one of the most *alive* people you could meet.'

The Queen went over and perched on the edge of the bed, until her hip protested and she took Philip's suggestion of a nearby armchair.

'Of course, we know who did it,' Philip said.

'Do we?'

'One of the family.'

'Mmmm,' the Queen said, which was her usual response when she didn't necessarily agree.

'It's as plain as the nose on your face. D'you want a handkerchief, by the way? Yours is glowing like a beacon.'

'No thank you. I'll manage.'

'It's always the family, one way or another. I pitied those wives of his. Not surprised they didn't last the distance. The man shagged half the county.' The duke was thoughtful. 'Or he owed money. He liked to give the impression of living off the fat of the land, but Abbottswood was hopeless

30

for farming. Too many woods and wetlands. I often wondered how he managed to heat his pink monstrosity of a villa. We flew over it this morning, did you notice?'

'Yes. I always thought it was rather pretty,' the Queen admitted.

'Pink's a *Suffolk* colour,' the duke protested. 'And did you spot those deer on the lawn?'

'Yes, that was very odd,' she agreed.

'Right up to the house. Eating everything in sight, I shouldn't wonder. God knows what that was about. Another of his godforsaken projects, no doubt. Do you remember the rock concerts? The commune? And that bloody book festival stuffed up the roads in half the county until the council shut it down. He was always in the papers for some violation. Didn't know what he was doing, didn't care who tried to stop him. I—' Philip was interrupted by a cough and for a while his body was convulsed with them. But the Queen noticed his eyes cloud as he recovered, and it wasn't just his cold that made him pause before he carried on. 'God, the man was butchered, Lilibet. Wasn't he?' As if it had really hit him for the first time. 'What did they *do* to him?'

In a dressing room at Clarence House near Buckingham Palace, where he was reviewing some of the evening dress suggestions of his valet, the Prince of Wales greeted a footman bearing a telephone (he did not believe in mobiles) and accepted a call from the Princess Royal.

'Charles speaking,' he announced crisply.

'Of course it's you.' Like their father, Princess Anne did not suffer fools gladly. 'Listen, have you heard about the hand on the beach?'

'No. What beach?'

'Snettisham. Found yesterday, identified this morning. It was on the news just now. We'll have to rally round Mummy. It's the last thing she needs.'

'What hand?'

'Ned St Cyr. Georgina St Cyr's son. That awful boy who used to chase you around the dining table at Sandringham.'

'He didn't chase me,' Charles protested.

'He did. Anyway, he's dead. Or minus an extremity at the very least.'

'Do they know how he died?'

'I assume losing your left hand doesn't help,' Anne answered caustically. 'According to the news, he's been missing for several days. Poor Astrid'll be devastated.'

'Astrid who? Why?' Charles asked, still getting to grips with the news. Anne was, not for the first time, three fields ahead and going at a gallop.

'Astrid Westover. Ned's fiancée, the one who reported him missing.'

'He was getting married again?' Charles hadn't seen the man for decades, and had only the sketchiest awareness of his circumstances.

'Yes. Third time. Or fourth. Zara knows her. She used to be an eventer. Good seat, terrible hands. I went to Pony Club with her mother, back in the Dark Ages,' Anne explained. 'Astrid's an interesting character. She's only in her thirties – younger than Ned's eldest. Zara says she's an influencer, whatever the hell that is.'

'I'd like to think ... someone like me, perhaps,' Charles suggested, aware that he was straying from the point.

'Take it from me, you are categorically not, and never will be, an influencer.'

'Really?'

'Don't worry, you're well out of it. According to Zara, it's all Instagram and filters and taking pictures of your breakfast.'

'Breakfast? And that influences people?' Charles pictured his boiled egg. *Did they paint them? How curious.*

'Apparently it influenced Ned. Although Astrid does it with horses. He tried to go out with me, back in the day, you know,' Anne added, pensively.

'Did he?'

'Said he'd take me to Corfu and show me a good time. I was tempted for about thirty seconds. He drove a Porsche Spyder and liked to think he was James Dean. He did look a bit like him in a good light, I suppose.'

'But you turned him down?'

'God yes! I took one ride in that Spyder and I swear he'd have killed me in ten minutes. Runs in the family.'

'Does it?'

'Absolutely. Think of his poor uncle Patrick in the Cobra. Anyway, Mummy'll be terribly upset. We'll have to rally round, as I said. Be supportive but not mention it. I thought I'd warn you.'

'Thank you.' Charles made a mental note to be as supportive as possible. 'By the way, what d'you think of an embroidered sherwani jacket for after dinner? Silk and cashmere. It's got quite a fashionable cachet, and it's also very comfortable.'

'Awful idea. Papa will have a fit. Bin it.'

Charles looked regretfully at the shimmering midnight-blue garment hanging in front of him. Anne was probably right. But when he was in charge at Sandringham, there was going to be a revolution in the indoor dress code that Beau Brummell himself would be proud of. Absently, he handed the handset back and returned to the matter in hand.

Thirty miles away from Sandringham, the daughter of the current Baron Mundy, Flora Osborne, had been contemplating the results of her labours in the flower room at Ladybridge Hall. She reached across a trug containing several large sprigs of holly and bunches of freshly cut mistletoe to answer the phone that she had placed out of reach of the splashing tap.

'Val! Is everything OK?'

'Are you busy?' her brother demanded as she tucked the phone next to her ear.

'Not exactly. Just finishing the greenery arrangements for the Long Gallery. It always uses up about six times as much foliage as I originally cut.'

'Have you heard about cousin Ned?'

'No, what? Have they found him? I was starting to get rather worried.'

'You should be.'

Flora's expression grew darker as she heard the news about the body part. She abandoned the holly she'd been holding and listened hard.

'Do they know where it went into the water?' Her voice was low, her mouth dry. She didn't know whether or not to be reassured by the answer that the police seemed to know very little at this stage.

'I was wondering . . .' Valentine said. 'Shall I call them? Explain about us? I mean, it'll look rather—'

'No,' she said firmly. 'It's none of their business where we go, what we do. None at all.'

'If you think so.'

'I'm sure of it.'

'If the police ask us,' he began tentatively, 'I suppose I can just say . . . I mean . . . we have nothing to hide.'

'Absolutely,' Flora agreed. 'But they won't ask, why would they? I only met him in June. You the same, I suppose.'

'Well . . . yes, but I—'

'Say nothing,' Flora insisted. 'It's not up to us to do the police's job for them. Now, let's talk about nice things. You're coming with us on the thirtieth, yes? And you're staying here overnight? Are you sure you don't want to come for Christmas? You're always welcome here, you know. Both of you.'

There was a brief bark of laughter down the line. 'I don't think so. Roland and I have plans. We're dining at Claridge's. Roland says he has a surprise for me.'

'You don't think . . .?'

'I think nothing, Florette. If anything happens, I'll tell you when I see you. Now go have fun with your greenery. Let Birnam Wood come to Dunsinane.'

Flora frowned. 'Didn't Macbeth die when that happened?'

'I was thinking more of the aesthetics. I know you don't do greenery by halves.'

'Val?' she said, uncertain of herself for the first time. 'Does it matter that I feel lighter? I've suddenly realised I do. Does that make me a bad person?'

'Nothing will make you a bad person,' he reassured her. 'Give my love to the girls. How's the old man getting on, by the way?'

'Still not well. It's like he's been knocked for six. He was even worse this afternoon. He spent an age in the chapel. Frankly, I'm dreading Christmas.'

Her brother's voice was kind. 'I'm sure you'll make it wonderful for everyone. You've got Mummy's template to follow. Just put your spin on it.'

'Sure,' she said. But she wasn't really listening. Her thoughts were still with the hand in the water. When the call ended she found herself washing her own hands under the freezing water from the tap, even though they were already clean.

In his cottage on the Sandringham Estate, Julian Cassidy swirled the tot of whisky round his glass, inhaled its peaty smell and downed it in a couple of gulps. This was his third and it was taking the edge off.

It was funny – you thought you'd reached your lowest ebb, and then something came along to make you sink lower. Julian felt as if the inrushing tide was washing over his head. On his bookshelves a thicket of Christmas cards were interspersed with others congratulating him on his New Job! and New Home! Many featured crowns and corgis. 'Proud of you, son.' 'Enjoy the moment.' 'Don't shoot any royals!!!! Haha!!!!!'

For a minute, he allowed himself to imagine how it could have been, sitting back on this sofa with a beautiful woman snuggled up beside him, a glass of wine, her body heat, a head full of plans and a clear, bright future.

Then the thought disintegrated. One minute was all it took.

He relived that moment again and again, as he had done since it happened. There was only one answer. He eyed the bottle. But he was distracted by a whimpering sound. Billy, his elderly black Labrador, was sitting at the door, eyeing it keenly, desperate to go out. Julian eased himself up off the sofa and accompanied the dog outside, where he nosed around in the bushes for a while before doing his business.

The sharpness of the night air brought with it a moment of clarity. He realised how fuddled he was. The only noticeable effect of the whisky had been to amplify his sadness. He would stick to wine from now on.

'Hey, boy,' he called softly to the dog across the garden.

Billy trotted back to him, his dark eyes glistening in the moonlight, full of love and trust.

'C'mon, let's go inside.'

Chapter 4

The next morning was Christmas Eve. After breakfast, warmly wrapped up in a tweed coat and fleece-lined boots, the Queen made a quick tour of key parts of the estate to wish season's greetings to the staff who were still at work. At least, that was the official reason. In reality, she was desperate to see the animals. From the cows in the barn to the mares at the stud, and even the pigeons in their loft at Wolferton, she didn't feel she was truly *here* until she had breathed in the bracing odour of cow manure and straw, or rested her hand on a warm and velvety equine neck.

Drawing up at the stud, she was pleased to see that her timing was good. As she got out of the car, she spotted the brood mares and their foals returning two by two from the paddocks in the huge, old walled garden, where they had been getting a blast of fresh air. She stopped to watch them briefly, enchanted as ever by the sight of the leggy foals, who had grown dramatically since the last time she saw them. Each one was the progeny of a line of distinguished race-horses. They weren't yet weaned, but already some stood out to her as potential champions. It took a combination of proportions, strength, character and temperament. Having watched foals grow up into racehorses for as long as she could remember, by now she had a sixth sense for spotting the perfect blend.

Estimate herself, who had recently been immortalised in bronze, drew up the rear with a foal who already showed a lot of promise. He had his mother's spark and ears that pricked with intelligence. The Queen called them both over and gave them all the Polo mints from her pockets. On her return to the house, she realised she was surprisingly tired, but rallied at the thought of the family members who were on their way. One was really so very *lucky* to be able to gather so many of them together – children and grandchildren, and now little great-grandchildren, too. True, right now the thought of a quiet afternoon in front of *Pointless* on TV had a certain appeal, but that was only the head cold talking. As soon as they arrived, she would feel better, she was sure.

From ten o'clock onwards, a succession of Range Rovers began delivering their contents to the front door in strictly managed order of seniority. The junior cousins were first, followed by her youngest son Edward, the Earl of Wessex and other Wessexes, large and small, then Andrew and his girls and, shortly afterwards, Anne and her husband, accompanied by Prince Harry, who had got a lift with them from St James's Palace.

The Queen tried not to think about the people who were *not* coming. Zara, her eldest granddaughter, such a lovely, *sensible* girl and a mother herself now, was not well. Also missing were William and his family, who had chosen to spend Christmas with Catherine's family in Berkshire. A Middleton Christmas was quite something, apparently. Full of jollity and good cheer. The Queen felt thoroughly put in her place when William had described it. In what way jollity and good cheer were lacking at Sandringham, she didn't know. However, a part of her rather admired her grandson for taking a stand. One needed fortitude for the job he would one day hold. It took a loyal spouse, too, and that necessitated care and compromise along the way. Catherine would have her family Christmas. The monarch would make do. There was always FaceTime.

Among the freshly polished royal vehicles, a mud-spattered old Subaru estate car incongruously drew up in the courtyard and its driver got out alone. The Queen happened to be looking out of the saloon window as he did so. She turned to the butler who was standing beside her.

'What's the chief constable of Norfolk doing here?'

'I don't know, ma'am,' he said, looking as surprised as she was. 'I'll redirect him round the back.'

The Queen shook her head. Surely the most senior policeman in Norfolk wouldn't visit Sandringham on a day like today unless it was very important? It must be to do with Ned St Cyr, and yet it had only been twenty-four hours since she had identified the hand. Was that enough for significant progress? She didn't know whether to hope or dread what he might say.

'Show him in, would you? One might as well say hello.'

The lugubrious, angular man who came in from the cold, shrugging off his waxed jacket and handing it to a waiting footman, looked astonished to be ushered into the saloon itself, and to find Her Majesty waiting for him. The circumstances were unusual, but this was by no means the first time they had met. Nigel Bloomfield had been head of the Norfolk constabulary for five years. He was a keen and thoughtful officer who had joined as the son of local farmers and risen quickly through the ranks. The Queen admired him for sticking with the Norfolk force and not seeking flashier jobs elsewhere. 'They call Yorkshire God's own county,' he'd said once, 'but we know where it is really, don't we, ma'am?' She was pleased that his loyalty hadn't held him back. He was well regarded among other senior officers she knew. She found him both imperturbable and affable, which was an attractive combination, despite his general demeanour of a disappointed bloodhound.

'Chief Constable! It's good to see you,' she announced. 'Very kind of you to come on Christmas Eve.'

He bowed at the neck, and apologised for his off-duty outfit of neatly pressed corduroy trousers and smart red jumper.

'I'm off to a carol concert later. My wife's singing with a choir in Burnham Market. I hope you don't mind, ma'am.'

'Not at all,' the Queen said. 'Very appropriate.'

'I was hoping to give your private secretary a quick update before Christmas. I got a bit held up, I'm afraid.'

'You'll have trouble seeing Sir Simon. He's in Scotland,' the Queen informed him.

Bloomfield frowned. 'He rang first thing to find out how the team were getting on, ma'am. He sounded very keen to know all the details. I assumed he was here.'

41

'Sir Simon's on holiday,' the Queen said sharply, making a mental note to tell the man in no uncertain terms, when he got back, not to do Rozie's job for her while he happened to be away. 'And I'm afraid Captain Oshodi, my APS, is getting ready to play football. My grandson has inveigled her on to his team. Can I help?'

Bloomfield took a couple of seconds to process the information. However, he gathered himself.

'Quite possibly you can, ma'am. You're familiar with the victim, I gather. I don't want to intrude into your day. I'm sure you must be . . .'

He was somewhat distracted by whatever was going on behind her – almost certainly one or several of her children and grandchildren popping their heads round the door from the armoury corridor that led to the drawing room, to see who on earth this new arrival was.

'You're right, we're very busy. But I have five minutes. Where can we . . .? Ah yes, follow me.'

In the company of the dogs, she led him to the far end of the room, where a doorway was almost invisibly silhouetted in the panelling beside the fireplace. It led to a small, dark, book-lined room with a desk. The Queen turned on the light and closed the door behind them.

'So. An update,' she said. 'How encouraging.' She didn't sit down, because stand-up meetings tended to be quicker.

Bloomfield was still adjusting to his surroundings. He paused to look down at his trousers, where Vulcan was energetically sniffing his leg, and bent to give the corgi a reassuring stroke. The Queen had a lot of time for people who instinctively fondled the ears of friendly dogs. He straightened. 'I wish I had better news, ma'am. Edward St Cyr was last seen in London on the fourteenth of December. My senior investigating officer is up there now. Mr St Cyr spent the night at his flat in Hampstead, prior to a meeting the following morning. He was certainly in a hurry. He was caught speeding twice on the A13 in his Maserati.'

'He was rather known for speeding, I seem to remember.'

'Ah. We can't say for sure if he attended the meeting on the fifteenth. However, he wasn't at Stansted Airport to meet his fiancée that afternoon. She couldn't get hold of him, so she reported him missing the next day, which by then was the sixteenth, eight days ago. We weren't unduly worried because he was known to go off grid occasionally. People go missing more often than you might think, ma'am.'

'Oh, I know,' the Queen said. She was familiar with the statistics, which were grim. It was alarming to discover how many of those who were subsequently found had good reasons for staying away.

'Of course, this identification casts a new light on everything,' Bloomfield said. 'The Maserati's still parked outside the flat; the friends have heard nothing; St Cyr's phone hasn't been used since he first went up to London. There's no record of him leaving the country. We're confident the DNA analysis will confirm the hand is his.'

'Oh, dear. Does anyone at Abbottswood have any light to shed on what happened?'

'No, ma'am. Mr St Cyr lived alone, unless his fiancée was visiting. There's a cleaning lady who comes in three times a week, a local cook who obliges on request, and a grounds-man who lives in the gatehouse, but he wasn't there.'

The Queen nodded. A few decades ago, a place like Abbottswood would have bristled with servants, but it didn't surprise her that Ned might rattle round his house these days. He was divorced, his children grown-up, and long gone were the days when the gentry could afford live-in staff, unless they found ways to make those houses pay. Which, as Philip had pointed out last night, Ned had serially failed to do. The poor man must have been quite lonely. She herself, she knew, would go stark, staring mad if left entirely to her own devices. She thrived on company.

'What was his meeting about? Does anyone know?'

'Not yet. It's marked in his diary as "RIP".'

'"RIP"? How unsettling.'

'Yes, ma'am. We have reason to believe it was a loca-tion. He used that sort of annotation for events in his diary. He seems to have gone out on schedule, expecting to come back. The breakfast dishes were still in the sink and there were no signs of violence. We'll find out what he was up to soon enough. We're checking local CCTV in Hampstead. Forensics are already hard at work on his home computer here at Abbottswood. He kept all his passwords on a sticky note he stuck to the monitor, would you believe? His secu-rity all round was very . . .' The chief constable sighed. 'You mustn't speak ill of the dead and so on, but I sincerely wish we'd had the chance to talk him through a few basic pro-cedures. Still, it speeds things up for us significantly. And it helps that whoever did this is making it easier for us, too.'

'In what way?'

'Well, the hatchet job on the hand, for starters,' Bloomfield explained. 'It was done, presumably, with the intention of making the body harder to identify.'

'It rather backfired in that case, didn't it?' the Queen observed archly.

He nodded. 'Precisely, ma'am. None too bright, our killer. Or killers, plural. They want the victim to be anonymous so they remove the, um . . . ah . . . distinguishing extremity, and decide to dispose of it out at sea. They put it in a plastic bag and instead of sinking to the seabed and being devoured by the creatures of the deep, it floats. It's washed ashore by the storm, and in an entirely avoidable irony, it's the only body part we have.'

The Queen winced. 'Where do you think the rest of him is?'

'Far away,' he said decisively. 'The whole idea was that nobody would think of St Cyr when they found the body. I imagine the, ah, head is not in good condition either. It could be buried the other side of London, or it might also be at sea. We may well find it washed up in Sweden in a couple of months. I'm sorry, ma'am. I realise he was a family friend.'

'Not exactly,' she said, reeling slightly at the thought of the head, which she hadn't considered. Ned's golden hair had always been a glory. 'We hadn't seen him for many years. But his mother was.' She glanced across at the spot on the floor where Willow, the last remaining corgi, was enjoying a patch of winter sun on the carpet. Georgina had been a dog person, too. Always English or red setters, glamorous

45

and slightly mad, always at least four of them. Thank God she was no longer around to hear any of this.

'I'm surprised,' she added, 'that the Met aren't dealing with the case, if Ned disappeared in London.'

'He was reported missing in Norfolk, ma'am. There was an exchange of views about it between the forces, put it that way, but my team prevailed. And despite the signs, I sense this is a Norfolk crime at its heart.'

'Oh?'

'The hand was found up here, after all,' Bloomfield pointed out. 'St Cyr grew up here, lived here, ran all his businesses from his place at Abbottswood. I knew him through his charity work. Always took a keen interest in what I was up to in my role as head of the Drugs Task Force. He was surprisingly well informed for a man of his—' He caught the Queen's eye and coughed again. 'Ahem . . . his generation. He let us use Abbottswood for meetings and events. It was obviously his home, not just some bolthole he used at weekends.'

'I see.' She wondered suddenly if the chief constable thought that one saw Sandringham as a bolthole. But surely not? So much of her family's life was bound up in it.

'Anyway, we'll know a lot more when forensics make their report,' he went on. 'I expect they'll give us an idea about what happened to him first and where the bag went in the water, too. It's amazing how much they can deduce from temperature and tides. The cold weather helps, of course. If the hand had been in that plastic bag under a hot sun it would have been quite a different story.' He saw the

Queen's bleak response to that last statement and sought to reassure her. 'I've got fifty people working on this night and day. Whatever happened, ma'am, we'll find it soon enough. I guarantee we'll have it wrapped up for you as quickly as any force in the country.'

The Queen sensed a note of competition in his voice. Norfolk was not, on the whole, known for its speed and efficiency. No doubt its major investigation unit could compete with the best in Manchester, say, or Edinburgh or Belfast, but as a county in general it had a reputation as slow and steady. Which was exactly how she liked it. Still, Bloomfield's intention was a good one, if slightly misplaced.

'Not for me. For his family,' she said. 'And for the sake of justice. Thank you, Chief Constable.'

She arranged for him to be looked after by the kitchen staff before heading off to his wife's carol concert. The investigation sounded as if it was in good hands, which was where she wanted it to stay. Finally, she could focus on her own family, who would be wondering what on earth had happened to her.

Chapter 5

In the festive drawing room, the recent arrival of Charles and Camilla meant that the family, such as it was this year, was complete. Those who were there soon fell into familiar patterns, built up over many years and generations. Outside, the traditional football match was already underway against the local village of Castle Rising, the Sandringham team of staff and groundsmen captained by Harry in William's absence. Indoors, the little ones gathered around the Christmas tree to hang the decorations that were set out for them in ancient cardboard boxes, some of which dated back to Queen Victoria, watched over by the painted pheasant on the drawing room ceiling. The Queen was content to observe from a nearby chair, sipping a hot tea and lemon and giving suggestions for where choice ornaments should go.

Anne came to sit beside her.

'Mummy, I'm so sorry.' Her tone was sombre.

'What about?'

'The hand!'

'Oh, that.'

'You must be feeling awful.'

'I wasn't.' For a pleasant half-hour, filled with children's chatter, the Queen had managed to put it from her mind.

'Did you hear that Astrid's gone missing too?'

'Who's Astrid?' the Queen asked.

'Ned's girlfriend . . . fiancée. Moira Westover's girl.'

'Oh, I see. How dreadful. How do you know?'

'It was on the radio,' Anne explained. 'We heard a news update as we were driving down. She was the one who reported Ned missing a week ago.'

'Oh, dear,' the Queen sighed. The chief constable hadn't mentioned it. Another complication. She thought of the Westover family. It was awful enough trying to deal with a difficult emotional situation, but to do it in the public eye made it more distressing. She knew better than anyone how that felt.

Presents were opened after tea, in the German tradition, preserved since Prince Albert's day. Four generations of royals gathered in the drawing room, in suits and smart dresses (there were more costume changes at Sandringham than during a busy West End performance). The early winter darkness emphasised the cosiness of a room lit by candles, lamps and a galaxy of fairy lights on the tree.

There was a great air of anticipation as the youngest children ceremoniously handed out parcels from the laden trestle tables. Not that any of the adults were expecting high-tech gadgets or vintage watches. The children's presents tended to be traditional and generous, but the rest of the family had long since learned that when you sit in a room surrounded by antique Venetian fans and one of the best Fabergé collections in the world, where the hostess has recently been presented with a life-size statue of one of her favourite race-horses, you couldn't hope to compete. Or rather, the competition was quite a different one: to see who could be the most entertaining on a budget. The winner (and the family were competitive to a fault, so there was usually a winner) was the one who came up with the best joke.

Last year's present from Catherine to Harry, a grow-your-own girlfriend kit, had been a particular hit. Harry himself was a master when it came to cheeky presents. The Queen greatly enjoyed the 'Ain't Life A Bitch' shower cap he had given her. He admitted that this time he had bought William a bald wig with an inch of hair fuzz around the edges, and was hugely disappointed not to get to see him open it.

Catherine's grow-your-own present to Harry would not have worked this year. His very-much-real girlfriend was in Canada working on her TV series, so he was here on his own, but he was so obviously in love it was cheering just to look at him. The tips of his ears turned pink whenever her name was mentioned. William would inevitably have teased him mercilessly about her, as an elder brother's right, so perhaps it was easier in that way at least that he wasn't here.

The Queen appreciated Harry's latest present to her, which was a floppy waxed fishing hat designed to make her look like a famous lady detective from the television. 'You're the spitting image,' he assured her. But actually, it was also very practical for bad weather, and reminded her pleasantly of her mother, who had a whole collection of hats such as these. 'I'll wear it when I solve my next case,' she joked, and everyone grinned at the absurdity of the idea. Which was rather reassuring.

Her favourite gift, though, came from the absent little Prince George. Along with a framed, indecipherable crayon drawing was a mug that made her laugh out loud as soon as she opened it.

'What is it?' Anne asked.

The Queen showed it to her daughter. It depicted a row of plump grey birds with green and purple markings at the neck. The message printed above them said, *I may look like I'm listening to you, but in my head, I'm thinking about pigeons.*

'Ha! Well done, Catherine,' Anne observed. 'I sense a mother's hand in this.'

'I think, actually, that drawing of his is supposed to be a pigeon,' the Queen reflected. 'I thought it might be a giraffe at first.'

'Definitely pigeon,' Anne agreed. 'A man after your own heart.'

Like her father and his father before him, the Queen was an ardent pigeon fancier. The family tended to think of it as her little hobby, but pigeon racing was a sport almost as old as Christianity. She had always liked the idea that the National Flying Club referred to pigeons. These birds could fly for thousands of miles with an unerring homing instinct that science was still exploring. Something to do with magnetism and iron filings in their beaks, apparently. And they were much cheaper than racehorses, and just as interesting to breed. The Queen was thoroughly looking forward

51

to sharing her hobby with her great-grandson. *Well done, Catherine, indeed.*

Afterwards, they all retired upstairs. The children were prepared for bed with the help of an assortment of nannies and stockings were hung in anticipation of a visit from Father Christmas, while the adults dressed for dinner. Tonight was the big occasion: black tie and evening gowns, diamonds and silk shoes, a chance to let loose in relaxed company, which was precious and rare.

Philip, showing enormous fortitude and the power of ibuprofen, arrived in the saloon for cocktails looking like a fashion plate. For her part, no amount of makeup and sparkles could disguise the Queen's pink nose and red eyes, and now her voice was becoming so hoarse she could hardly talk. However, a little Dubonnet Zaza cocktail with a twist of orange helped her see the world in a rosier light.

Charles made his way across the saloon towards her and she raised her glass to him. The cocktail was hitting the spot.

He looked at her slightly mournfully. 'I wanted to let you know, I understand how bad you must be feeling.'

'Don't worry. It's just a cold. I'll feel better tomorrow.'

'No, I meant about the hand.'

'Oh.'

'On the beach.'

'Mmm.'

'I've been thinking about it all day.'

'Ah.'

52

'But I promise we won't talk about it.'

'Good.'

'Did you know,' he added, after a minuscule pause, 'that the police were searching Ned's place in London? I saw it on the news while I was getting changed.'

'Oh, are they?' the Queen asked, adding firmly, 'Isn't Harry looking well?'

'Is he? Yes, I suppose he is. They were wearing hazmat suits. You know, those white ones like beekeepers' outfits.'

'Who?'

'The police. In Ned's flat in Hampstead. Goodness knows why, given the hand turned up in Norfolk. I was wondering if it might be a kidnap attempt gone wrong. Do you remember that Getty boy's ear? Horrendous business. Got lost in the post. You could hardly make it up.'

'No, you couldn't. Ah! Sophie!' The Queen rather desperately hailed the Countess of Wessex, Edward's wife, who was halfway across the room. 'Are the children all right? Did they enjoy the day?'

'Oh, absolutely.' Sophie joined them, wearing a slub silk evening gown that the Queen was pleased to note she had seen before; she didn't approve of clothes horses and waste. 'Did you hear the news about the missing man?' Sophie asked. 'He lived near here, didn't he? I was just talking to Mrs Maddox about it and she said her daughter used to work at the Fen-Time Festival on his estate a few years ago. She met Stephen Fry there. D'you know, I think she had a bit of a thing for him?'

'For Stephen Fry?'

'No, Edward St Cyr. I don't think I ever met him. Did you know him well?'

Mercifully, the gong went, which meant dinner. The royal couple led the other adults into the dining room. Its pistachio wall colour, known as Braemar green, had been chosen by the Queen Mother to remind her of a favourite Scottish castle. It gave the room a jolly, feminine air that summoned up Mummy's spirit and sense of fun. The Queen had once overheard a guest suggesting it looked like an ice-cream parlour at Harrods, but surely that wasn't a bad thing? As always, the room was lit by candles alone, whose flickering glow, she hoped, could make even the most ravaged of cold-ridden faces look reasonably attractive. An artificial silver Christmas tree twinkled near the window. The wine was excellent and the venison was cooked to perfection. But every time the conversation veered away from the St Cyrs, it somehow veered back.

'Of course, it's a raging husband the police should be looking for,' Andrew suggested. 'Ned St Cyr famously had an eye for a posh girl in jodhpurs.' He grinned at his sister, who told him to shut up.

'Was he an artist?' Camilla asked. 'They said on the news his London place was an artist's studio.'

Anne started to explain, digging back in her memory to her teenage years. 'Ned's *father* was the artist. Simon Longbourn? Or Paul? I don't remember. Mummy, what was Georgina's husband called?'

But nobody could remember, or rather, they couldn't agree. Simon, or possibly Paul, had given Georgina the surname

Longbourn on her marriage during the war. They had all lived at Ladybridge Hall together, along with Georgina's younger sisters and her dashing little brother, Patrick, and Ned had been Ned Longbourn until the age of eight when Paul, or possibly Simon, divorced Georgina and fled to Greece, where he painted and drank until the drink finally killed him and young Ned inherited the studio flat in Hampstead and the captain's house on Corfu. It was questionable whether Georgina noticed. She was always more interested in her horses and helping her father look after the estate. After the divorce, she reverted to her maiden name and Ned took it too. He'd inherited his mother's red-gold hair and Roman nose, her charisma, her love of fast cars, her occasional temper, her charm . . . The two properties were the only things his father ever gave him, as far as they knew.

'After her father died, Georgina bought Abbottswood,' Philip explained, 'Nice Regency villa. Not on the scale of Ladybridge, obviously. The Yanks had had the place during the war and the house was a wreck, but the grounds were good. Designed by Repton, apparently.' Philip's knowledge of the house and its surroundings surprised no one at the table. If he was interested in something he tended to know everything about it, and local architecture was one of his hobbies. 'Georgina retired there like something out of Dickens, though she was only in her forties. Only rode to hounds and hardly spoke to anyone. She never forgave her cousin Ralph for casting her out of Ladybridge when her brother died and he inherited instead. Though what else he was supposed to do, God knows.'

'Couldn't she have lived on the estate somewhere?' one of the younger princesses asked.

'Possibly. But you didn't know Georgina. She was the eldest child, the only one with any common sense, and she'd been practically running the estate for years. She'd have been staring down the new baron's ruddy neck and second-guessing every decision he made. I'm not surprised Ralph practically bankrupted himself to get rid of her. Ned never forgave him, either. Ralph died forty years ago, but if *his* hand had ended up in the water . . .'

The Queen shot her husband a look.

'What kind of person was he?' Camilla wanted to know.

'Ned? Wayward,' Charles said with some disdain.

'Headstrong,' added Philip.

'They're saying he was a visionary in the servants' hall,' Sophie Wessex suggested, which caused all heads to look at her. 'That's what Mrs Maddox was telling me. He'd started this new project to turn Abbottswood into a nature refuge. He was planning to make it a centre for endangered species.'

'Oh?' Philip said, frowning. 'I hadn't heard.'

'It was a recent thing. Mrs Maddox sounded quite excited. As I say, I think she's a fan.'

Beatrice, sitting across the table from the Queen, looked confused. 'If he lived quite close, how come Eugenie and I never met him?'

'Or me?' Harry agreed.

'We rather lost touch over the years,' the Queen said vaguely.

'Ha!' Philip said. 'You mean, he dropped us like a hot potato.'

'He dropped *us*?' Beatrice asked. 'Seriously?'

'He grew up as Little Lord Fauntleroy at Ladybridge, then, after he and Georgina got chucked out, he went off to Greece, had an ersatz epiphany and came back a bloody communist. He saw us as fuddy-duddies. Too straight down the line for his bohemian tastes. He loved your great-aunt Margaret. We preferred Ralph's son Hugh. Dull but stable. You know Hugh. Dresses like a scarecrow, farms sheep and writes about John Donne. It was Lee, his wife, we were particularly fond of, mind you. Very attractive blonde from Yorkshire. Green-fingered girl. She died in the summer. Much too young.'

'My age,' Charles observed, swilling his claret around his glass before finishing it in a gulp and gesturing for a refill. 'We shared a birthday. We always used to send each other a basket of hyacinths.' He looked wistful. 'Ned introduced her to Hugh, I think. Thank God she didn't end up with him.'

'Didn't you say Ned tried to go out with you, Mummy?' Peter Phillips asked Anne.

'Mmm, he did,' Anne agreed. 'Ned didn't drop *me*. But he was very unpredictable. Mad, bad and dangerous to know and all that. Abbottswood was famous for rock concerts in the seventies. I think Led Zeppelin played there once.'

'Gosh!' Beatrice was impressed.

'Mind you, he settled down eventually,' Anne said. 'The last time I saw him was at a country fair a couple of years ago, looking at vegan dog food.'

'I heard his disappearance might be to do with drugs,' Eugenie suggested. 'That was on the news, too.'

'Well, it wouldn't be him taking them,' Anne said firmly. 'One of his best friends overdosed in Greece and Ned became evangelical about it. He made Abbottswood a sort of rehabilitation centre for a while.'

'Until one of the inmates practically burned the place down,' Charles reminded her.

'Hmph!' Philip snorted. 'He was good at attracting acolytes; not so good at actually providing them with decent therapy. He was always trying out some hare-brained scheme and going off half-cocked. Half Don Juan, half Don Quixote. He never could see a thing *through*.'

'He sounds interesting,' Beatrice said with a grin.

'He *was* interesting. Too interesting,' Philip grumbled. 'That was his problem. Too busy trying to impress his mother.'

'How very Freudian,' the Queen said, fairly certain that this was the correct use of the term, and also that it might encourage Philip to drop the subject at last.

Luckily, the dining room doors opened at precisely this moment to allow a procession of footmen to deliver towering individual chocolate soufflés dusted with icing sugar and decorated with filigree chocolate holly leaves. There were suitable noises of appreciation and conversation moved on to other things. This meal was one of the Queen's favourites of the year, and finally she could get on with enjoying it.

Chapter 6

The following morning the Queen felt worse.

Her head hammered. She put it down to the champagne, and possibly the Zaza cocktail. She could barely open her eyes.

In the corridor outside her room, children raced up and down, triumphantly calling out 'He's *been*!' to one another before being loudly shushed. Meanwhile, there was something the Queen needed to do. Whatever it was, she couldn't do it.

Lying in bed, eyes closed, she tried to think. It *couldn't* be down to the drink. She hadn't overindulged, not really. Not nearly enough to feel like this, anyway. And it couldn't be her head cold. (What *was* it she was supposed to be doing?) Philip was a day ahead of her in that regard and he'd looked and felt much better last night. In fact, he'd said he was looking forward to getting some fresh air this morning at the early service.

Her eyes shot open. The dull morning light was blinding. *No!*

She sat up sharply, before woozily collapsing back into her pillows.

The early service! This was Sunday, and Christmas morning. She was supposed to be at St Mary Magdalene's at nine for private worship, and back at eleven for the public service and the family walkabout. It was more than a tradition, it was a *duty*, and she had attended the eleven o'clock service either here or at Windsor every single year of her reign, without fail. It was simply impossible to imagine not attending. What would her grandmother, Queen Mary, say?

She sat up again and tried to call for her maid. She still had about an hour to get ready. But her voice was barely a croak and she had to ring the bell. The doctor was called by video link, swiftly diagnosed full-blown flu and forbade her to leave the house. Philip, who was already dressed and breakfasted, took one look at her and agreed, which was most disheartening. So did Charles, who was so astonished at the news of his mother being incapacitated that he had to come and see for himself. Really, her bedroom was turning into Piccadilly Circus, or something out of *The Madness of King George*. If she hadn't been almost incapable of speech, she would have had quite a lot to say about it.

Eventually, after a large breakfast and a short walk for the children to burn off some energy after their stocking-opening shenanigans, the rest of the family disappeared for a blissfully quiet couple of hours to go to church and talk to the crowds. If it had been possible for the Queen to feel more dreadful than she did at the thought of letting down the visitors at the gate, who had been waiting for hours in sub-zero temperatures to see her, she would have done so, but instead she took her time getting ready, accompanied by her dresser and the sound of carols on the radio.

She took the chance to write a brief note to Moira Westover, whose daughter Astrid had so mysteriously disappeared, and to Hugh St Cyr, Ned's cousin at Ladybridge Hall, commiserating on 'what must be most unsettling times for you all'. She wanted to say *your bereavement*, but they didn't know for certain yet that it *was* a bereavement. Anyway, poor Hugh had grief much closer to home to contend with, since the death of his beloved wife just short of their golden wedding anniversary. Whereas he hadn't spoken to Ned for years, as far as she knew. Was it harder, she wondered, to lose someone who had already made themselves absent from your life? There were no heart-warming memories, no consolation of shared experience. It was easy to tell yourself that it didn't matter, but was it true?

Later, the rector arrived to give her private communion – there were advantages to being head of the Church of England – and everyone reconvened in the dining room for a meal of roast turkey, seven types of organic vegetable from various royal farms and gardens, a flaming Christmas pudding and, for those with the stomach for it, plenty of fine wine and champagne. There were party crowns and, by tradition, the Queen was the only one who didn't wear one. As a girl, she had found it so very funny when her father didn't and everyone else did. They finished just in time to gather round the television set in the saloon at three, to watch the message she had recorded earlier at Buckingham Palace.

'I looked perfectly well then,' she said, observing herself from her vantage point on the nearest sofa.

'That was before the little Petri dishes got going. Which one of you buggers was it?' Philip demanded, glancing round.

'You look lovely now,' Sophie said gamely. You could always rely on Sophie to say the right thing, even if in the teeth of the evidence.

Familiar with what she was going to say to the nation and the Commonwealth, the Queen let her gaze drift from the television to a small gap in the panelling, marking the hidden door. The room where she had spoken to the chief constable was the one where her father and grandfather used to record their Christmas messages for the radio. They were broadcast live to an empire that seemed to power the world. How quickly that idea had become history, and both her life and her father's had been spent managing the transition.

For a moment, she pictured him beside her again, his hand reassuringly on her shoulder. These feelings didn't completely fade, even after so many decades. He had died in his bedroom upstairs, aged only fifty-six, and she had been far away, in Africa. Halfway across the world.

'Mummy, are you all right?' Anne asked.

'It's just this dreadful flu. Pass me my handbag and I'll find a handkerchief.'

'One thing you can be sure of,' Mrs Maddox said to a select audience in the housekeeper's sitting room a few hours later, 'it wasn't one of the family.'

Mrs Maddox was a commanding presence, with an inscrutable expression and a helmet of immaculately cut, bobbed hair that made her look uncannily like Anna Wintour – should the editor of *Vogue* ever forgo sunglasses and don a festive plastic tiara. The resemblance had been noted by many a Sandringham guest, so often, in fact, that the family now took bets on how long it would take someone to mention it.

'What? A prince, you mean?' one of the butlers asked, to brief sniggering, quickly shushed.

'No, really, Mr Roberts! One of *his* family.'

This evening, the housekeeper was holding court with the household staff while the royals, for a brief moment, looked after themselves. Rozie, who had spent the day missing the spice and flavour of her mother's cooking in her family's flat in West London, and the equal spice of her cousins' friendly, bickering conversation around the table, was grateful to be asked along. Technically, she was too senior to join the 'downstairs' staff, but at Sandringham such distinctions seemed to shift like the tides.

'Why's that, then?' the butler asked.

'Because,' the man sitting beside Rozie said, 'if you want to inherit, you need a body.' This was Rick Jackson, one of the Queen's long-standing protection officers and chief inspector at the Met. 'Or you have to wait seven years before you can declare the man dead.'

Mrs Maddox nodded. 'Precisely, Mr Jackson. So, anyone hoping to inherit from Mr St Cyr would be trying to *provide* an identifiable body, not hide one.'

'So where d'you think it is then?' a lady's maid wondered.

'Me personally?' Jackson queried. 'Limed. In a quarry somewhere. I think the hand was a trophy. Then they got scared they had it, so they threw it away. Or they got told to. There are a million better ways of doing it, though.'

'Surely not?' Mrs Maddox interjected. 'Mr St Cyr was hardly some sort of gangster. If you go back enough generations, I think he's related to the Queen.'

'That's hasn't stopped anyone before,' Jackson pointed out. 'In some periods of history, it was a motive.'

'It needn't have been for the inheritance, mind you,' Rozie mused, returning to the original point. 'There are other reasons for killing a relative.'

'True,' Mrs Maddox agreed. 'But I can't see why anyone would want to in this case.'

'Three bitter divorces,' the lady's maid pointed out.

'Yes, but the last one was twenty years ago,' Mrs Maddox observed. 'Poor man. He was unlucky in love. He told me about it one evening at the festival. He lost the love of his life at twenty-one and never really loved a woman again. He was a true romantic.'

'Not exactly,' the lady's maid scoffed. 'The way he treated his wives was shocking. My friend used to work for Christina, the third one. He had this system. When he came to get divorced, he suddenly had no money. He was living on thin air, no savings, practically bankrupt, and he couldn't afford to give them a decent settlement. Then as soon as everything was finalised, back came the nice cars, the trips to Greece to his old house, which was now owned by a friend of his. Convenient.'

Mrs Maddox looked disapproving. 'I can't imagine him doing that. He talked so fondly about all his children.'

The lady's maid shrugged. 'Easy to do that when you're not paying for their keep. He told them it was good for them to look after themselves, like he'd had to. Those poor kids. But I agree with you, Mrs Maddox, this isn't a woman's crime.'

'What's a woman's crime when it's at home?' the butler asked. 'Some of the nastiest murders in history've been done by women.'

'Name one.'

The butler thought for a minute. 'John the Baptist. We saw the play once. Salome did the dance of the seven veils and when she was asked what she wanted, she said John the Baptist's head. And she got it, on a plate. I remember those veils.'

'Sure,' Mr Jackson said from beside Rozie. 'But I bet it was a man that cut it off and gave it to her. Women tend to be more impulsive. Or more indirect.'

'Women tend to be the victims,' the lady's maid put in gloomily.

'Actually, they don't,' Mr Jackson said. 'Overall, victims of homicide are eighty per cent men. But those killed by a partner are eighty per cent women, I'll give you that.'

'That's it!' Mrs Maddox announced, unknowingly mirroring the Queen's reaction. 'Enough murder talk on Christmas Day. Now, will somebody make me a negroni and let's talk about something else?'

Chapter 7

After a feverish night, the Queen woke early. The sky beyond her bedroom window was a watercolour wash of pink and lavender, infused from below with frosty light. She sat quietly against her pillows for some time, waiting for her headache to abate and grateful, for once, that there wasn't room at Sandringham for her personal piper.

Downstairs, the more active members of the family were gathering for a hearty fry-up, ready for the traditional Boxing Day shoot. Some of the women would be joining the men, while others had breakfast in their rooms and took the chance to recover from two days of festivities. Shooting was largely a man's sport anyway, in the Queen's experience. At least, it had been in her father's day.

This morning, the royal party assembling in the gun lobby would be a slimmed-down version of Sandringham in its pomp. Since Philip's heart operation he travelled as an observer only. William was still keen on the tradition, but of course he wasn't here. And Harry had developed a sensitivity to blood sports and wasn't going out with the guns today.

The tide of history was on Harry's side, she thought. When she and Philip were young it had seemed quite natural to combine a love of field sports and wildlife conservation – necessary, even – and yet that combination had now become a paradox. Charles, aware of this, had given up the hunt and tried to be seen less and less with a shotgun in his hands. The Queen wondered where this loss of tradition would stop. So much of the countryside worked the way it did, with hedgerows and copses as cover for birds, because sportsmen kept it that way. What would happen without keepers and sporting farmers to look after it? By the time little George took over, would it be one big theme park with 'royalty' rides, or, God forbid, a massive golf course with sterile putting greens?

At least there was one advantage to Harry's sudden aversion to blood sports: it meant he could keep her company and help her with the jigsaw. She was looking forward to hearing more about the girlfriend. Her grandson's general air of bonhomie reminded her somewhat of herself when one of Philip's letters arrived after the war. It was cheering to see him so happy. She had never doubted the essential, transformative effect of love.

Rozie was woken by the alarm at 7 a.m. Heavy curtains blocked out the sky, and it took her a moment to remember where she was. She needed a pee and a drink of water. She needed to be elsewhere. She probably shouldn't have brought that second bottle of champagne up to the room last night.

As she sat up slowly to examine the extent of her hangover, a heavy arm threw itself across her from the other side of the bed.

'Don't go.'

'I have to,' she said, remembering the late-night text she had received from Sir Simon. 'You, do too. You're the one who set the alarm, remember?'

'Yes, but it's so comfortable.' The owner of the arm had the same peevish stubbornness of her sister when Rozie used to try and wake her up to go running in the mornings.

'Prince Philip'll be expecting you.'

'I can dress very fast. I'm sure we've got twenty minutes to spare.'

'I can dress fast too, but I've got to get back to my room, remember?'

'Borrow something of mine,' he grumbled. 'We're the same kind of size.' He nuzzled her shoulder, but she wouldn't be persuaded.

It was tempting, though. Henry Marshal-Ward was a captain in the Coldstream Guards, fit in every sense, with a cushy staff job as a temporary equerry to the Queen. Rozie didn't have time for a full-on boyfriend and Henry didn't come with strings attached, so occasional hook-ups suited them both. Especially here, where he had a room inside the main house, within drunken staggering distance of the servants' hall last night, while she was billeted in the overflow accommodation on the estate, half a mile down the road. However, royal shoot attire was very strict, even for observers like her, and it didn't include black lace bodycon party dresses or a boyfriend's borrowed tracksuit. She needed to go and change.

Sir Simon's drunken text from the night before suggested that he, too, would be nursing a hangover this morning. He'd been talking to one of the ghillies in Balmoral, who had heard on the grapevine that the Sandringham shoot would contain some friends and neighbours of the family, to make up for missing royals:

> *There's a possibilility likelihood that one or more of these people may be connected to St Cry. Find out what you can. Be discreet. We may need to do some damage control later. Good lick.*

Rozie reached over to switch on the light. As its glow caught the Roman profile and the tousled curls of his strawberry blond hair, she was reminded of her Google Images search from three days before.

'You're not related to Edward St Cyr, are you?'

'The missing man? Um, yuh,' Henry said. 'I think he's like my second cousin twice removed. I'm related to most people, though, one way or another, if you go back far enough.'

'I bet you're not related to my family,' Rozie challenged him.

'Well, no, I don't have any ancestors in Lagos that I know of. Wouldn't swear to it, though.'

'You don't have a ring like his,' she observed.

'No. We're the Shropshire branch of the family. It's the Norfolk St Cyrs who go in for the bloodstone ring. We always thought big stones like that were rather naff.' He raised his left hand, which bore a small gold ring on the little finger, similar to many that Rozie saw on the hands of royals and senior household staff.

'So is it naff *not* to wear a ring?' she asked, looking at her own long, nimble fingers.

'No,' Henry told her, tracing one of his fingers down her arm from shoulder to wrist. 'I like your fingers bare. Like this bit.' He slid his hand under the sheet.

She threw a pillow at him and crawled out of bed.

The shooting party set out together across the estate in a motley collection of Range Rovers, Land Rover Defenders and an ancient shooting bus, in the direction of Wolferton, towards the marshes. To avoid paparazzi lenses, they drove down a series of tracks made for military vehicles during the war, observed only by a hovering kestrel and the occasional pheasant that whirred up from the ground like a helicopter before breasting the hedgerows on the breeze.

Overnight, a hoar frost had layered every twig, leaf and seed head with heavy ice. The almost horizontal rays of a pale sun, penetrating a light layer of low cloud, made the wide fields of stubble glint and twinkle. Rozie could see why the royals got out of bed for this. In fact, she felt sorry for anyone who had chosen not to come out with them. If there was a way of doing it without dressing up in tweed and shooting the funny, silly, colourful pheasants out of the sky, she'd be all for it. Not that she would share that particular train of thought with anyone here.

She stood at the edge of the field where the first drive was due to begin. The guns were having their safety briefing on one side while the observers and pickers-up shared conversation and slugs of sloe gin in a huddle on the other. Henry, her equerry-with-benefits, was among the guns. Everyone seemed to have been to school with one another, or knew one another's parents. Like Henry, they had all been on shoots since childhood and knew exactly what to do. Rozie knew her way around a rifle, but had only started rough shooting with shotguns in the summer, and never on anything as formal as this, with whistles and clickers and pegs to show each gun where to stand, and matching pairs of shotguns that cost more than her university education. It was like going back a century in time.

'Hullo. How are you getting on?'

She looked round to see the friendly face of Lady Caroline Cadwallader, the Queen's lady-in-waiting, hands thrust into the pockets of her tweed jacket.

Rozie explained her mission from Sir Simon.

'In case it's one of us, d'you mean, who did it?' Lady Caroline asked.

'No, just—'

'It is, isn't it? You want to spare the Queen embarrassment. Well, I knew Ned, so you can put me on your list, but I hadn't seen him in an age. We moved in the same circles as teenagers. Our mothers came out together.'

'Came out?' Rozie asked.

'As debs, not lesbians,' Lady Caroline clarified breezily. 'In 1939. What a year. So many of the men they danced with that summer were dead five years later. One of my uncles was shot down over Belgium and another was lost in the North Sea. Georgina's father was never the same. He came back a shadow of the man they sent to war. Anyway, what was I saying?'

Rozie reminded her, and Lady Caroline peered out across the field.

'Ha! I don't *think* the Queen's set are the sort who have people dismembered. We've entertained the odd guest at Buckingham Palace I've had my doubts about, but that was official business.' She surveyed the line of men and women taking up position at their pegs. 'To be honest, most people you can see probably are connected to Ned one way or another. I mean, take that man there.' She pointed to a broad-backed, middle-aged man positioned just beyond Prince Charles. 'That's Gerry Harcourt-Worthorpe, the Earl of Mayfield. He married Ned's first wife, Nancy, after Ned took up with the nanny.'

'Oh, right. Is Nancy here too?' Rozie wondered.

'No, no. She went off to New Zealand. The marriage to Gerry was pretty awful, I gather. She married a sheep farmer and third time lucky, as far as I know. Ned's eldest boy and girl are proud New Zealanders these days. The boy builds bunkers for billionaires. I can't remember his name. Fascinating job, though, don't you think? When the apocalypse comes, all the private jets will be heading to Auckland. Gerry might be one of them. He's one of those few old-money people who actually still possess it. His parents were frightful snobs. They used to refer to the Queen and Prince Philip as the German and the Greek. Although, strictly speaking, they should have called Prince Philip the Dane, I suppose. The Greeks had sort of borrowed the Danish royal family because they didn't have one of their own. Who else?' She scanned the line of guns until she got to the end and handed Rozie her binoculars. 'Ah, and see the woman two pegs along, in lilac tweed, with the fur-trimmed hat?'

'Yes.'

'I assumed it was a novelty outfit the first time I met her. That's Helena Fisher. You wouldn't think so to look at her, but she's a phenomenal shot. She's half Swedish, half American, and she was on the national Olympic team, I can't remember which. Her husband Matt runs Muncaster, which is the next estate along. It's between here and Abbottswood, so I assume they knew Ned quite well.'

'Oh, right.'

'Ned was very charismatic and Helena's charming and attractive, so if he had anything to do with it . . . She's much younger than him, of course. She can't be more than forty-five. But, as we know, age was no barrier to Ned's interest in a woman. Matt's an average shot, so he's over with the pickers-up somewhere. I overheard Prince Philip saying he felt obliged to invite them because we poached his bean counter for the estate. I think that's the bean counter there, see? At the end of the line, in the bright yellow ear defenders. You could see them from space! I assumed Prince Philip meant he was an accountant, but apparently he really does count beans.'

'Why?' Rozie asked.

'He's some sort of conservation manager. His thing is organic farming. Of course, that's catnip for the Prince of Wales. He has to show how good the organic yields are or something. Hence—'

'He counts them. Not individually, I presume,' Rozie said.

'By the tonne, I imagine,' Lady Caroline agreed. 'And blackcurrants, too. Did you know they supply them for

73

Ribena? I'm surprised he's shooting with the guns today. Staff don't usually . . . But I'm sure Prince Philip has his reasons. And that's it, as far as I know,' Lady Caroline concluded. 'Oh, look, they're about to start and the duke is glaring at me because I'm talking.'

She gave Rozie an unrepentant grin and headed back to the group of wives and other guests who were watching from a suitably safe distance. Rozie noticed the bean counter with the yellow ear defenders had turned his head and was looking in her direction. It was a little unnerving. Had he not seen a six-foot black woman in tweeds before? She stared back at him until he looked away.

After the third drive, Rozie decided she had had enough of tweed for the day. She was contemplating the long walk back across farmland and paddocks to her lodgings, when a Range Rover stopped beside her. Princess Anne was at the wheel.

'Oh, good! It's you,' she said. 'Hop in.'

Rozie did as she was told.

'I was hoping to catch you,' Anne went on, negotiating the car down the muddy track. 'Any more news from the police?'

'Not that I've heard,' Rozie said.

'Lady Caroline mentioned that you're on the lookout for potential murderers among us.'

'Not exactly, ma'am. I just thought it would be useful to know who knew the victim.'

'Do they know what Ned was doing in town?'

'Not yet.'

'I wonder if it was a gangland thing,' Anne said. 'Ned mixed with some dodgy types back in the seventies. It's not hard to picture them luring him to London. Though God knows what for, after all this time.'

'It's interesting that whoever did it came back to Norfolk,' Rozie said, glancing beyond the stubble and dykes towards the marshes that led to the Wash. 'Something must have drawn him here.'

'Lunch!' Anne declared.

Up ahead, an isolated building too small to be a house, and too delicate to be a farm building, stood solitary behind a sea of winter wheat. Already, various cars were disgorging their occupants on the track nearby and Anne swung her Range Rover alongside them.

'You'll join us, I take it?' she asked as they got out.

'I was going to head back. I don't think I—'

'Don't be silly,' Anne said. 'You're here now. Come on.'

They walked into the relative warmth of the building, at one end of which a team of chefs stood guard over a vast array of cold meats, pies, hot soups and sizzling sausages. Guests were already assembling around a long table, laid with silver cutlery and cut glass. Anne was hailed by various people and left Rozie to her own devices. Henry wasn't there yet, but she noticed Matt Fisher and the Earl of Mayfield sitting next to Prince Philip at the far end. Bearing in mind what Sir Simon had said, Rozie joined them.

The conversation was something to do with new opportunities for farmers now they weren't going to be 'tied up in

Brussels red tape'. The Earl of Mayfield, fuelled by Bloody Marys and red wine, was holding court.

'Of course, if people like Ned St Cyr had their way, poor bastard, we wouldn't have farms at all. It would all be trees.'

'What?' Prince Philip asked.

'Didn't you know? He was trying to take his land straight back to the Middle Ages. I think he may actually have gone insane. It's this new fad that involves letting your grounds go to rack and ruin.' He speared a sausage with a furious fork. 'The idea is you let the place run wild. No mowing, no management. Makes the countryside look a bloody mess. There's a place doing it not far from us. They get *deer* in to manage the advancing forestation, if you can imagine that.'

'Ah, I see,' Philip said. 'He was *wilding*. I know a bit about that. Explains the deer. I had the impression Ned was setting up some kind of zoo.'

'You might as well call it that,' the earl said dismissively. 'They want half the country to be wooded over and wild animals left to roam it. They're supposed to look after themselves, summer and winter, without needing food or vets or accommodation. And somehow they don't breed themselves into starvation. Of course, the natural way – the medieval way – would be wolves. It honestly wouldn't surprise me if Ned intended to reintroduce those, too. And meanwhile, the land is turned to scrub.'

'I've been looking into the idea of wilding,' Philip mused. 'It has its merits – if done in the right places.'

'You don't really think so?' the earl asked, astonished.

'That so-called "scrub", as you put it, blackthorn and dog rose, is a haven for wildlife. Some extraordinary results have been achieved in Holland. Several species are coming back from the brink of extinction.'

'Norfolk is the breadbasket of England, for Christ's sake. You can't feed the nation on blackthorn and butterflies.'

'You can't feed a nation without pollinators,' Philip said. 'They absolutely thrive in these places. It's fascinating.'

'Ha! You sound like your son, sir,' the earl said with a smile.

Philip's gaze was cool. 'We have more in common than you may think.'

The earl caught a hint of steel in his voice and his florid face flushed further. 'No doubt,' he muttered, dropping the subject. They returned to the topic of Brexit. Rozie, who had more than enough of that in her day job, quietly left them to it.

The racing had just finished on Channel 4 when the shooting party got home, fresh-faced, tired and happy, eager for hot baths and tea. Philip found the Queen in the drawing room, soothing her throat with honey in hot water after an enjoyable afternoon shouting at the television set with her fellow racing aficionados. Having complained vigorously about the noisy Nerf gun battle raging along the corridors – which the Queen found rather unfair, in the circumstances – he was keen to update her on his day.

'Extraordinary end to the fourth drive. Cassidy, the new bean counter, is a liability. He shot for Oxford, which is why I agreed he could join us today. I was hoping to see a fine performance. But he only got one bird in four and he practically shot Helena Fisher, who was on the next peg.'

'What?'

'An idiotic misfire. The fool forgot to check if both barrels had fired before swinging his gun around prior to unloading.'

'Was anyone hurt?'

'No, but no thanks to Cassidy. You should have heard the beasting that Helena Fisher gave him. Vocabulary of a Royal Marine. Impressive. But that wasn't the most interesting thing. I discovered what Ned's been up to. He was on a mission to manage his land with the help of wild animals. It's known as *wilding*. I've been researching a bit about it recently.'

'Wilding?'

'According to the head keeper, it was the talk of the Fens in the summer,' Philip said. He explained how it worked, and the use of wild animals to keep encroaching vegetation at bay.

'I see.'

'Helena Fisher filled me in on the details. Ned, being Ned, was intoxicated by the whole thing. Instead of waiting and planning like any sensible person, he'd ordered the animals in by the truckload. Beaver, boar, those deer we saw . . . To absolutely no one's surprise, they got through his inadequate fencing in minutes, and they've been making his neighbours' lives a misery. The beavers flooded half of Matt Fisher's beet crop at Muncaster. There was an incident with wild boar, too, would you believe. They dug up every bit of lawn around the house. Left it looking like the Somme, two days before he was due to hold his daughter's eighteenth in the garden. He threatened to kill Ned to anyone who'd listen.'

'I'm sure he didn't mean it,' the Queen said.

'Really?'

'Nobody would kill their neighbour because of a few wild animals, Philip.'

'What do you mean? Show me a landowner whose fields have been turned to ponds by overactive beavers, and I'll show you a man bent on homicide.'

'In theory,' she agreed. 'But he wouldn't actually go through with it.'

'The trouble with you, Lilibet, is that you're too forgiving. You overestimate the human spirit.'

'The strength of the human spirit is what keeps me going.'

'Matt wasn't the only one, though. They were queueing up to criticise. Farmers don't want the land turned into forest.'

'You'd hardly kill someone for growing trees, either.'

'D'you think? They kill locals by the dozen for trying to stop 'em being chopped down in the Amazon. Happens every day. It's an international disgrace.'

How had they got from Abbottswood to the Amazon? the Queen wondered. When he was in this sort of mood, her conversations with her husband could be stretching.

'Mind you, it wouldn't be a farmer,' Philip went on. 'Too many other ways of disposing of the body parts. Take pigs, for example. Or a midden. Or a slurry pit. He wouldn't have needed to resort to plastic bags in the Wash.'

'Philip! I'd rather not have this conversation, and especially not just before dinner. Ned was such a charming little boy.'

'He bloody wasn't. He was a rascal. Anyway, it can't have been Fisher because he's been in Barbados since the beginning of December,' her husband concluded. 'Only got back the day before we arrived, and that was after the storm. Unless he ordered a hit while he was away and they brought the hand down to prove they'd done it and lost it somehow.'

'Philip! I mean it!'

Her page interrupted them to tell her that her APS was on the phone. She walked over to the old-fashioned instrument on a table near the door and picked up the receiver.

'Yes? What is it?' There was a long pause while she listened. 'Ah. That was quick. Are they sure? Thank you, Rozie.' Sad and somewhat disturbed, she put the phone down.

'News from the chief constable?' Philip asked.

'Yes. They've brought a man in for questioning who calls himself Jack Lions. He's Ned's son from his second marriage – the one with the nanny. Rozie will have more details in the morning.'

'So they've got him!' Philip looked mildly triumphant, as if their recent conversation hadn't happened. 'You see? I told you. It's always the family.'

Chapter 8

The arrest had been sudden and violent.

As always, a full raft of papers was delivered to Sandringham in the morning and laid out in the saloon for everyone to read. Several featured news of the arrest in a suburb west of London, accompanied by old photographs of a semi-shaven, surly, long-haired man, unmistakably a St Cyr by birth, with his tall, rangy frame and strawberry blond curls, dressed in dirty clothes and heavy boots, marching for climate change or posing with a spade in a shady allotment, looking as if he may have been planting tomatoes or burying something unspeakable in the dirt.

'Poor bastard,' Philip said, brandishing the *Telegraph* at the others over coffee after breakfast. 'Ned, I mean. Georgina must be turning in her grave.'

'Has he actually been charged?' Anne asked.

'Not yet. But according to this kiss-and-tell so-called friend—' Philip waved the paper again '—Lions was a magnet for trouble right back to his school days. Expelled for taking cannabis. Fell in with a crowd of drop-outs and eco-warriors. Hasn't held down a proper job for longer than a few weeks. Unless you count teaching drumming in a tent at music festivals, which, frankly, I don't.'

'Why did he do it?' the Queen wondered.

'According to this, he was mentally unbalanced. Psychotic episode, they're suggesting.'

'Don't those episodes happen quite suddenly?' she asked. 'I thought Ned had been invited to a meeting. It sounded rather organised.'

'Who knows? Perhaps the boy lost his temper. If he was on drugs, he might have been capable of anything.'

'Hmmm.'

'Anyway, the whole thing's done and dusted,' Philip said. 'I'm glad Bloomfield has it squared away. Good man.'

The group spent several minutes discussing what might have driven a blood relative to such an act of unspeakable violence. The Queen, who found it all extremely unsavoury, eventually had to put her foot down and insist that they refrain from discussing murder over coffee. She had a strong suspicion that everyone resumed the subject, though, as soon as she departed, coughing and aching, for the relative peace of her office overlooking the garden.

After two days off, which was as many as she ever took, it was back to the business of being Queen. However, her official paperwork was thin, as most Government officials were still on holiday. She had finished it and was surreptitiously catching up on a couple of stories in the *Racing Post* when Rozie arrived, skirting round the dogs' elaborate feeding stations in the office in order to reach her desk.

'The chief constable rang again just now, ma'am,' Rozie announced. 'He's offered to update you on the Lions arrest in person. He said he's going to be in the area in a couple of hours. He could drop by, if you like.'

The Queen pursed her lips. 'Oh, he could, could he? Hasn't he seen enough of Sandringham recently? I think we can spare him a second trip.'

Rozie nodded. 'Yes, ma'am. I'll get him to—'

'Wait.' The Queen relented. She still found it extraordinary to think that one of Georgina's grandsons could have killed her only child. It was heartbreaking, but she wanted to try and understand it. 'You might as well let him come. I wouldn't mind a word or two.'

'Certainly.'

'Oh, and, Rozie . . . do explain to him where to park this time.'

The Queen met Bloomfield in the Long Library, which sat behind the dining room and overlooked the ponds beyond the lawn. Its book-lined walls gave few clues that it had started life as a bowling alley. Her great-grandfather was not entirely serious when he was Prince of Wales. The Queen had to admit to herself, she would have rather liked a bowling alley. The books that replaced it had been chosen for the attractiveness of their gilded spines and she had yet to read most of them.

'Horrible business, ma'am,' the chief constable agreed. He was in uniform this time, perched on the edge of his chair, as lugubrious as ever. 'We're still getting to the bottom of it. Lions is as guilty as sin. You can tell he wants to talk, but he won't.'

'Have you charged him with his father's murder?' she asked.

'Not yet. We're working on it. Give the team twenty-four hours and I think we'll be ready. All very sad. I don't think he meant to do it. Now he's stuck with it for the rest of his life.'

'I see that he'd changed his name.'

'Ah! Well, that's a bit of a clue,' Bloomfield said. 'He was christened Orlando George Ellington Longbourn St Cyr, but he changed it by deed poll to Jack Lions ten years ago. His mother's maiden name. It was a mark of estrangement from his father. Of course, Edward St Cyr had done a similar thing himself, in a way.'

'He had,' the Queen agreed.

'Anyway, Lions wanted nothing to do with the whole St Cyr connection. When his schoolmates were going to university, he was living in a squat. The thing is, though, his mother became addicted to prescription drugs. Jack wrote to his dad in a fury several months ago because St Cyr refused to help with her latest rehab stint. Jack pointed out St Cyr is on the board of three anti-addiction charities. St Cyr wrote back saying if he needed cash, he could get a job on his rewilding project.'

'Did he?'

'After that, they spoke by phone. I doubt Lions wanted his opinions recorded. You ask for a parent's love, and they offer you outdoor labour at minimum wage.'

'How did you find him?' the Queen asked.

'He was always on our radar. For a man born with the proverbial silver spoon, he has quite a criminal record.

Taking vehicles without consent, possession of Class B drugs, affray . . . He started off as a hunt saboteur but he's been involved with increasingly extreme fringe elements on the animal rights front. But what clinched it was the RIP meeting in the diary.'

'Oh?'

'This is where we give thanks for the wonders of modern technology,' Bloomfield said proudly. 'A cross-check of the number plate recognition cameras showed that on the fifteenth, a van belonging to one of Lions's close associates was parked behind a building occupied by Rich Indie Productions in Soho. RIP. You see, ma'am?'

The Queen was quite capable of working out a three-letter acronym. Her life revolved around them, after all. 'Yes, Chief Constable. I do.'

Bloomfield noted a mild tone of irritation in her voice. 'Of course. Anyway, the owner of the van, a man called Simon Lefevre, did two years in jail for firearms offences. The next day it was caught on camera again, heading west out of London on the A4, with none other than Lions himself in the passenger seat.'

'I see.'

'That's why we had to make sure the arrest was done safely. We couldn't be sure Lions wasn't armed. We'd have arrested Lefevre, too, but he's disappeared, along with the van. We'll find him soon enough.'

The Queen accepted that this was very diligent deskwork by the vast team who were working on the case. She was fascinated by how it was attention to the small details, such as vehicle number plates of an associate – not even the main suspect – that enabled a breakthrough. The crime shows she watched on television usually involved brilliant sudden deductions, but the reports she read in her papers often featured almost impossible amounts of data, patiently filtered by unsung heroes at their desks. Even so, 'parking nearby' and 'driving west' didn't constitute conclusive proof of guilt in her view.

'Has Mr Lions admitted anything?' she asked.

'Not yet. But his alibi fell apart straightaway. He claimed to be at home all day with his girlfriend and their baby. His phone records supported it, but unfortunately for him, her mother put up several videos on Facebook of herself with her daughter and baby granddaughter at a pub in Nottingham. That's the thing about parents on social media – you can't trust them. I think it's only a matter of time before we get a full confession. As I say, Lions needs to talk, you can feel it. You know, I feel almost sorry for the lad. New partner, young baby . . .'

'And you think he did it in a sudden rage?'

'I doubt he intended violence, but something snapped and he lost it. If he had a knife on him, it's easy to do something you regret. Happens all the time.'

And then he had the presence of mind, the Queen thought, *to make sure his phone records did not betray him, before taking the body to Norfolk – for reasons unknown – and dismembering it. His own father.*

'I see,' she said sadly, though she didn't, really.

'Drugs,' Bloomfield said with sombre finality. 'He was worried about his mother, but he seems to be in denial about

86

his own addiction. He was almost certainly under the influence when he acted. I've seen it so many times. It's nice to think he'd get some help in prison, but he won't. Cutbacks. But that's politics, ma'am. That's for the home secretary, not me. Anyway, I mustn't keep you.'

After he'd gone, she reflected on what the men and women of the police forces must see, day in, day out, to make it easy for them to imagine a man dismembering a parent in the way he suggested Jack Lions had done, when she could not. Not at all. She also found it difficult to be pleased that they had got their man. An image of the new mother and her child refused to dislodge itself from her mind, especially at this time of year, when a newborn baby was very much the theme. All she could see was a wasted life and a missing father, and that was nothing to be glad about.

Chapter 9

The next couple of days between Christmas and New Year were busy ones for Mrs Maddox, as some guests left to visit family elsewhere and others arrived to take their place. Philip got steadily better. He spent time closeted in his own library with Charles, the estate manager and the newly hired bean counter, discussing the future of Sandringham, which would soon be under his son's control. Voices were raised and fists were thumped during the more dramatic moments. The Queen knew that Charles found the whole thing exhausting, but his father thrived on it.

Rozie stared at herself in the mirror of Henry Marshal-Ward's little wardrobe. The plain blue dress was from an upmarket retailer called Fold that her sister used for special occasions. The neck was high, the silhouette demure, and the skirt came down to her calves. Her shoes were modest ballet flats. She missed her normal uniform of pencil skirt and heels. This dress had the advantage of being quick to put on, though. At Sandringham, you had to learn the art of the rapid change.

'How do I look?' she asked.

Henry, who was busy doing up the buttons of his sexy dress uniform, glanced up to give her the once-over.

'Like a very expensive nun.'

She sighed. 'Is that a good thing?'

She was learning, once again, about the shifting tides at Sandringham. Normally there was a clear distinction between senior household staff and their royal bosses. It was old-fashioned and hierarchical and to start with it made Rozie feel uncomfortable, but it kept things simple. However, on days like today, when the Queen was throwing a small drinks party and there were too many guests for the family to entertain easily, it became a question of all hands on deck. Many of the junior royals had already left to visit other family and friends, so Rozie and Henry would be expected to make small talk with the guests who might otherwise feel left out. She hadn't felt this nervous in months.

'Just put on a high voice and say, "And what do you do?"' Henry suggested with a smirk. 'Tell them . . .' he did the voice again '. . . "I've just shagged Her Majesty's assistant equerry and he was very good in bed."'

She shot him a look.

'It's a Sandringham tradition,' he protested.

'What, shagging equerries?'

'Shagging people you can't keep your hands off. What do you think the guest lodges in the grounds were for?'

'Guests of the shoot?'

'Mistresses. Mistresses who could shoot were ideal.'

'I wonder what they think of me,' Rozie mused. 'At my lodgings, I mean. Constantly not turning up for breakfast.'

'I wouldn't worry about it. What happens at Sandringham stays at Sandringham. Are you ready?'

Rozie wondered what her mother would think, seeing her daughter on the arm of a Guards officer, ready to go and mix with royalty. Her grandfather had started out in Peckham, washing bodies in the mortuary. *His* daughter had got a nursing degree and was a respected community worker. Rozie had already turned down a proposal of marriage from a viscount, but he was incredibly drunk and said how much she reminded him of Grace Jones – which could be a compliment coming from some people, but felt pretty racist under the circumstances. Perhaps today she'd be sharing a sherry with a murderer. Sir Simon was right: you never knew what to expect in this job.

Today's pre-lunch drinks was one the Queen had been slightly dreading, not helped by the lingering effects of her cold. It was a chance to see friends and neighbours, but it was difficult to know what to say when one of these had recently lost his beloved wife and his estranged, dismembered cousin was in the news. The Queen wanted to show her support to Lord Mundy, but she was more of a doer than an orator, and she was never quite sure what to say.

Charles, much to his credit, had intuited something of the sort and offered to postpone his trip to Scotland for Hogmanay, so he could be at her side for their visit. He had been a big fan of Lee's, too.

'Are you sure you're up to this, Mummy?'

'Of course,' she told him, stoically.

She had wondered if the baron would come at all, and for much of the party there was no sign of him. Lee had always been the more social of the two, and it was possible he had decided to stay at home with his beloved sheep. And then she spotted him at the far side of the saloon, heading towards her, accompanied by his two children, who were in their forties, and a man about his son's age whom she didn't know.

Rozie had told the Queen about Hugh's frailness on the phone before Christmas. Even so, his appearance was quite shocking. He looked hollowed out by grief. His son Valentine towered over him, of similar build and looks, with the prominent St Cyr nose and piercing blue eyes, but still fit in middle age. He was nervously twisting the bloodstone signet ring on his little finger. Valentine saw the Queen looking and clasped his hands behind his back.

'It's so kind of you to invite us, Your Majesty,' his sister Flora said, curtseying unselfconsciously and bobbing up to flick a tendril of hair out of her eyes. 'Isn't it *dreadful* about Uncle Ned? And Mummy gone, too. I can't tell you what a nightmare Christmas was.' She grinned ruefully. 'Anyway, how are you?'

Something about her over-bright eyes suggested the pain behind her smooth civility. It was Flora who had the vim, the Queen sensed, just like her mother. She looked like her mother, too, beetle-browed, with rosy cheeks and a ready smile, her unruly brown hair flecked with grey. The Queen assured her she was very well, thank you, which was a lie, but the only possible reply in the circumstances. Philip grunted about feeling like death, which was more honest, but unhelpful.

'May I present Roland Peng,' Valentine said.

At which the attractive, beautifully attired man beside him bowed neatly and murmured, 'Your Majesty.' He seemed polite and un-starstruck, which made him promising company.

'Roland's staying with us for the weekend,' Flora explained.

'My business partner,' Valentine clarified.

'Another horticulturalist,' Flora added, smiling. 'Like Mummy.'

The Queen turned to the man in question. 'Oh, really? And what exactly is it that you do?'

'I grow plants without soil or daylight,' Mr Peng said with a smile and a raised eyebrow, as if anticipating surprise. 'At least, I invest in businesses that do.'

'Ah! Hydroponics!' The voice was Charles's, and the Queen glanced round to see him stepping in to join them. 'How fascinating. Where are you doing it? I gather they can grow salad in the desert. Are you having much success?'

'As a matter of fact, we are,' Peng said, his smile broadening at a fellow plant-lover. 'We have sites in Nevada and California. So far it's going very well.'

'And you do all this from Norfolk?'

'No,' Peng admitted. 'From London and Singapore. I have family there.' He turned to the Queen. 'My grandfather shares a passion with you, ma'am,' he told the Queen.

'Oh? Not salad in the desert, I take it.'

'Not at all. He's a fellow pigeon fancier. I know you keep a loft here. My grandfather has bought one of your star pigeons at auction, China Blue.'

'Did he? How wonderful. I remember China Blue. How is she getting on?'

'Very well. He's busy breeding champions from her.'

The Queen certainly *did* remember. After a stellar racing career, the prize pigeon surprised everyone by selling at auction for a six-figure sum. Pigeon prices were escalating at unheard-of rates. Roland Peng's grandfather clearly had expensive hobbies. It might explain his grandson's ease in the setting of Sandringham. They chatted briefly, but Roland had the good manners to notice that the Queen really wanted to talk to her friend, Hugh. He made his excuses and guided Valentine to the next group, where the Queen saw Rozie seamlessly engage them in conversation. She learned fast, that girl, the Queen noticed with satisfaction.

Lord Mundy, who had been silent up to now, shuffled forward to stand beside his daughter.

'I'm so sorry about Lee,' the Queen murmured, focusing her attention on him and taking the opportunity to say it in person at last. 'I wish I could have been at her memorial service. I gather it was very moving.'

The baron's eyes glazed with tears. 'It was. We filled the church with every flower from the garden. Every last one. We could hardly fit them in, could we, Flora?'

'No,' Flora said, without elaborating further. Her brittle brevity was eloquent enough. The Queen's heart went out to the girl.

'How difficult for you all.'

'Actually,' Hugh said, 'there were some silver linings, of a sort. Ned came to the funeral, which was very big of him.

93

The first time he'd seen us in a quarter of a century – the first time he'd spoken to me in person for longer than that. But he'd got in touch when Lee was very ill.'

'Did he? Sounds unlike him,' Philip said.

'I think he was softening as he grew older,' the baron suggested. 'And he had intimations of his own mortality. He was suddenly concerned that he might not be welcome in the family vault. But I assured him he was. Bygones, and so on. On the financial front, I'm afraid I was less forthcoming. He asked for help with his rewilding affairs, but I simply couldn't oblige.'

'Oh, goodness, no,' Flora chipped in. 'The hall's a money pit. We spend our whole lives trying to think of ways to keep it from falling down. Thank God for the gardens – the visitors provide most of our income in the summer. But we're going to have to give in and open up the interiors as well next season. I'm working on it now. It'll be all health and safety, green gloss and a cake shop.' She made a face of comic despair.

'Ah, yes,' the Queen said, thinking of her own visitors' centre down the drive. 'We know all about that.'

Flora's eyes widened with a flash of embarrassment that quickly passed. 'Of course you do, ma'am. We must come to you for advice. You do it so beautifully.'

'Flora's doing a magnificent job,' her father said. 'In fact, Lee and I talked about letting her inherit Ladybridge when the time comes.'

'Ned was horrified,' Flora said. 'You'd think he'd have been the first to approve. If *his* mother had been allowed to inherit, he'd be in charge now himself. Perhaps he wouldn't have gone off the rails so much.'

'That's rather what we thought.'

'He was awful to his children, so neglectful. Even so, to think what that man did!' she added furiously. 'His own son! I mean, can you *imagine*?'

No, the Queen couldn't.

'I can't stop thinking about it,' Flora went on. 'He must have been high on drugs or something. And we're actually related. It's quite terrifying, really. You do wonder if such things are genetic, don't you? You just can't help it. We saw Ned just before he disappeared and you'd think he had another twenty years in him.' She looked at the royal couple shrewdly. 'Or thirty.'

'You saw him recently?' the Queen asked.

'We met up a few times. We were just starting to mend fences. Not literally. Ned and broken fences seemed to be a bit of a theme lately. We had lunch the day before he vanished. The police were horribly suspicious. A couple of them came round, took one look at the armoury in the hall and asked us a thousand questions. They seem to think we might have grabbed a halberd from one of the walls, dashed up to London and—'

'Were you aware of the recent pigeon club scandal, ma'am?'

The Queen, who had become absorbed by this sudden talk of Ned's last known movements, was shocked to find Roland Peng standing in front of her again, leading her gently but firmly away from the others.

'No,' she said, somewhat annoyed. She could see what he was doing: deliberately trying to distract her from the upsetting thought of Ned's last hours. And she *was* upset, but right at that moment she was as gripped as anyone else.

Anyway, it was too late. Roland had her cornered now, and told her a long and involved story, told to him by his grandfather in Singapore, about drug gangs in the UK who bought their way into pigeon racing clubs so they could use the sale of prize pigeons for nefarious money-laundering purposes. Roland wondered if the practice had yet reached Norfolk. She assured him it hadn't. The fellow pigeon fanciers she encountered in East Anglia were some of the most straightforward people she knew. By the time she had reassured him not to worry, Hugh St Cyr was talking about the future of British farming in the wake of the loss of EU subsidies, and the conversation had moved on.

When the front door was shut behind them, Charles came to join his mother in the saloon. 'Well, that went better than I feared. Poor Hugh, though. He looked practically at death's door.' And, as if prompted by that thought: 'You're not too exhausted, are you, Mummy?'

'No, I can just about stand, thank you,' she told him drily. 'So tell me, what was Flora saying about Ned's visit? I was distracted by pigeons.'

'Nothing much. Only that they must have been some of the last people to see him alive. Papa asked point-blank if they had an alibi for the next day – I *think* he was joking – and Flora said she and her father spent several hours with the vicar, so unless he's in on it . . . Anyway, it doesn't matter, does it, because the police have their man, thank goodness.'

The Queen nodded. She still wasn't so sure.

Chapter 10

Her suspicions proved correct. When Rozie arrived in the office with the boxes the following morning, she announced that Jack Lions had been released. Perhaps 'parking nearby' had not been enough of a reason to detain him. Given his relationship to the victim, the Queen was relieved. She saw this as a positive development, although no doubt Bloomfield and his team would be disappointed.

However, as they were preparing to entertain their guests in the ballroom for New Year's Eve, Rozie updated the royal couple with some worrying information.

'Apparently Mr Lions has given the *Sunday Recorder* an exclusive interview, ma'am. It will be in the paper tomorrow. They wanted to let us know, because your name will be mentioned.'

'Mine? Why?' the Queen wondered.

'They wouldn't say. They were only informing us as a matter of courtesy.'

'Do you have any idea what it might be?'

Rozie had just had a short and difficult conversation with the chief constable, who in turn had just had a short and difficult conversation with his team at the major crimes unit HQ. Both were sorry. It was maddening that the Queen had been landed in it like this, with no warning at all.

'It turns out that Lions *did* have an alibi for the fifteenth,' Rozie explained.

'A good one?'

'Er, yes, ma'am. It was provided by a Met officer who was working undercover with a group of animal rights activists. He recognised Mr Lions from a news item about the arrest. It turned out he was at a meeting in North London all day, to coordinate a campaign against a couple of medical laboratories. The Met officer saw him there in person. CCTV footage confirmed it, and once they presented him with the evidence, he admitted it straightaway.'

'Why not say so before?' Prince Philip wondered. 'Surely planning to attack a laboratory is better than being accused of chopping up your own father?'

'Yes, sir,' Rozie agreed. 'They thought Lions seemed to be spinning out his detention deliberately. Apparently, he had a huge smile on his face when he made his admission. As if he had scored some sort of point.'

'What sort of point?'

Rozie shook her head. 'I asked, and they don't know.'

The Queen pursed her lips. 'Given what he was really doing, I think I have an inkling.'

She sighed and hoped it wouldn't be as bad as she thought.

It was worse.

INNOCENT MAN HELD FOR SANDRINGHAM MURDER

HEAVY POLICE TACTICS TO PROTECT QUEEN'S CHRISTMAS

JACK LIONS – HOW I WAS SNATCHED TO SPARE HM'S BLUSHES – FULL INTERVIEW INSIDE

Nobody dared read the tabloid in question too ostentatiously in the morning, but surreptitiously, it was snatched up and perused by everyone in the house.

'The bastard!' Philip said, the first to voice his opinion. 'The absolute bastard.'

'It had nothing to do with you!' Sophie Wessex complained to the Queen, affronted on her behalf.

'Those pictures of Bloomfield arriving at Sandringham on Christmas Eve . . .' Anne pointed out tersely. 'Not ideal.'

'They like to give the impression that we orchestrated the whole thing!' Philip exploded. 'Or at the very least that the police are our toadies, rushing around to save our reputations as if the country is some sort of tinpot dictatorship. All we ever do is cut bloody ribbons at their bloody police stations. And give them medals for saving the public's bloody lives. *Bastard*,' he muttered again.

The Queen was the last to see the paper, having over-exerted herself the night before, and spent the morning incapacitated by the remnants of the flu. At ninety, her body occasionally reminded her that she needed to take care of it.

The paper didn't help. The extensive exclusive interview with Jack Lions was splashed across pages four, five and six, accompanied by several photographs of Sandringham House, herself at a window (taken about ten years ago in Scotland), as if she was spying on events through a curtain, the chief constable arriving at Sandringham in his Subaru, and an alarming image of several officers of the Met Police in full body armour, as if dozens of them had been dispatched to drag Mr Lions into the street.

It was the day after my first Christmas with my girlfriend and little baby girl, who was born six weeks ago. The birth was horrendous and Alana was still recovering. We were just starting to put all that trauma behind us when there was a battering at the door and the next thing we knew, the room was full of police shouting and my tiny little girl was screaming. I was picked up by a draconian squad of officers who bundled me into a van . . .

. . . They got me in a cell and you could see they didn't have anything on me. They just needed somebody, fast, that they could pin the blame on because my dad's severed hand was found on the Queen's sporting estate . . .

But it wasn't! she thought. However, that was beside the point.

. . . No question of letting me grieve for my father, who I'd just discovered had been kidnapped and dismembered. In fact, he'd told me about a new project to save the countryside that we were going to work on together. We'd been talking about it for weeks. My father had seen the light about his duty to the planet. We had reconnected. My life was going to turn around and now it was shattered. The police didn't care. They spent endless hours questioning, trying to break me, so I could be the scapegoat and they could look good in front of a very rich old lady whose family has been responsible for the deaths of millions of innocent animals for the last thousand years. In fact, they hustled me out of my flat the very same day the Queen and her family were blasting hundreds of pheasants out of the sky at Sandringham . . .

And there it was: the reason for the failure to produce an alibi earlier, the waiting, the triumphant smile on his release. Vandalising a laboratory was small beer in the mind of an animal rights activist compared with dragging the royal family themselves into the debate. The next four paragraphs were about previous kings and their love of hunting, coupled with images of various family members on a stag hunt near Balmoral and King Edward VII shooting a tiger from the back of an elephant. In Mr Lions's circles, he would be a hero.

Back in the saloon, everyone was nervously waiting for her reaction, which was silent, but dour.

'It's outrageous,' Edward said. 'What are we going to do about it?'

But they all knew the answer: never complain, never explain. However difficult, frustrating and infuriating that could be.

'Should we call Sir Simon?' someone asked.

'No,' the Queen said decisively. 'Rozie can deal with it. She knows the form.'

'This won't be the end of it,' Anne muttered.

The Queen agreed. Cold-ridden and otherwise occupied, she had hoped she could avoid involvement with this case. Now, the press had placed her at the heart of it, whether she liked it or not.

PART 2
A RACING CERTAINTY

Chapter 11

Sir Simon Holcroft lay wide awake in his bed in London, after a long and complicated journey down from The Highlands. The private secretary had left his wife Sarah in the charming Balmoral cottage to finish their holiday alone. The Queen needed him at Sandringham, that was obvious. She hadn't actually contacted him to say as much, but everything was clearly falling apart in his absence. Body parts in the mud . . . newspaper interviews . . . the Queen's absence at church on Christmas Day. The winter visit was Not Going As Intended. It was New Year's Day and he itched to be back at his desk, on the phone to the people that mattered, sorting everything out for the Boss and showing Rozie how it was done.

He had already had a long conversation over the phone with the chief constable of Norfolk, during which Sir Simon had made his displeasure quite clear. Ditto with the editor of the *Recorder*. The palace had always had a tricky relationship with the newspaper: one minute they were rhapsodising over the colour of the Duchess of Cambridge's latest dress, and the next they were running an exposé on palace expenses and rumours about ructions among the staff.

The newspaper interview with Jack Lions had been particularly difficult. Especially with its picture of the chief constable himself visiting Sandringham on Christmas Eve. Someone should have stopped that from happening. It made it look as if the police were in the palace's pocket, which they most certainly were not. Although, admittedly, the chief constable had been very helpful on the phone.

But more than that, Sir Simon longed to be useful in the matter of the missing person. When it came to the matter of crime in the Queen's vicinity, he had recently proved that he had a talent for rooting out perpetrators. He wasn't sure what it was – perhaps a skill he had unwittingly picked up in the navy or the Foreign Office. Her Majesty must be feeling particularly vulnerable at this time. He wanted to be there to protect her. It was really quite a surprise, actually, that she *hadn't* asked him to cut his holiday short. Even so, he pictured her relief when he finally got to Norfolk.

On Monday, 2nd January, another article appeared in the *Recorder*.

THE DISAPPEARING QUEEN

For the second Sunday in a row, Her Majesty was missing from the usual royal line-up at St Mary Magdalene Church at Sandringham. This is unprecedented for the elderly monarch, who hasn't missed a service in decades. Royal sources say she has a bad cold, but rumours have it that she is upset by the violent death of family friend Ned St Cyr, whose dismembered hand was found within walking distance of the Sandringham Estate. Locals are concerned for the Queen's health, but say the plucky monarch will 'get through this somehow' with her usual Dunkirk spirit.

'What fresh hell?' Philip asked, scrumpling up the page in question and chucking it in the direction of the fire. 'What "locals" are concerned for your health? Who in God's name calls you "plucky"?'

The Queen was too irritated to reply. She decided to take her mind off it by visiting the horses in the stud.

Drawing up outside the mare barn in her favourite Land Rover, she found the immaculate yard empty. It had been a last-minute decision to come, and no one walked over to greet her. She didn't mind – in fact she was rather relieved. She didn't quite have the energy yet for a discussion of every mare's and foal's progress with the manager: she just wanted to greet some old equine friends, hand out some festive mints and get back to the warm.

Leaving her protection officer at the car and walking across the frosted cobbles, she paused by the tack room to catch her breath, cough, and curse the flu for making her feel so light-headed. A glossy, coal-black cocker spaniel puppy looked up at her. He was sitting alone, waiting for his owner. The Queen was impressed by how well behaved he was, and bent down to stroke his eager head. Through a gap in the tack room window, she could hear a female voice was talking about parasites. She idly wondered if they were discussing equine diseases. When it came to horses, she was always keen to learn.

'Shhh, you can't say that!' a male voice was saying.

It was the 'shhh' that caught the Queen's attention. She stopped and listened properly.

'But that's what I'm *saying*.' It was a girl's voice, soft and melodious, but loud enough to carry. 'They feed off us. We pay for them, and they get to live in their fancy houses and race their horses, and own all the shit in the world. And we just let them. It blows my mind.'

Oh. That kind of parasite. Honestly!

'He's, what, nearly a hundred. She's just as bad. They're practically nineteenth-century.'

'*Shhh*. Stop it! They aren't!'

No they aren't, the Queen thought crossly. *We're as twentieth-century as you can get*. She had lived through three-quarters of it, before cantering through a decade and a half of the new millennium. Young people needed to learn more history.

'Well, they are. I mean, I bet I could run this estate as well as she does,' the girl went on. (*I bet she couldn't*, the Queen thought.) 'Better. I wouldn't kill half the bird life, for a start.'

'Yer talking squit,' the boy said.

'*You*'re talking squit. All you see is the bling and the nice little job, but think about it. They won the lottery when they were born. And we bow and scrape to them like they earned it just because their ancestors killed a bunch of people in the Middle Ages. It's like, we give all the rich people all the stuff

– the influencers, the billionaires, the celebs, the royals, whatever – we let them take everything and we effing *admire* them
for it. We give them our attention. It's like "You've got more
than me so you're better than me. What else can I give you?"'

'Shut *up*, will yer?' the boy's voice growled, taut with
urgency. The Queen recognised it as that of Arthur Raspberry,
a local lad from the estate who they had taken on as a groom
last summer. 'They pay our wages.'

'Not mine,' the girl said.

'You don't work, remember? Mum's and Dad's and mine.'

'Only because they own effing everything. If they just
minded their own business, Mum and Dad could work for
themselves. And I can guarantee you Dad wouldn't be fat-
tening birds for them and their fancy guests to kill for the
sake of it.'

'Everything gets eaten,' Arthur said.

'Like that makes it better,' the girl scoffed. 'It's not just
the pheasant that get killed, it's the predators that take the
chicks. It's a wonder anything survives.'

'They love animals, and you know it.'

'Yeah, stuffed in a pie or stuck on the walls.'

'I hope I'm not interrupting.'

This last voice was the Queen's. She had walked round
and was now standing at the door to the tack room. Two
pale young faces stared out at her, with identical hazel eyes
framed by long blond lashes, startled and horrified.

'You have a very well-behaved puppy,' the Queen
observed. One might as well start on a polite note, and it
was the only one she could think of.

The girl, who wore a rainbow fleece over sky-blue leggings that matched her hair, slithered down from the high shelf where she'd been sitting. When she reached the ground, she blinked, and said, 'He's my auntie's. I'm looking after him. His name's Nelson.'

'Your Majesty,' Arthur prompted her under his breath.

'Your Majesty.' The girl's expression very much said, *And you know how I feel about that.*

'I came to see Estimate,' the Queen explained. 'Don't worry, I know where to go.'

If anything, young Arthur's face paled further. He stood rigidly to attention. 'I'll come with you, ma'am. I mean . . . I don't need to be here. We were just . . .'

'Talking politics,' the Queen put in for him. 'I must say, I wasn't sure your generation did that anymore. It's quite reassuring. In a way.'

The girl continued to stare. Then, as if she'd suddenly remembered, she stuck one boot-clad foot out behind her and bobbed into an inelegant curtsey. Aware of the absurdity of it all, she suddenly grinned.

'Awkward,' she muttered. Her eyes gleamed with a defiant naughtiness that reminded the Queen very much of her sister Margaret at that age – or indeed any age. It was always difficult to remain cross with Margaret when she herself was smiling and sunny. The Queen wondered if this girl had a similar effect on her long-suffering family.

At Estimate's stall, the retired racing champion was grateful for a Polo mint. The Queen spent a little while congratulating her on her new life as a mother. But she hadn't

forgotten the recent exposition of her own family's iniqui-
ties. The young groom hung back wretchedly. She felt sorry
for him.

'Was that your sister?' she asked.

He hung his head. 'Yes, ma'am. Her name's Ivy.'

'I see. I thought you looked alike. What a spirited girl.'

'Yeah, kind of. Did you hear much of what she was on
about?'

'I think I got the gist of it,' the Queen told him. 'She's not
a royalist, I take it.'

'Not as such.' Arthur twisted his limbs in paroxysms of
embarrassment. 'She dun't mean it. I mean, she does, but she's
seventeen. She's like that about everything, ma'am, a bit over
the top. It gets her into trouble. It's why she hangs around with
the horses even though she's not supposed to. But she's so good
with them, it's like . . . it's like telepathy or something. And it's
the only thing that de-stresses her. She's been kind of wound
up since our auntie's accident. And then she found that hand.'

The Queen stared at him. 'It was your sister who found it?'

'Yes. On the beach. She thought it was a starfish or something but . . .'

'Poor girl. What a shock.'

He winced at the memory. 'Yeah, it was. She was pretty
freaked out all day. She locked herself in her room for hours.
She would've gone to our auntie's, but she can't.' He looked
hopeless and frustrated. The absence of the aunt was obviously causing problems.

'Did you say your aunt had an accident?' the Queen
asked gently.

111

'Yeah. Her name's Judy, ma'am. Judy Raspberry. She's the treasurer at the Women's Institute. You've met her a few times.'

The Queen's annual trip to the WI in West Newton, a nearby village on the estate, was one of the highlights of each winter visit. 'Yes, of course I know Mrs Raspberry. What happened?'

The groom ran a distracted hand through his hair.

'Hit-and-run, the week before Christmas. It happened in Dersingham, where she lives. She was lying in the road for ages before someone found her.'

'How bad was it?' the Queen asked anxiously. She was very fond of Judy Raspberry, who was one of the lynch-pins of the WI and much else besides. They had tasted many a Victoria sponge together, watched many a dog show, remarked on the beauty of many a flower arrangement. She was a talented pigeon breeder and her birds had beaten the Queen's in a couple of races.

'Very bad,' Arthur said dully. 'She's in a coma, at the Queen Elizabeth.'

The local hospital was named after the Queen's mother. One became used to being buildings and ships eventually.

'Oh, I'm so sorry.'

'Ivy took it harder than me,' Arthur went on. 'She never really liked it at home. Mum kept going on at her about school until she went half mad with it. But Auntie Judy got it. She was somewhere Ivy could go, you know? And now it's all gone to shi—Gone bad, ma'am.'

'It must be a huge worry for you all.'

112

He shrugged. 'Coming here helps. Like I say, it calms me. Ivy, too. Thanks for not minding. So she can stay? Keep coming over, I mean?'

'Yes. If she can pull her weight here, as you say.'

'No question, ma'am. She's got a gift with animals. Horses and dogs especially.'

'Then this is where she should be.'

The Queen thought about Judy Raspberry all the way back to the house. A coma! The poor woman! Lying alone in the road until she was discovered. Was she still conscious at that point? And two young people who clearly needed her help. Judy was a woman in her fifties: at that age when everybody needs you – parents, children, workmates, pets . . . At WI meetings, she was always the person everyone turned to if the lights failed or the guest speaker was late or somebody went off with the key to the loo. Her stories about it afterwards were a riot. How would they cope without her? And what about Arthur, and his forthright little sister? It was the deepest fear of many women, the Queen knew: not being there for the people who needed them. She understood it well.

'Feeling better?' Philip asked when she got back.

'Up to a point.' She told him about Mrs Raspberry and then, to lighten the tone a bit, about Ivy in the tack room.

'Good God! On our own estate! We should have her horsewhipped.'

'I told her brother she can help out with the horses. I think it will do her good. She was the one who found the hand, by the way.'

'Ah! So we have her to thank for all of this,' Philip grunted.

The Queen pursed her lips. 'If you mean for alerting the police to what happened to Ned, then yes. Otherwise, we might never have known.'

'I mean for making us suddenly wonder if all our friends and neighbours are stone-cold killers.'

'I never did,' the Queen assured him.

'I still do,' he muttered. 'And by the way, Simon's back. He wanted to surprise you. And by the look on your face, he did. Ha!'

Chapter 12

Her private secretary had put on weight in Scotland, as he usually did. Joining her in her study fifteen minutes later, he looked well fed to the point of rotundness. Were those jowls, emerging gently from under his naval-officer jaw? *Age comes to all of us eventually*, the Queen thought. *Just you wait.*

'I hope you had a pleasant holiday?' she asked.

'Magnificent, Your Majesty. Just what the doctor ordered. Thank you very much.'

'And yet you're here so soon?'

He straightened somewhat, perhaps catching the glint of steel behind her question, and blustered something about how good it was to be back in the saddle, which was an odd phrase to use for one of the few members of her Private Office who didn't ride.

'I'm sorry I wasn't around to help you when the unfortunate hand was found.'

'I seem to recall that you were, remotely,' the Queen said, with the same edge to her voice.

Sir Simon missed the edge. 'Talking to the chief constable, you mean, ma'am? It wasn't a problem, I assure you.'

The Queen explained to him that it was, rather, and he was slightly chastened. However, he soon perked up when he explained he'd been catching up with Bloomfield again this morning.

'There was a packet of drugs missing from the bag on the beach, ma'am, judging from the way it was packed. His officers are making enquiries about what happened to it. But if anyone offers you cheap cocaine, you'll know where it came from.'

'Very funny, Simon.'

He straightened his face. 'And there's an update on where the plastic bag went in the water. The currents and tides in the Wash are a complicated study. I won't bother you with—'

'No, do,' the Queen said. 'I'm interested.'

He seemed surprised. 'Certainly. Well, if I've understood it correctly, then generally, there's a tidal drift on this coast that runs from north to south, but among the swirling waters of the bay, on our little stretch of the Wash it ends up running south to north. The forensic team modelling suggests the bag's likely to have been deposited in the Great Ouse near King's Lynn, a couple of days before the storm. That would make it some time between the nineteenth and twenty-first of December, four to six days after Mr St Cyr disappeared. The hand was in good condition before it went into the water, so the question is, where it – and he – was during those four to six days.'

'I see. Do they have any thoughts?'

'It looks as though it might have been in cold storage. It makes it harder to work out at which point it was detached.

116

And that still leaves the question of why. Bloomfield is edging towards thinking that it might be a professional job after all. They have several lines of enquiry. Mr St Cyr had a certain amount of debt, for example; he liked to gamble.'

'I remember,' the Queen said. 'He played cards for money here sometimes. He was very good at it. We had a roulette table once and he was glued to it all night.'

'There's a team looking into his finances. No obvious communication yet regarding large wagers that might have got him into hot water. No sign of unusual withdrawals from his bank accounts. Or at least, there were many, but lately they were almost exclusively for things like electric fencing and wild ponies. I can find out what that was all about if you—'

'I know what it was,' the Queen told him. 'Rewilding.'

'Re . . .?'

'Look it up, Simon. It's been the talk of north Norfolk. The duke thinks it's the next big thing.'

'I will, ma'am. "Rewilding".' He made a note. 'Meanwhile, they're searching Abbottswood itself for the body, in case the trip to London was some sort of double bluff. Then they'll move on to Mr Fisher's estate at Muncaster.'

The Queen's eye roll did not escape her private secretary.

'He did threaten to kill Mr St Cyr more than once, in front of witnesses,' he reminded her.

'Yes, but honestly, Simon. Mr St Cyr had that effect on some people. He wasn't the easiest neighbour.'

'Well, quite.'

The Queen sighed. 'Anyway, I gather that Mr Fisher wasn't in the country on the fifteenth.'

'No, he wasn't, ma'am – but then, nor is he the kind of person, I think the reasoning goes, to do his own dirty work, so to speak. Which becomes rather difficult for us.'

'Oh?'

'The last person Mr St Cyr called before he left for London was Julian Cassidy.'

'Mr Cassidy? Our new conservation manager? The bean counter?'

'Yes, ma'am. As you know, he was working for Mr Fisher until November. I understand there were various disputes about the land. Mr Cassidy was seen scuffling with Mr St Cyr in the car park of the Horse and Hound in Castle Rising in early December. Mr St Cyr didn't press charges, but there were several witnesses.'

'Oh, dear.' The Queen sighed. 'How unfortunate. Do we know why?'

'Not really. He claims it was a parking dispute.'

'But the police think Mr Cassidy might have killed Ned on Matt Fisher's behalf, even though he stopped working for him several weeks before. I must say, Simon, that sounds incredibly unlikely.'

'They don't know what to make of it at the moment, ma'am. He doesn't have an alibi for the fifteenth, unlike Mr Fisher. He did try to punch Mr St Cyr. But it seemed out of character.'

'That's a relief. We're not aware of other violent incidents, are we? Is this something we need to worry about?'

'Not as far as we know. I've had a quick chat to the estate manager. Cassidy's references were immaculate, and in the way of these things, the staff know several people who've

118

known him for years, back to his days as a biology student at Oxford. He was known for rescuing injured birds and hedgehogs and so on.'

'Really?'

'Yes. There was quite a female following who thought of him as a bit of a St Francis of Assisi. They may not have known that he went shooting at weekends. He has a reputation for being laid-back, if anything.'

The Queen tried to picture the bean counter storming down to London from Sandringham with murderous intent . . . But of course, it wouldn't have been 'storming': Ned was lured there, it seemed. It would have been planned. That was even harder to imagine. One didn't want to harbour a cold-blooded murderer on one's estate, but she really didn't think she was.

Sir Simon was followed shortly afterwards by Mrs Maddox, who was armed with the week's suggested menus for approval. The housekeeper saw the Queen's dark expression and asked if she could help.

'Not really,' the Queen admitted. 'It's been an interesting morning. Actually, there's one thing. Do you know how Mrs Raspberry from the WI is getting on? I gather she's had an accident.'

Mrs Maddox was north Norfolk born and bred, and thought it a personal affront if she didn't know what was going on in any village within a twenty-mile radius.

'Oh, that! It was awful! We did wonder whether to tell you, ma'am, but we didn't want to worry you so close to Christmas, with you so busy in London, and then with your cold. It was very upsetting. She was tossed into the air like a rag doll. Not that anyone saw it directly, but she must have been, the way she landed in that bush. My niece works at the ICU at the Queen Elizabeth. She got the shock of her life when they brought Judy in. All over knocks and bruises and a gash on her head . . . How anyone could drive away from that . . .? It's wicked. May he rot.'

'I spoke to her nephew at the stud,' the Queen said. 'His sister seems to rely on her.'

'I'm not surprised. Judy's wonderful with the teenagers. Not just her own, who've left home now, but all of them in the villages round here. Setting up clubs, you know, getting them holiday jobs, like with the Fen-Time festival, when it was running. Anything to keep them out of trouble. She sponsors a *lovely* refugee family from Syria. She spent months fundraising to make sure they had everything they needed. And I don't know what the parish council would do without her.'

'Is there a Mr Raspberry?' the Queen wondered.

'There *was*. He sold wood-burning stoves in Burnham Market. Ran off with a woman from Blackheath.' Mrs Maddox sniffed. Her look of disdain suggested she thought as little of south-east London as she did of men who ran off with the women who lived there. 'Judy was too good for him. Any man would be lucky to have her, *if* she had time for him.' The housekeeper stopped short and blinked away tears. 'Anyway, thank you for the menus, ma'am. I'll let chef know.'

The Queen got up and stood at the window, brooding. What a winter this was. Two people injured – one of them almost certainly dead – and it struck her how both of them had been described as particularly alive. Philip had said it about

Ned, and Mrs Maddox had said something similar about Mrs Raspberry. They shared a certain bloody-mindedness, which she rather admired, an antipathy to drugs and a willingness to get stuck in. They knew each other through Ned's festival. She wondered idly if they were friends.

She returned to the memorandum from the Cabinet secretary on her desk but her mind went back to Judy. At the last WI meeting, they had discussed an article Judy was writing for the *Flying Post* about Norfolk's pigeons in the war. They had played a critical role delivering messages to and from the Front for the Signal Corps. The birds were decorated for their bravery: no fewer than thirty-two had won the Dickin Medal. Several had undoubtedly saved lives. Judy's knowledge and curiosity on the subject was impressive. Even though it was a part-time interest for her, she had a journalist's instinct for getting to the heart of a story. Another string to her bow.

The Queen caught sight of the mug that little Prince George had given her for Christmas. *I may look like I'm listening to you, but in my head, I'm thinking about pigeons.* Who else had she been talking to about them recently?

Then she remembered. Gradually, her curiosity turned to a prickling sense of dread. It wasn't a suspicion, exactly. Just a twitch. A worry. A series of connections.

She reached for the telephone on her desk, which sat beside a picture of a small man in a white coat, standing in front of a table of silver cups he had won for her with champion birds. The operator asked where to direct the call.

'I'd like to talk to my loft manager,' she said.

Chapter 13

The job of royal loft manager came with a house near the abandoned railway station at Wolferton and a pigeon loft in the garden for two hundred birds. The loft itself had recently been refurbished with ventilated roofing, nesting boxes and perches, and awnings under which they could sunbathe in the summer. In pigeon terms, it was as lavish as Sandringham. The man who got to manage such lavishness was a friendly Lancastrian called Stephen Day, whose cheerfulness belied a cut-throat competitive spirit that made him an excellent choice for the job.

After a minute or two, his warm, Christmas pudding of a voice came reassuringly down the line.

'Happy New Year, Your Majesty. And what can I do for you?'

'I wondered if you might know anything about money laundering, Mr Day.'

'Ha! You're talking to the wrong person, ma'am. I can just about manage online banking. Is that any help?'

'Money laundering through pigeon clubs. Someone was talking to me about it at New Year. From what I can remember, there are gangs that buy into the clubs so they can sell

122

prize birds at below their value and record a higher price in the accounts. I think that's it, anyway.'

'Why would they do that, ma'am?'

'So that any illicit money could disappear in the difference between the two. I assumed at first that you wouldn't be able to hide much money that way, but then I realised how much auction prices have rocketed recently. I found it rather alarming. So you aren't aware of anything like that happening round here?'

'I had no idea you were such an expert on crime, ma'am. It's news to me. I can't see that happening in East Anglia.'

'That's what I thought, too, to start with.'

'I can ask around, though, if you'd like.'

'If you wouldn't mind.'

'I'll tell you who'd know, mind you,' Mr Day reflected, 'except she's not around at the moment – and that's Mrs Raspberry. She talked to a lot of people for that article she did for the *Flying Post*. If something odd was going on, she'd know.'

The Queen's heart sank. This had been her suspicion, too, or part of it.

'I heard about her accident,' she said.

'Horrible, isn't it? He just drove right off and left her, whoever he was. There's quite a few round here would like to get their hands on him.'

'Was she researching anything in particular, do you know?'

'Ah! I know what you're thinking. Was she doing anything that might have caused the hit-and-run?'

This was exactly what the Queen had been thinking, but before she could resolutely deny it, Mr Day continued, 'We had the same idea, my wife and me. Judy said she was working on a new piece, based on something she'd seen at the beach. Not to do with money laundering, I don't think, but it might have been to do with drugs. She was very exercised about them.'

'Did she try and tell the police?'

'Ah, therein lies a tale, ma'am,' he added. 'Not a very happy one.'

'Oh?'

'We don't know. We were wondering about it all over Christmas – what if she'd got into hot water and the hit-and-run wasn't an accident? My wife was very worried, so she rang the police to ask if Judy had said anything to them, and the desk sergeant told her not to worry, they were on to it.'

'Oh, good.'

'Ah, but . . . So, my wife has a friend from her yoga class whose son works at the police HQ in Norwich, and she's a *bit* of a gossip, if you don't mind me saying so . . .'

'Ah.' The Queen tried to sound both disapproving and encouraging of gossip in all its forms.

'*She* said her son told her they were saying at the HQ that Judy was one of those silly women always trying to give the police information and expecting them to jump to it, but the accident was clearly just that, an accident, because of where it happened in the bend in the road. It wasn't something you could engineer, they thought. They were just annoyed anyone thought they weren't doing their job.'

'How very unfortunate.'

'It was a bit. They don't realise that people talk to each other, that's the problem, ma'am.'

'It is indeed. Mrs Day must have been upset.'

'She was furious. That's the last time she tries to help.' He moved on. 'But don't worry, as I say, I'll ask around and find out for you about this gang business. Birds sold on the cheap, you say? Sold on the "cheep"! I think there's a Christmas cracker joke in there somewhere. As soon as I hear any more I'll let you know.'

'Thank you, Mr Day. That's very kind.'

'Will you be coming over soon, ma'am, to visit the loft? You wouldn't believe it, but my wife's invested in a still and is making some rather impressive gin. We'd love to offer you a jigger or two to try, if you're amenable.'

'You have a very inventive family,' she said, impressed as always by the industry and ingenuity of her tenants.

The Queen put the phone down and gazed out of the window again. Then she picked it up one more time and asked the operator to put her through to Rozie.

Rozie had been in the middle of some paperwork, but she was pleased to get the call. In London there was always something to grab her attention but here, in the depths of the country, and with Sir Simon now taking all the interesting phone calls, she had never felt so far away from the centre of the action. From her mother's chatty texts about excursions with friends to West End theatres and Soho restaurants, to friends' Instagram images of pools and ski slopes on far-flung holidays, she had the feeling the world was somehow carrying on without her. Norfolk had its attractions, but an open field, however beautifully lit by the rays of a setting sun, was never going to beat a poolside bar in St Barts.

'I think I might have a little job for you,' the Queen said, when Rozie arrived at her study.

Rozie positively grinned. 'Of course, ma'am. What can I do?'

The Queen outlined her concerns, and the recent conversation with Mr Day.

'I'd like you to look into it for me. Privately.'

Rozie thought she detected a certain glint in the Boss's eye that she hadn't seen since they'd left London.

'With pleasure, ma'am.'

'And I think I know someone who might help.'

Chapter 14

That afternoon, Rozie closed her laptop and told Sir Simon that she was going out for a run. This wasn't unusual: she worked hard to maintain her levels of fitness from her army days. Today, she covered the mile or so from the gates of Sandringham to the village of Dersingham, down the long alley of copper beeches and along the verges and paths beside the road. It was dusk and there wasn't much traffic aside from the odd red double-decker bus – which came as a surprise to Rozie, so far from London – and a couple of mud-splashed four-wheel drives. Given the reason for her visit, she was very careful to stand right back as they passed by.

She noticed, as she passed, how the mathematical neatness of the grass and hedges of the estate gradually gave way to the rougher walls and lumpier fields of the village. She hadn't realised how quickly she had become used to the standards of the Sandringham groundsmen. The estate had a film set quality to it: everything always tidy and in its place.

Beyond its boundaries, the winter gloaming cast a grey pall over the paddocks and the church. Rozie passed the Feathers pub, named after the three-feathered badge of the

Prince of Wales, and a few buildings further along she came to the little knapped flint cottage the Queen had asked her to visit. The light peeping through its windows cast a friendly glow. She waited for a while, listening to the sound of a dog enthusiastically barking, until eventually the door was opened.

'Hello!' the occupant said.

'Hello, Katie.' Rozie grinned.

The other woman's cropped auburn hair framed a wide, freckled face and clear, clever eyes behind stylish glasses. She was a few years older than Rozie and dressed for leisure in yoga pants and a red jumper featuring white sheep that looked like something Princess Diana might have worn. The dog leaping up behind her was a young dachshund, glossy and keen.

'So it's happened,' she said, standing aside to let Rozie in.

'Yeah.' Rozie nodded and walked inside.

The last time they met, Katie had been handing over the role of assistant private secretary to Rozie. After that, she had dropped off the radar. This was unusual for the Royal household, where people tended to stay in touch unless there had been some sort of scandal. There had been mutterings about Katie 'dropping the ball' among some members of the household, but nothing major. According to Sir Simon she had had 'a few mental health problems', but he hadn't gone into detail and Rozie had had too many other things going on to pay much attention. Until this morning, when the Boss had mentioned her out of the blue.

You can trust Katie, she had said, with a sharp look from behind the bifocals that Rozie had learned to interpret. It meant, *You can trust Katie with secrets, and specifically what I'm about to tell you.* Rozie dealt in secrets all the time and most of them could also be shared with Sir Simon. A small number could not. The look behind the bifocals this morning suggested that what the Queen then told her was among the latter type.

'So, Boss thinks the killer's in Dersingham?'

'She thinks they *might* be,' Rozie said.

By now they were standing in the cottage's little kitchen. Katie was pouring boiling water onto a fragrant selection of oriental leaves in a glass teapot while Rozie finished outlining the Queen's concerns. It was Katie's predecessor, Aileen Jaggard, who had initiated Rozie into the secret club that all APSs, past and present, belonged to. It transpired that they were the only people the Queen trusted to help her with her little sideline in 'problem-solving', as she liked to put it – or successfully investigating crimes, as Rozie had subsequently discovered.

'And it's to do with pigeons?'

'Or drugs, or both,' Rozie said. 'She's keeping all options open at the moment. It may be nothing.'

'It's not usually nothing,' Katie muttered.

'Did you help her a lot?' Rozie asked. 'This way, I mean.'

Katie reached into a cupboard and took a couple of delicate, handmade porcelain teacups from a shelf, arranging them carefully on the tray beside the pot. 'Once or twice,' she acknowledged. 'But never murder. How about you?'

'A couple of times last year. Not that you'd know the Boss did anything. One man got knighted. Another got a medal. She likes to keep a low profile, doesn't she?'

Katie grinned. 'It's like Bletchley Park in the war. Or the first rule of Fight Club. Have you met the others yet?'

Rozie shook her head. 'The other APSs, you mean? Only Aileen.'

'I met them all at a get-together they were having at the Ritz,' Katie said, avoiding Rozie's eye and rearranging the cups. 'They were such amazing people. One of them actually did work at Bletchley and she was totally with it still, and fabulous. I could see myself like her one day, you know, this kick-ass old lady like the one in Jenny Joseph's poem who will wear purple and a red hat.'

Rozie didn't know the poem. She made a mental note to look it up when she got back. Katie led the way into the living room, small and neat and lined with as many books as could fit. There was a small study table in one corner, with yet more books piled up on it. The dachshund waited for Rozie to choose a seat and then jumped up to sit beside her.

'Ignore Daphne,' Katie told her, putting the tray down on a small coffee table and curling up in the chair opposite them. 'She just wants to be cuddled and admired and getting it twenty-four-seven from me isn't enough.'

Rozie was happy to oblige the wriggling puppy. She hadn't grown up with dogs, but she was generally fond of them, and she was certainly used to them by now.

'She was a present from the Boss,' Katie explained. 'To keep me company.'

Rozie wondered why the Queen had thought Katie needed a dog. She knew that she had been a high-flying civil servant in the Home Office before taking on the APS job. Usually, people did it for several years before going on to greater things. Rumours abounded as to what the 'mental health problems' might have been. Sir Simon had respected Katie's privacy, so Rozie did, too. If Katie wanted to explain, she would. In any case, they had other things to talk about.

'Have you met Judy Raspberry?' she asked.

Katie smiled. 'Have I? I'd been here for about seven minutes when she arrived with a pot of home-made vegetable lasagne, in case I was vegetarian, and a bag of sausages and bacon, in case I wasn't. A week after I got Daphne, she invited herself over for tea and took a look around. The following day she came laden with dog paraphernalia. There was a harness to make the lead more comfortable, a dog bed, a ball-thrower and some old towels for rubbing her down after walks. Judy said it was all going spare, but I swear she bought the harness specially.'

'Is she like that with everyone?'

'Not necessarily. I've heard that if you get on the wrong side of her you'll know about it.'

'On the wrong side of her how?'

Katie cupped one of the teacups in her hands and breathed in the steam. Her clean-living lifestyle was very noticeable after Sandringham, where the gin would be flowing freely by now.

'There were a couple of cars that used to park near the crossing place for the school, so the kids couldn't see the traffic easily. The owners received warning notices from the council. Rumour has it – which I believe – that Judy worked out who was doing it and put in a call. She doesn't put up with what she calls "nonsense".'

'But you don't know about anything she was currently worked up about?'

'Not beyond the usual, no. You said it might be to do with Edward St Cyr. What makes the Boss think the two are connected?'

Rozie pursed her lips. The Queen had not been specific when she had outlined her concerns this morning. 'The coincidence of timing, for a start. Judy was knocked over five days after Mr St Cyr disappeared. And it's something to do with who Judy is. The Boss has this sixth sense for dangerous women.'

'You think Judy's *dangerous*?'

'To the wrong person, maybe. You said she won't put up with "nonsense". She'll take on anyone who threatens the school kids' safety. Perhaps she took on someone with more at stake than she realised.'

'And Mr St Cyr took on the same person?'

Rozie shrugged. 'That's one of the things we need to find out. If the police were worried, they'd be investigating already. I can't raise the issue with them until we have more to go on. Maybe he and Judy weren't exactly working together, but she discovered something that would make her know who to suspect when he disappeared. Or, as I say, maybe it's nothing. We need more than feminine intuition. The Boss doesn't like to do anything until she's sure of her facts. Talking of which, do you know where the accident happened?'

'Sure. I can show you, if you like.'

They finished their tea and took the dog, in her harness, for a walk past the row of cottages and a little tea shop, to the end of the road, which formed a T-junction with the main road through the village. Katie pointed out the sharp bend twenty yards to their right, and the place beyond it where Judy had been found.

'She was on her way home from a WI meeting in West Newton,' Katie said. 'Funnily enough, it was to go over the arrangements for the Boss's visit in a fortnight. One of her friends dropped her off back here afterwards. Judy usually got out by the Scout hut, near my cottage, and walked from there. The lane to her house is round the corner, see? The way she was lying, it was clear she was hit by a car travelling out of the village, so it wouldn't have seen her until just before the impact.'

Rozie tried to see a way in which the car could have known in advance where Judy would be. She failed. If you wanted to stage something that looked like a genuine accident, this was the perfect place to do it.

'She wasn't found for at least fifteen minutes,' Katie said. 'Luckily, the woman who spotted her is the local GP so she got good care until the ambulance came. It could have been fatal if she'd been there much longer.'

'Did she usually cross in that place?'

'Probably. I've done it myself. You don't exactly get rush hour traffic in Dersingham. You can normally hear cars coming a mile off, especially in winter. But if the car was going fast . . .'

'Was there any CCTV?'

Katie laughed. 'In north Norfolk? I think there's a camera in Fakenham but I'm not sure. And nobody remembers anything out of the ordinary. If they did, I'm sure they'd have said something.'

Rozie stared back down the main road. It was difficult to imagine a car being parked far enough away to build up enough speed to do damage, and yet close enough to time its impact precisely. If it had suddenly revved up, surely it would have attracted attention, even in a sleepy village like this?

Katie carried on. 'I know you're going to ask if it's possible to find out when the meetings are, and it is. They're on the WI website, so any local who knew where to look could've worked out roughly when Judy would be coming back. But she often stayed on to chat to people. You wouldn't be able to know exactly when she'd get here. And how would you guess when she'd cross the road if you couldn't see her until you rounded the bend?'

'Mmm,' Rozie agreed. 'You'd need someone loitering at the bend. They'd have to make a phone call to the driver just as Judy approached.'

'Wouldn't that be obvious?'

'Not if they had earbuds in. It would look as if they were just muttering to themselves.'

'I can ask if anyone spotted a loiterer,' Katie offered.

Something had been puzzling Rozie. 'How?' she asked.

'How what?'

'How do you ask a village? How d'you know so much already?'

'Oh!' Katie smiled. 'Well, you could just mention some-thing in the queue at the Co-op. That usually does it. Or you mutter under your breath in the tea shop, or after church. But I use A Load of Balls.'

'Sorry?'

Katie's grin widened. 'They're a WhatsApp group of knitters. I joined a few months ago. Judy suggested it, not surprisingly. They incorporate the Sweary Stitchers, who do embroidery, and the Happy Hookers, who crochet. The Sweary Stitchers are the best. They can teach every stitch in the book, but they tend to use them for swear words on little samplers and patchwork. It gets the rage out of their system.'

'There's rage round here?'

Katie gave Rozie a piercing look. 'Of course there is. Grief. Frustration. Getting ill. Growing old. There's a lot of rage in the countryside. But turning it into samplers is really therapeutic. They have their meetings in different people's houses, so it's good for seeing other people's taste in kitchens and furniture. Judy suggested the group to me, not surprisingly. Anyway, between them all, they know most things. That's how I heard about the hit-and-run.'

'What do they think happened?'

'Oh, they honestly think it was an accident. Some idiot boy racer. Judy was wearing a dark coat and hat, which wasn't very clever of her, especially on a dark winter evening, but you don't necessarily think about neon and safety clothing when it's a five-minute walk, do you? They've got their theories on what happened to Edward St Cyr, too, by the way.'

Rozie frowned. 'You haven't asked about that?'

Katie shook her head. 'I didn't need to. They've got theories about everything. The general consensus is that he isn't

135

dead at all. He somehow managed to amputate his hand – and to be fair, they know a few farmers who've done that by accident in various bits of farm machinery, so it's not impossible – and he left it on the beach.'

'Like leaving your clothes in a little pile?'

'Exactly. So he could go off and start a new life. They're fascinated by him. He's like the local celebrity – apart from the Boss, of course, but she keeps her head down. He did the opposite. There's nothing they don't think him capable of.'

'Even so . . . his own hand. That's a bit extreme, isn't it?'

'It's extreme, whoever did it,' Katie pointed out.

Chapter 15

After a decent night's sleep, the Queen woke up with a sense of energy and purpose she hadn't felt for a while. Today, William, Catherine and the great-grandchildren were due to visit. She tried not to rush through the box of Government memoranda, notes from the Foreign Office and other assorted paperwork, but an objective observer would have noticed that she read it faster than usual – starting as always with the papers at the bottom, on the basis that these were the ones the Cabinet Office least wanted her to see.

She was done with it all so quickly that there was time to fit in a ride. The first one she had the energy for since she arrived. She asked Rozie to accompany her. The Queen had always been impressed that a young woman who had grown up on a council estate in the middle of London had somehow found the resources to ride. Not only that, but Rozie had competed for the army. The girl had grit, which was good.

They met up at the stables before setting off together across the paddocks, where a light blanket of snow was marked with the tracks of hares and rabbits. The Queen thought it might be nice to bring little Prince George here later. But now she was grateful to have the opportunity to talk to Rozie undisturbed.

'How did it go yesterday?' she asked.

Rozie was equivocal. 'Katie showed me where the hit-and-run happened. Either it really was an accident, or it was very cleverly staged.' She explained about the crossing place.

'So it would be difficult to do it deliberately?'

'Yes, ma'am. You would need at least two people and some decent planning. Even so, it's hard to see how you could get the timing right. I did wonder,' Rozie added, 'whether there might have been an accomplice standing by the edge of the road, ready to give Judy a nudge if necessary.'

The Queen nodded gravely. The scenario seemed to fit, in an odd sort of way, with the nature of Ned St Cyr's murder as she understood it: sudden violence, masked by the careful impression that nothing unusual had happened at all.

'Can you ask Katie to find out if Judy is being safely looked after in hospital? I assume she doesn't know what it was that Judy was writing about?'

'Not yet, although it might well have been drugs-related. Judy was definitely worried about drugs in the area. Katie's going to make some discreet enquiries. She's checking Judy's social media accounts, too. It's possible she mentioned something on Facebook, for example.'

'Good.'

It astonished the Queen that so many people, even sensible middle-aged ones such as Judy Raspberry, chose to live their lives online. She flinched whenever her family's private moments were shared without permission and dissected by strangers. Why would anyone willingly submit to this scrutiny? And yet millions did, and many of them obviously got comfort from it. She had tried to understand, but it was still beyond her. However, Rozie was adept at using it to their advantage when there was a problem to solve, such as this one, so for that she was grateful.

'We might speed things up by gently finding out if Ned had approached the chief constable about any concerns,' she suggested. 'Mr Bloomfield runs the National Drugs Task Force.'

'I'll ask.'

Unless Ned was on the wrong side of a drug deal, the Queen thought. He had not been entirely law-abiding in his youth. But Anne was so certain he was anti-drugs, and the Queen trusted her daughter's opinion.

'From what I know of Ned, I can imagine him starting out along official channels, then getting frustrated and going it alone.' She paused and turned her pony for home. Reluctantly, she added, 'There's one more thing.'

'Yes?'

'Julian Cassidy. I gather the police are interested in his activities. He obviously had some sort of quarrel with Ned. I doubt we have reason to be worried, but let me know if you hear anything.'

'I'll see what I can find out, ma'am,' Rozie assured her.

The Queen returned to the house in a cheerful mood. She had no idea if the prickle under her skin was right, but at least she was doing *something*. The Cambridges would be here any minute, and that hideous cold was finally retreating.

For the first time since her arrival her sinuses were clear and her body was, relatively speaking, free of aches and pains. She didn't exactly skip down the corridor to the staircase to get changed out of her riding togs, but there was definitely a spring in her step.

Chapter 16

A quiet moment with her lady-in-waiting before lunch the next day brought with it the answer to one mystery, at least.

'I think you ought to see this,' Lady Caroline said.

The Queen looked up from a copy of *Country Life*, where she had been reading a rather poetic article about water voles. Lady Caroline had been going through the Queen's personal correspondence to pick out letters and notes that required her attention. 'Mmm?'

'It's from Astrid Westover, of all people.' Lady Caroline made a face. 'Would you like me to read it out to you? I'm tempted to do it in a funny voice, but that would be terribly *rude*. Especially after everything she's been through. It's quite tragic, of course.'

'What is?'

'The missing hand business. And she's so very young really. I suppose that explains it. But *honestly*, you'd think she'd know better. She writes like something out of a Mills & Boon. Except they were better written. I used to love Mills & Boons at school. One of my friends wrote some of them under a nom de plume. I—'

'*Do* get on with it, Caroline.'

'Yes, ma'am. So sorry. Of course.'

Lady Caroline read aloud:

Thank you so very much for your kind letter to my mother. She was utterly charmed and I know she's writing to Your Majesty separately. I just wanted to let you know how touched I am that you're thinking of me and Ned my darling fiancé. I'm sure you must have been worried about what had happened to me but I wanted to reassure Your Majesty that I'm fine and I'm staying with Mummy out of the way of the press who are so odious, as I'm sure you know, and were making all sorts of hurtful comments about our age gap and me marrying him for his money, which is the opposite of the truth. I just couldn't face them so I came here to join Mummy at Guist, not so very far from you at Sandringham.

Your Majesty is so kind to think about Mummy, who sends her love. Darling Ned talked about you a lot and his happy days at Sandringham where Your Majesty treated him like a second son. I know he wanted to show me those special places where he grew up.

I simply cannot begin to take in what's happened to the person who I was going to share my life with. Ned was a pure ray of light, as I'm sure Your Majesty knows. We were due to get married in six weeks. I'm lost without him and the only thing that helps is to talk to other people who knew him and understand. As someone who knew him from childhood, I'm sure Your Majesty must feel the same way too.

With great fondness, and wishing you a happy 2017,

Your obedient servant,

Astrid

'How astonishing,' the Queen said.

'Isn't it?'

'So that's why the police weren't unduly worried. They must have known.'

'Lying low. I can't say I blame her,' Lady Caroline said. 'All that press attention would be awful. Even so, she's quite bold, isn't she? Shall I do the usual? "Her Majesty would like me to thank you for your letter . . ."'

'Yes. And do say, again, how sorry we are. I think that should be enough.'

But the letter became a topic of conversation again over a game of charades in the saloon after dinner. Lady Caroline had joined the family and guests, who by now included the young princesses and an eclectic assortment of old friends. While everyone was working on the film, book and TV titles to put in the hat, Lady Caroline turned to the Queen and said, 'The cheek of that girl! Astrid Westover. I still can't get over it. Can you?'

Lady Caroline had a loud voice, honed on many a lacrosse pitch in her youth, and everyone's ears pricked up.

'Ooh! Astrid? Who was marrying Ned St Cyr?' Beatrice asked. 'What did she say?'

'She made it very clear,' Lady Caroline suggested, 'that she would like to visit Sandringham. Didn't she, ma'am?'

'Yes, she did, rather.'

'I've never seen so many hints. I half expected her to say she was popping over in the morning for a chat.'

'Oh, can we invite her?' Eugenie asked. 'She might know something about what happened.'

'What a gruesome subject,' the Queen said. 'Especially for someone so close to Ned.'

'But she *wants* to come. Perhaps she *wants* to talk about it.'

'I should think she just wants a decent recce round the house and a chance to see us all doing the jigsaw,' Philip observed, with great perspicacity, in the Queen's opinion, especially given the chief constable's recent visit.

'You could always ask her and see,' Beatrice suggested.

'I must admit,' Lady Caroline said, 'I'd love to see if she's as forward in person as she is on paper.'

'I'm not sure it's a trait I want to reward.'

'You have to give her brownie points for chutzpah,' Philip conceded.

'Come on, Granny!' Eugenie pleaded. 'The poor woman's *bereaved*. We'd be *helping*. Could she come soon? We've only got a few more days before we're due at the chalet.'

The Queen intended to remain firm. She did not invite people to join the family just because they had expressed an interest in doing so. If she did, she would need a place the size of several Wembley Stadiums. However, she was an indulgent grandmother. Perhaps vestiges of her jealousy of Georgina St Cyr's closeness to Ned remained. Before the last port decanter and cocktail trolley had circulated, she had somehow agreed to let the family 'help'.

In hiding as she was, Astrid Westover's diary was otherwise empty. She arrived for morning coffee forty-eight hours after being invited, before the young princesses headed off for their skiing holiday. She emerged from her car wearing a multi-hued faux fur coat that the girls instantly recognised from a popular fashion brand created by one of their friends, and paused with her back to the house for a moment, unaware that the family were watching from one of the windows in the saloon.

'I think she's taking selfies,' Eugenie said.

'Someone will have to tell her not to post them.'

When she entered the saloon, the Queen was fascinated to see that, close up, she looked as flawless as an airbrushed model in a magazine. Whatever makeup she was wearing, it seemed to smooth her face into doll-like simplicity. Her forehead was unnaturally unlined and her lips had the fish-like appearance that the Queen was increasingly noticing among her younger female acquaintances. Sophie Wessex had told her this was a 'trout pout', and the Queen had yet to be convinced that the exaggerated contours were preferable to one's natural flesh and bone. She wondered what Astrid looked like underneath. However, the girl had great poise and, taking in the roomful of waiting royals, she sank into a deep curtsey.

'Your Majesty,' she murmured, in a deep, contralto voice that the Queen had not expected. 'Thank you so much for the invitation. I brought you jam.'

Astrid dug around in the basket-like handbag she had brought with her and handed two jars of something rather gloopy and disconcertingly violet to the nearest footman. Like many before her, she must have read that Catherine, the Duchess of Cambridge, had won over the family with her first Christmas present of home-made jam. Many was the jar the Queen had received since. She was rather wary of them. The thing was, Catherine was really quite good at making jam, and that was a key feature.

'So *this* is where Ned grew up.' The contralto voice vibrated with emotion, as Astrid raised her eyes to the tapestries on the walls, the minstrels' gallery, the royal portraits. 'Do you know, even just being in this room, I can feel Ned's presence?'

The Queen saw Philip's eyebrows rise by about a millimetre. She hoped her family would behave themselves.

'Well, he spent a *little* bit of time here. A very long time ago.'

Astrid continued to drink in the room, squealing slightly when her eyes lighted on the grand piano.

'There's the jigsaw! You still have one! Ned told me all about it. He adored Sandringham. It was such a special part of his childhood.'

'How well did you know him?' Philip asked. 'I mean, how *long* did you know him? He wasn't always a fan of ours.'

'Wasn't he?' Astrid looked surprised. 'I'm sure he was. He talked about you a lot. He said you were brilliant farmers. Very forward-thinking especially for people of your generation. He said sometimes the older farmers are the best, because you've seen everything.'

Philip and the Queen exchanged a look that Astrid didn't catch.

'Would you like some coffee?' the Queen asked. 'I think it's ready in the drawing room.'

It was, along with a selection of freshly made biscuits and pastries, and the remaining guests, who were as keen and curious to see Astrid as she was to see them. Soon, she was sitting at one of the card tables, nibbling at some lavender shortbread biscuits and effectively holding court.

'Ned said you're doing interesting things with the estate,' she said to Prince Philip. 'To make farming more sustainable, I mean.'

'Did he notice?'

'Oh, yes. He was very curious. He grew up with the farm at Ladybridge, of course. But Abbottswood wasn't the same at all. The land is all wood and wetland, and Ned couldn't bear to chop the trees down. Some of them have been there for four hundred years.'

Philip nodded. 'I've been saying as much. So he had this rewilding idea.'

'Actually, I was the one who suggested rewilding to him,' Astrid said. 'I heard all about it on a work trip to Europe. Ned looked into it and he was so *excited*. It was our way of connecting with the land spiritually, you know?'

There were general non-committal noises round the room.

'He wanted something for his children to be proud of. That's why I was so certain the police had the wrong person when they arrested his son. I met Jack at Abbottswood when he came down to talk to Ned about the project. He was the sweetest guy, so supportive of what we were trying to do. It was really beautiful. I was hoping he might come and work with us.'

'I don't understand. I thought he hated his father?' the Queen said.

'They had a strained relationship,' Astrid admitted, 'but Ned was working hard to build bridges. We did a lot of therapy together at this fabulous retreat in Kerala last year. He wanted to reach out to all his children, and grandchildren, too. When he knew Jack's girlfriend was pregnant it changed everything. It's all about what you hand on, isn't it? We wanted it to be a place of growth. Nature was in charge. Ned was very Zen. You should have seen him do the lotus position.'

'I'm profoundly glad I didn't,' Philip said, with feeling.

'I heard he was mellowing,' the Queen suggested. 'So Lord Mundy's daughter told me.'

'Oh, yes, he was! That was lovely. So sweet of them to invite him to Lady Mundy's funeral. His mother's buried at Ladybridge and it meant he could go and visit her, which was more important to him than he let on, I think. He tried to reach out to everyone, really. And he wanted rewilding to put north Norfolk on the map.'

Philip raised an eyebrow. 'I rather thought Sandringham did that.'

'But it was so *difficult*. People just don't understand. Every project has teething troubles. I mean, there were incidents with the boar and beavers and the deer, but they were *accidents*. Ned didn't *mean* them to escape. If you knew how many thousands he spent trying to keep them in! Matt Fisher and his wife did everything in their power to shut the project down. I don't think they forgave Ned for the boar digging their lawns up just before their daughter's birthday party. They just didn't get it, Ned *treasured* the land. The boar are transforming the landscape at Abbottswood. Or at least, they were, until we lost them.'

'I bet they were,' Philip muttered.

'The beavers were a *bit* of a mistake because it's astonishing how easily they get past any enclosure, but they created

148

this beautiful sort of wetland area before they escaped. You should come and visit. Except—' Astrid broke off. 'I don't know what's happening to it now. I had this whole brand set up to market the project on social media. To get a fan base going, you know? We were even in early talks with Channel 4. Ned was supposed to pick me up from the airport and drive me to Abbottswood so we could shoot some videos to show them. We texted about it the night before. He said he couldn't wait to see me . . .'

'Did he really just disappear?' Eugenie asked.

Astrid nodded. 'I wasn't worried at first. I kept thinking I was about to see him any second. I rang his mobile from the airport. He'd warned me it might be out of power, which it was, so I rang Abbottswood . . . the same. There isn't a landline at the flat. I was kind of pissed off with him then. Which is just so . . . kind of . . . tragic now.'

'No, it's understandable,' Beatrice agreed. 'So what happened?'

This was 'being helpful', the Queen assumed.

'I got a taxi to the house and I was so sure he'd be in the kitchen, making supper and sorry for forgetting. But he wasn't there. The dogs were howling. The sitting room was completely trashed and I assumed there must have been burglars . . . I had the most awful, awful visions, but it was just the dogs. Ned must have forgotten to shut the kitchen door properly and he hadn't put their toys out for them. Gwennie goes absolutely crazy without her bunny. And they were starving, poor things.'

'Had he just left them for all that time?' Eugenie asked. She, too, was a dog person.

The Queen had been wondering about this. She knew it was absolutely not the most important thing, but surely he hadn't just abandoned them?

'No! They're used to being alone at night sometimes. The cleaner normally feeds them and lets them out in the mornings if we're not there. Ned had left a note on the table, but it wasn't her day. He wasn't thinking straight. Anyway, I went outside, thinking he might have gone to check on the deer or something and fallen over or . . . I don't know. It was pitch black. I couldn't see anything. I called and called. The next day I waited, but nothing, so in the afternoon I called the police. They told me not to worry, but of course I *did* worry. I took his spare key to the flat and drove up that night, but there was no sign of him, just breakfast things in the sink, as if he expected to come back and wash them up. Those texts on my phone . . . They're the last thing I have. I keep reading them over and over.'

Astrid stopped suddenly. Had her facial muscles been able to express emotion, it would have been dismay. The Queen felt slightly guilty she had underestimated the strength of the bond between Ned and his young fiancée. There was real affection there, and a sense of common purpose. She knew how that felt.

'It must be very difficult,' she sympathised.

Astrid nodded. 'It helps that I have the dogs. They miss him as much as I do. Gwennie, she's the setter – he always has one to remind him of his mother – she won't be consoled. She just lies there, looking at me. They all know something's wrong.'

Several pairs of royal eyes looked at Astrid sympathetically, because they completely got it about the dogs.

'Something must have been eating him up. The way he was speeding up to London and he *promised* me he wouldn't anymore because he had so many points on his licence and he couldn't live without the car.'

'Did he seem stressed out?' Beatrice asked.

'No! But I guess he must have been. Maybe he was trying to hide it from me. I mean, I know he had a lot on his mind. I assumed it was to do with the breakout of the boar because there had been the horrible business with Mrs Fisher's cockapoo.'

'Goodness!' the Queen said. 'What happened?'

'Oh, that was awful. The boar broke out about a month ago, and they were just rummaging about in the bushes, like they do, not doing any harm to anyone, but the dog came over to investigate and wouldn't leave them alone and in the end . . . Well, they're wild animals, after all. They do what they do.' Astrid shrugged. Then she noticed several pairs of royal eyes now staring at her in horror. She blushed. 'It wasn't their *fault*, is what I mean. Apparently, they still see dogs as wolves. It's a protective instinct.' She stuck out her chin. 'And that awful man from Muncaster threatened to kill him, which was so unfair. Ned was devastated about the dog, naturally. He adored them.'

At which point Astrid did something none of them expected. Her eyes welled up and she cried ugly tears that dislodged her mascara, unable to help herself.

'I . . . I'm s-sorry!' she gasped. 'I don't know what I'm d-doing!' She tried to cover her wet cheeks with the back of a clenched hand. A footman stepped forward with a napkin for her to use as a handkerchief, but she shook her head.

'I'll be fine.' She took a deep breath, managed a weak, shaky smile and glanced across at the nearest large object, which was a screen of Venetian fans. 'Those are lovely. Do you collect them? Are they eighteenth-century?'

At that moment, the Queen was reminded sharply of Astrid's mother, Moira, who had the same disconcerting core of steel. Moira had always dealt with her late husband's famous drinking habit by pretending it didn't exist. She had clearly brought up her daughter in a similar vein. But the Queen could see that behind the carefully filled façade, poor Astrid was devastated. She was clearly devoted to Ned, and the life they had planned together. She would have made a good match for him, despite the age gap. Perhaps, under her influence, they might even have found their way into Sandringham life again. Another party organised by Ned St Cyr would have been quite something.

She didn't share any of these reflections with Astrid. They would hardly have been helpful. But she offered to ask the chef to share the lavender shortbread recipe with her, and assured her that they were very much looking forward to sampling the jam.

Chapter 17

S ir Simon and Rozie were both working late. Last January, Rozie remembered, he had tended to switch off his monitor at about 5 p.m. before calling his wife in London for a chat, making the most of the winter holiday lull before everything ramped up again in February. This year, Lady Holcroft was still in Scotland, but that didn't explain the worried look on the private secretary's face and the large pile of reading material he was working his way through.

'Anything interesting?' she asked, poking her head around his door.

'Not unless you find the supplementary information to the Government's appeal to the Supreme Court against R. Miller versus the Secretary of State for Exiting the European Union interesting,' he said, rubbing his eyes. He looked up. 'It's all extremely important, but it stopped being interesting eight hours ago. I'm lost in Euro-speak. But I'll get there.'

'Do you need to?'

'I do. The PM tried to invoke the royal prerogative to trigger our departure. Her whole "Brexit means Brexit" thing. We rather care how the royal prerogative works. But in this case, Brexit means . . .' He indicated the two-foot high pile of papers on his desk. 'I'm not sure anyone knows exactly what it means at the moment. Meanwhile, the PM's secretary rang. She wants to talk. This is ominous.'

'Why?' Rozie asked.

'Because it means she's been thinking over Christmas.'

'Isn't that a good thing?'

'Not necessarily, no. Prime ministers with too much time on their hands tend to have bad ideas and discuss them with the wrong people, thus rendering them infinitely worse.'

'I'd have thought the rest and relaxation would do her good,' Rozie ventured.

Sir Simon scoffed. 'If she rested or relaxed, I might agree with you. But they never do. Or at least, not since Macmillan. They call in their special advisers for table suppers and sometimes their supporters for grand dinners, though I'm not sure how much of the latter she does. They game every scenario and overthink everything. If the Boss had her way, she'd take each one out fishing so they could kick back and get a little perspective.'

'I can't see Theresa May fishing,' Rozie said with a grin.

Sir Simon nodded and sighed. 'That's the trouble. Neither can I. I sense this pile of papers is going to get higher over the next few weeks. I need to have some clue what I'm talking about.'

'Do you want me to read them for you? Or some of them at least?'

'No, I'll do it. I have a few meetings lined up in town next week. I might as well look as if I know what I'm talking about. You go home.'

He gave her a friendly smile. Rozie smiled back, but she felt excluded. She had enjoyed her brief moment at the top of the Private Office food chain, when she got to read all the international intelligence. Now her job felt more mundane. She couldn't even entertain herself with Henry, who had rotated duties with another officer for a couple of weeks. She wished Sir Simon goodnight and headed out.

Rozie's accommodation was in a Victorian lodge a fifteen-minute walk from the house. It had been used to house kings, queens, dukes and mistresses over the years, and most of them, Rozie thought, must have found its dark walls and heavy furniture as oppressive as she did. However, her room was large, the bed was comfortable, and anything could beat the tiny boxes they had given her in the army.

Currently, the two overflow guests who shared it with her were a classical composer and his opera singer wife. They were down for a few days and spent the evenings playing party games and treating their royal hosts to classical music and old Beatles pop tunes on the piano in the saloon. Which meant that Rozie had the place to herself. She planned to use the large mahogany dining table to spread out her notes on the Queen's calendar for the next few months, so she could colour-code the events according to how much preparation they needed. *What happens in Sandringham stays in Sandringham*, but a lot of the time it was just paperwork.

The job took longer than expected. She lost track of time but knew it must be around midnight. The playlist of Fela Kuti and Nina Simone playing quietly on her phone in the background had repeated itself at least a dozen times. The wind was up tonight and something outside was flapping with a dull, irregular rhythm. Distracted, she pictured ropes loosening. It took her back to her army days, when everything had to be battened down tight. Eventually, she couldn't bear the distraction any longer. She took the heaviest torch she could find in a cupboard in the hall, grabbed her coat, shoved her feet into the first boots that would fit and went out to investigate.

The lodge shared a garden with a little cottage that had once been used by the servants of the royal guests. Rozie knew it had been given to the bean counter while he looked for somewhere more permanent. She had tried twice, now, to talk to him about his story of the scuffle in the car park, but either he wasn't at home or he was avoiding her. Rozie remembered the way he had stared at her at the shoot. She hadn't been worried at the time; now things were more complicated.

The noise seemed to be coming from an open lean-to with a cast-iron roof attached to the cottage. Shining her torch inside, Rozie saw that it housed some rusting garden equipment, a small boat under canvas and a vehicle under a plastic tarpaulin. The problem was obvious: the tarpaulin had come loose on one side. Rozie wondered why the frantic flapping sound didn't drive Cassidy as mad as it was driving her. The sweep of her torchlight revealed a bungee cord lying on the ground that must have been used to hold the cover down, stretched under the car from one side to the other. Without it, the loose plastic revealed a modern Land Rover Freelander four-wheel drive.

Rozie was surprised by this. Plenty of her army friends had kept vehicles at home this way – but usually because the car was sporty and delicate, or because it was old and liable to rust. This one was neither. She was surprised that Julian wasn't driving it. It would make much more sense on these roads than the little Nissan she'd seen parked at the front, which had the look of a hire car. *Why keep a decent vehicle under canvas if you . . .?*

Before she finished the thought, her torch was lighting up the pristine driver's side of the engine grille. She unhooked the remaining bungee cord, pulled back the tarpaulin and shone her torch on the Freelander offside corner. Her heart rate leaped as she saw the way the headlamp unit jutted at an unexpected angle. The whole corner of the chassis was crushed, and the bumper panel below it was hanging half off. There was a large, crumpled dent in the bonnet. *A dent*, Rozie thought, *about the size of a small, adult woman.*

The headlights of a distant car lit up the treetops as it approached. Rozie could hear its engine above the wind. She reached into her coat pocket for her phone to take a picture of the damage – but her hand found nothing. The car drew closer. Her phone, meanwhile, must be on the dining table where she had left it, playing 'My Baby Just Cares For Me' to an empty room.

Rozie turned off her torch and waited. The car moved on. She was about to head back to the lodge when she heard pounding feet, and looked round to see a large black shape heading through the darkness for her at speed. *Shit!* He had a dog. Of course he did. Everybody had a dog round here. It stopped in front of her and barked fit to wake the dead. She tensed every muscle, waiting for Julian to appear.

Except, he didn't come. Rozie noticed for the first time that the back door to the cottage was wide open. A thin light poured out from an inner room. The old Labrador seemed agitated. She could have sworn that, if anything, it was asking her to come inside.

Given what she had just found, common sense said to run and call the police. However, there was something wrong about the way that back door was wide open in the dead of winter. Her army training told her to assess the situation for risk, and investigate.

The curtains to the room beside the kitchen were only partly drawn. Torch in hand, her senses on hyper-alert, Rozie crept towards the window and peered through. The room beyond was similar to Katie's living room in size, lit by a single table lamp with a wonky shade. The floor near the lamp was littered with dirty plates and a couple of empty wine bottles on their sides. She could just make out the stockinged feet of a man lying prone behind a battered sofa. The dog had gone back inside to sit beside him.

Rozie cautiously followed. The open door led into a small kitchen, where a shotgun lay on a table next to a neat array of cleaning rods and oils. More empty wine bottles neatly lined the skirting board in double rows. Beyond them, an open door gave on to the living room. Rozie saw the man as soon as she entered. She crouched down by his head and took in the pale, unshaven face.

So *this* was Julian Cassidy. Rozie recognised him now. The last time she had seen him, he had had a light beard and he had been rifle shooting beside her at the Queen's Prize at Bisley, about five years ago. She wasn't surprised he'd remembered her: black women tended to stand out in the rarified circles of rifle competitions. White men not so much. Cassidy had been friendly, she remembered, and as handy with a rifle as she was. Even though they hadn't won, they had celebrated hard that day.

She placed her fingers against his neck and found a faintly beating pulse. Whatever had happened to him, he wasn't going to do her any harm, tonight at least.

Chapter 18

The Queen looked up from the last paper in her boxes and watched as a swirling, eddying cloud of knot birds made its way across a pale grey sky. The little sandpipers, named after King Canute of advancing tide fame, always amazed her with the complicated patterns they created overhead, forming living shapes that bent and melted in front of one's eyes. They were a reminder of the limits of a sovereign's powers, and also the great outdoors, and the fact that she wasn't in it. The latter was a situation that she decided to remedy.

Along the corridor, the main reception rooms were quiet. The family and their guests, it seemed, were all outside already. She had assumed they were all on a happy hack across the fields, only for Mrs Maddox to inform her that the younger ones had gone shopping in Burnham Market. The constant desire to be in small, enclosed, overheated spaces was something she had never fully understood, when one could be spending time instead with animals. No matter. It gave her an excellent opportunity to visit the stud again.

As she knotted her headscarf under her chin in preparation for leaving the house, she wondered idly whether poor, nervous Arthur Raspberry would be there, and thought back to his redoubtable little sister, Ivy. She had been at the beach at Snettisham, of course, the fateful day of the hand washing up on the shore. The Raspberrys and Snettisham . . . Judy was not the only member of the family to see something interesting on the beach. The Queen pictured the scene after the storm, with the plastic bag bobbing on the water, and the terrified girl. That was the day the drugs washed up, too, not all of which were recovered. Sir Simon had mentioned that a package had gone missing from the bigger bag. But after Ivy's discovery, the beach would have been full of police officers and forensic teams. That mental image gave the Queen pause for thought.

It was *possible*. Unlikely, but possible. The more she thought it through, the more possible it seemed. Tightening the headscarf knot in place, she headed outside with greater purpose.

The Land Rover was waiting for her in the forecourt, but her chief personal protection officer was not. Normally, when she was preparing to go out, he lurked outside, ready to accompany her in the car or follow on as required, but there was no sign of him She turned to the nearest footman.

'Do you know where Chief Inspector Jackson is?'

'Do you mean Inspector Depiscopo, ma'am? He took over your protection from Mr Jackson yesterday. I'll find out for you.'

The Queen berated herself for forgetting. Her PPOs regularly rotated shifts and Jackson had gone back to London yesterday. Jackson, she had known for years, but Depiscopo was new. He was part of a Government scheme to save money by rotating officers across a range of VIPs. So far it had annoyed all concerned and cost a fortune in additional overtime, because traditional royal PPOs didn't think of their role in strict terms of 'on' and 'off', but the new policemen definitely did. Nor did they understand where to be and when, and how one liked to work. She waited impatiently for a couple of minutes and decided to drive the Land Rover by herself.

'He knows where to find me,' she said tersely.

The footman gulped and nodded. Tony Depiscopo wouldn't be making that mistake again.

At the stud, the Queen spent some pleasant time watching the mares with their foals in the Walled Garden. Like her, the foals had an official birthday in addition to their real one, and theirs was always the first of January. One of the jobs of a breeder was to encourage them to be conceived in time to be born as early in the year before as possible. Estimate's foal, for example, had been born in the early spring, which was ideal. He would be well established before he raced as a two-year-old – assuming he was good enough to do it. Judging from his proportions, his movement and that intelligent flick of his ears, she had high hopes for him. But her thoughts were elsewhere this morning.

She was pleased to see that Arthur was among the grooms. As they prepared to walk the horses back to the yard, she asked him to stay behind, near the statue of Persimmon, whose winnings on the track for her great-grandfather had paid for the magnificent Walled Garden itself. The poor boy looked chalk-white with lack of sleep. She had seen him this way at the stables, too. At the time, it seemed natural that he should be anxious about his aunt and his little sister; now she wondered if it was something more.

'How is Mrs Raspberry?' she asked. 'Is there any news?'

Arthur looked astonished to be asked.

'She came out of the coma a couple of days ago, ma'am. But she's got no memory of that day. She's covered in bruises. Dad didn't want us to go and see her, but we had to. I mean we wanted to.'

'Well done. I'm sure it must have been very comforting for her.'

'She looked . . . bad, ma'am. Thin. Her face all purple and yellow . . . And, you know, tubes and things.'

'Give her time. She'll heal. She might lose her confidence a little,' the Queen added, having seen enough riding accidents to know. 'But you can help her by keeping her company. I sense you'll be good at it.'

'Er, OK. I'm not sure about that.' The troubled look on his face was evidence of a confidence crisis of his own.

'I've been thinking about your sister's discovery on the beach,' the Queen went on.

She saw his whole body tense. 'What, ma'am? I mean, why? I mean . . .?'

'I wondered if she had gone there alone that day. It's a very long walk to Snettisham from West Newton. That is where you live, isn't it?'

'Yes, ma'am.'

'So I wondered if someone had driven her. And they might have been on the beach with her. And they might have seen . . . all sorts of things . . . while they were there. Before the police arrived, I mean.'

The poor boy was practically blue. The Queen had considered that it was three to one she was probably wrong, but now it was odds-on she had pictured the scene correctly.

'I-I dunno. Maybe someone drove,' he said. 'I can ask.'

'Do you drive, Arthur?'

He tried to swallow. His throat was dry. 'I . . . Sometimes.'

'Around that time, a packet of drugs went missing from the bag that washed up. The police know, because of the way the bag was packed. You've probably heard about it because I understand they've been trying to track it down.'

He stared.

'I suppose someone *might* have come across it before Ivy got there . . .' she suggested.

He nodded eagerly.

'. . . But it was early in the morning, so perhaps they didn't. Anyway, whoever found the bag acted rashly, on the spur of the moment. They made a very stupid choice. Perhaps they were coerced.'

'I don't know what you're—'

'The thing is, I do *hope* that it wasn't anyone who worked for me. Because that would make things very difficult. One likes to give people second chances. But if they have drugs on them, or hidden somewhere . . .'

Arthur's mobile face was a picture of panic. If he was seeking to go into a life of crime, he was singularly ill-equipped for it. The Queen carried on.

'On Sunday, I'll be attending the eleven o'clock service at Flitcham. My protection officers always sweep it very thoroughly before I arrive. If something were to be left there anonymously, it would be found. I think it belongs with the rest of the contents of that bag, in police custody, out of harm's way,' she rounded up. 'Don't you?'

He nodded.

'I like to give people second chances, but not third ones. I'm glad we've had this little chat, Arthur.'

He stared at her wordlessly, before accidentally curtseying and bolting for the yard.

'Will he do it?' Rozie asked.

They were supposed to be discussing the Queen's calendar. Rozie had noticed some interesting potential issues with the schedule. However, as so often during this visit, they had got sidetracked.

'We shall see. I might have got the wrong end of the stick,' the Queen said. 'He couldn't have been looking at me like that out of politeness. But I think so. Yes?'

'I just can't believe . . .'

Rozie said it as respectfully as she could, but she still couldn't finish the sentence. The Queen could tell she didn't believe one might suspect someone had stolen a packet of drugs, and was giving them a get-out clause.

'If I'm right about him, and the packet were to be discovered, his career will be quite over before it's begun. He's a promising groom and a hopeless criminal. I really don't think it was his idea.'

'If it was someone else's,' Rozie said, 'won't they mind when the drugs are handed in?'

The Queen had considered this. 'He can truthfully say he didn't have a choice. And nobody has lost out – the drugs were found accidentally, after all. But I certainly don't want one of my employees hanging on to them.'

'No, ma'am. I see that.'

'I do hope he has the good sense to wipe his fingerprints off the packet. Anyway, enough of that. How have you got on?'

'Katie has some good news,' Rozie said.

'Excellent.'

'She tried to see Mrs Raspberry in the hospital but it was impossible,' Rozie said. 'She's on a special ward and visitors are tightly controlled. She's pretty safe for now.'

'Thank goodness. What else?'

'I've made some progress. Not the type you were hoping for, though, ma'am.'

'Oh?'

Rozie realised this had become a bit of a refrain. She told the Queen about the discovery of the dented Freelander. And the fact that she had found Julian Cassidy, practically comatose with drink, on his living room floor, surrounded by empty wine bottles.

'The bean counter?'

'Yes, ma'am.'

The Queen tried to puzzle it out. This was a shock. Several shocks. What did *he* have to do with Judy Raspberry? He was the one person she was sure was not involved. And all those bottles . . .

'Have you reported it? The car, I mean?' she asked.

'There's no point,' Rozie said. 'The police already know. He was clever. I found out he reported it himself, two days later. He said he'd hit a deer that suddenly leaped out at him on the road to Muncaster, and it had made him crash into a tree. The second crash was real enough. He got Helena Fisher to back him up. She said she was driving the other way and saw it happen. They even called someone out to try and find the deer and put it down humanely.'

'No injured deer was found, I assume,' the Queen said.

'No, ma'am.'

'You saw the damage to the car. Does his story seem plausible?'

Rozie sighed. 'Just about, I suppose. I don't believe it, though.'

'And he'd been drinking?'

'Heavily. And repeatedly. You don't get through all those bottles in one night.'

The Queen grimaced. 'First the scuffle with Ned. Now the wine. We had high hopes for the bean counter.'

'If he did hit Mrs Raspberry, I don't see how he could have done it deliberately.'

'Hmmm,' the Queen said. 'Not alone, certainly.' And yet, he seemed to be drinking himself into oblivion. She was reminded of young Arthur for a moment: another hopeless criminal who couldn't live with himself. Still, why on earth would he do it?

'There's something else, ma'am. On the subject of Helena Fisher.'

'Hmm?'

'The police found the body of a wild boar buried on her estate yesterday. It was shot with a rifle, right between the eyes.'

'One of Ned's boar?' the Queen asked. 'I gather they'd gone missing.'

'It looks as though they escaped into Muncaster's woods. Helena Fisher says she was walking with her dogs and one of them disturbed the boar somehow, and it didn't survive the attack.'

'The cockapoo,' the Queen said to herself.

'She was worried for the others. And herself. She admitted asking Mr Cassidy to help her, because her husband was away and he was the first person she thought of who has a rifle. They apparently hunted the boar down together the next day. I know he's good enough to have done it, and not that many people are.'

'Why didn't she simply get Ned to take his animals back?'

'She said she didn't trust him not to let them escape again. Relations had broken down. She was angry and upset and did the first thing that occurred to her. That's her story, anyway. Cassidy backs it up.'

'They're quite a double act, those two,' the Queen said thoughtfully.

Chapter 19

The house party at Sandringham got through a few bottles of its own that evening. After breakfast the next morning, while several of the guests were sleeping it off, the Queen took the dogs for a walk on her own so she could think. A circuit of the lakes generally suited this purpose. They weren't large – more oversized ponds, really – and had been created with islands, rockeries and rich planting, so the eye would always have something to admire. Her great-grandfather once said he would have liked to be a landscape gardener if he hadn't been king. The Queen did not personally agree, but thought what a jolly job it must be: out in the fresh air much of the time, surrounded by nature, making things. She had yet to meet a landscape gardener whose company she didn't enjoy.

Yesterday, she'd asked Mrs Maddox whether there were any rumours about Mrs Fisher and the bean counter. Astrid Westover had suggested 'the awful man from Muncaster' threatened Ned because of the death of Mrs Fisher's cockapoo. The Queen had assumed Astrid was alluding to Matt Fisher, but now she wondered if the 'awful man' was Cassidy, and Astrid had been referring to the scuffle in the pub car park that Sir Simon had mentioned. It is quite an emotional involvement, to shoot a boar and then threaten a man because the animal has caused the death of your ex-employer's wife's pet dog. Then to hide a damaged car and get that same ex-employer's wife to confirm when the accident happened. The Queen was starting to see Cassidy with new eyes.

The housekeeper had readily confirmed the Queen's suspicions. According to the servants' hall at Muncaster, the affair had started in the summer. Apparently it was in revenge for Mr Fisher's relationship with his art adviser. The Queen reflected that one missed all the country gossip when one was in London. Although, of course, the city was a rumour-factory of its own.

So, Cassidy and Mrs Fisher were much more than casual acquaintances. It must indeed have been Cassidy who threatened Ned over the poor cockapoo. The Queen thought about Ned's dogs, too, and the chaos in the sitting room at Abbottswood after his disappearance, which the police seemed unconcerned by. Then there was the telephone call to Julian Cassidy for no obvious reason, the day before he disappeared. None of it connected and it was quite exhausting to try and fit it all together. The only reason she had got involved at all was because she felt certain that the hit-and-run on Judy Raspberry was important, and that it *didn't* have anything to do with the goings-on at Muncaster. One liked to think one's neighbours and staff were not homicidal. Now, if anything, she had more evidence than the chief constable that they might be. Perhaps she should leave it to the police after all. But people kept telling her things.

She was halfway round the ponds when she was surprised to see a young person of indeterminate sex in jeans and a

170

hoodie walking rapidly towards her. Closer up, the flash of a blue fringe under the hood reminded her that this was the redoubtable Ivy, Arthur's sister, whose views on royalty the Queen had not forgotten.

'Good morning,' she said, somewhat stiffly. Young people, or old people for that matter, tended not to run up to her at will.

The girl was slightly out of breath. She grinned. 'I found you! Great! Hi! ... Your Majesty.' She dropped into a belated curtsey that was more of a knee-bend. 'Can I join you for a sec?'

'I suppose you can,' the Queen agreed. She narrowed her eyes. 'Aren't you supposed to be in school?'

The girl gave her a brazen stare.

'Inset day.'

The Queen wasn't sure exactly what that was, but could tell from the tilt of Ivy's chin that it wasn't true anyway.

'Willow's looking a bit tired, isn't she?' Ivy said. 'D'you want us to slow down so she can manage?'

'Do you know my dogs?'

Ivy looked surprised. 'Of course I do. I help walk them sometimes. That footman who usually does it likes to have a crafty cigarette. He doesn't think they need much exercise, but I do. I give them an extra ten minutes for him.'

'I had no idea,' the Queen said, nonplussed.

'Look, don't tell him I told you. Anyway, that wasn't why I wanted to talk to you. I know what you think about my brother.'

'I'm not sure you—'

'He's a diamond. You probably think he's a bit iffy because of me. I was rude to you at Christmas and I didn't mean it and I'm sorry. I just go off a bit at times. Arthur really loves his job. He's good at it. He needs it. He doesn't do drugs, ma'am, seriously.'

'How did you think I—?'

'I heard him telling the chickens at home. Don't ask. You and me talk to the horses. He talks to the chickens, OK?'

'What did he tell them?'

'You think he stole those drugs from the beach and he took them, but he had to, ma'am. He was with this stupid boy called Josh who was in his year at school. I'm telling you 'cause you don't tell anyone, right?'

'It depends,' the Queen said cautiously.

'Well, you can't tell them this because if you did, Josh would kill me.'

'Really?'

'OK, so not literally kill me,' Ivy amended. 'He's just a dopehead who thinks he's Jay-Z. But I can trust you. You know about the packet and you could've . . . Well, Arthur could be in jail now or something. Josh literally told him to look after it for a bit, till the heat died down. You saw what it did to Arthur. He can't even sleep. He's *terrified* of drugs.'

'That was rather my impression. Did Arthur tell the chickens all this?'

'No, not about Josh. I saw them on the beach together with the bag, after I found the hand. When I was on my way to tell them about it and give Josh's puppy back to him, before it ate something stupid and killed itself.'

'Is he a friend of yours?' the Queen asked. There was a heat to Ivy's tone that suggested something more than mere acquaintance.

'No way! He's a creep. Auntie Judy caught him dealing on the beach. She was writing a piece about it 'cause the police weren't doing anything. She told me to stay away from him last year. Should've listened. Josh is fit, but he's useless,' she added finally. 'I liked him once. He took me to the hides and said he wanted to show me the birds . . .'

Her voice tailed off and she stared up at the turrets and chimneys of the house in the distance ahead of them. The Queen sensed she wasn't really looking. A pall of sadness hung over her. The Queen had seen it many times before and it bore all the hallmarks of young love gone wrong. Josh was a love rat. So *that* was what went on in the hides – or at least part of it.

'I should've expected it, I s'pose,' Ivy went on, moodily. 'He takes after his dad. Maybe it's the dad Auntie Judy's worried about. It makes sense.' She grimaced. 'Him being a mass murderer.'

'What?' The Queen wondered if she'd misheard. 'I don't think you mean that, surely?'

'I totally do. He works on the turkey farm on the road to King's Lynn. They slaughter them in their thousands before Christmas. Josh laughed at me about it. He knows how I feel.'

This, too, was not quite what the Queen had been expecting. Though perhaps it should have been. Local Lotharios and turkey farmers. They were hardly the drug barons and people traffickers she had been anticipating.

'I hope you don't apply your "mass murderer" label to all livestock farmers,' the Queen said lightly, mindful that she was one herself.

Ivy missed the connection, or didn't care. 'I do. That's why I'm vegan. That, and because it's better for you. Mum kept saying I'd grow up stunted. I'm the fittest in the family.' The Queen was slightly piqued about the mass murderer suggestion. Vegans could be very aggressive in their views.

'Not everyone wants to eat that way or knows how to,' she said.

'Ignorance is no excuse,' Ivy said dismissively. 'They should educate themselves on what happens in abattoirs.'

'Abattoirs are a lot kinder than a fox in a chicken coop,' the Queen countered. 'Or would you have foxes turn vegetarian, too?'

'It's in their nature,' Ivy protested.

'And not ours?'

'We grew up. *We* evolved,' Ivy said, with the passion of youth. 'Our brains are a hundred times bigger than a fox's. We know enough to recognise cruelty when we see it. Or some of us do. We're not all Neanderthals anymore, though you look at the way we're destroying our own planet, you wonder.'

'It's obviously something you feel strongly about.'

'Don't you?' Ivy asked.

'Actually, I do,' the Queen said, somewhat relieved to have moved from veganism on to safer ground. 'So does my husband. We have great hope for your generation. You understand the issues better than anyone.'

Ivy tossed her head. 'That's what they tell us at school. I hate it when people say that. Like climate change and deforestation and all of it's our generation's problem to solve, when we had nothing to do with it. Your generation created the mess; you should be the ones to fix it.' She glared. 'Ma'am.'

The Queen didn't mind the girl's attitude and was glad there weren't any eager courtiers around to leap, unnecessarily, to her defence. In fact, she admired Ivy's spirit, and her unguarded honesty. It was vanishingly rare for her to be challenged in this way by one of her subjects, or indeed anyone other than Philip in a bad mood, or Anne in a very bad one.

'Did you know Ned St Cyr?' she asked, not in the spirit of enquiry this time, but out of curiosity. 'You sound as though you have a lot in common.'

'Yeah, I did,' Ivy said. 'Auntie Judy introduced me. She thought I might like to work on the rewilding thing.'

'And did you?'

Ivy rolled her eyes with frustration. 'I was going to, after my exams. It's like literally the last chance we've got to save the planet. The way it's going, it's dying. Mr St Cyr was fighting for the future. If he'd carried on, people would've been coming from all over the world to see what he was up to.'

'I'm not sure about *that*.'

But Ivy's eyes lit up. 'Yeah, definitely. It's incredible how many varieties of birds and butterflies you can get almost overnight on a rewilding project. Species like turtle doves you thought were gone forever . . . they're suddenly back. And nightingales. If you have wild pigs like Mr St Cyr did . . . maybe not *boar*, exactly, but Tamworth pigs like he should

175

have used if he wasn't being such a di—an idiot. The pigs dig up the ground and the new plants that grow provide the seeds the birds need and it's all there, just waiting.'

The Queen watched the girl's expression transform as she spoke. The habitual surliness was replaced by shining-eyed conviction and a reasonable mastery of her facts.

'You describe it quite compellingly,' she admitted.

Ivy shrugged. 'It doesn't matter now. Someone else'll take over. The land will be smothered in pesticides and the poor soil'll be forced to produce bad food until it's nothing but dust.'

This was not a thought the Queen wished to linger on. She always liked to find hope if she possibly could.

'Perhaps you should be a professional rewilder,' she suggested.

Instantly, the surliness was back. 'You need land for that . . . ma'am. Like yours.'

'Landowners need managers and experts to advise them.'

'Yeah . . . well. I don't want to be an *adviser*. I want to make something of my own.'

The Queen looked across at her, head down, striding forward. 'I don't doubt you will.'

They were nearly back at the house.

'Thank you for joining me. That was very interesting,' the Queen told her.

'No worries, ma'am,' Ivy said, with a lopsided grin. 'Thanks for looking out for my brother. You won't regret it.'

This 'ma'am' had come naturally, the Queen noticed. She felt, if not exactly honoured, then certainly gratified. Ivy was something of a wild creature herself and such gestures had to be earned.

On her way inside, she encountered Philip returning from a visit of his own to friends in the Fens. They paused together in the entrance to the saloon, where the jockey's weighing scales still stood that had once been used to ensure guests of her great-grandfather were suitably well fed. She told Philip about Ivy's passionate stance on livestock, because she wanted to see how far he could raise his eyebrows.

'Pah! Does the girl want us to live on lentils?'

'I think she does.'

'And who will grow them? Could she bear for the precious little things to be harvested?'

'She would manage,' the Queen said drily.

'I heard a very funny joke about lentils and chickpeas at Christmas. Gerry Harcourt told me. What's the difference between a lentil and a chickpea? You wouldn't pay a hundred pounds to have a lentil—' He stopped abruptly, mid-flow. 'Never mind. Actually, I heard about a man in Suffolk who's going to grow them commercially next year. Interesting crop. I must talk to Charles about it. Mind you, I suppose if Miss Ivy Raspberry had her way, even Sandringham would end up as a wild reserve.'

'I rather think so.'

'How will Charles and William support seven hundred people if they can't work the land, I ask you? Or shoot? God, by the time we get to poor George the place will be nothing but a glamping fest for butterfly fanatics – if he's lucky.'

Philip spat out the words, but he grew thoughtful. The Queen sensed he would rather love being outdoors, surrounded by butterflies. He certainly had on various trips to the jungle they had enjoyed during their royal tours. It was better than her vision of theme parks and golf courses: a sign of the return to the wild nature of their youth, when the countryside was messy and teeming with life, before all the hedgerows were scrubbed out and fields enlarged to feed the nation, and drenched with the pesticides of which Ivy Raspberry so vehemently disapproved.

'I'm off. I have work to do,' he said, shaking off his brief reverie and heading towards his library.

The Queen went upstairs to change. By the time little George was in charge, it would be entirely up to him how to run the estate, of course. One left it in as good order as one could, and hoped for the best. Who would win? she wondered. The farmers who wanted every bit of utility from ever-depleted soil, or the wilders who seemed to think the nation could live on bees and birdsong? She could see that both had the best interests of the land at heart, and one could only hope they would find a way of working it out together. It saddened her, and struck her as somewhat ridiculous, that they were constantly at each other's throats. They were really so close to each other in what they loved and cared about, if only they knew.

Chapter 20

On Wednesday, the Queen had her first encounter of the new year with the Prime Minister. It was just a phone call at this point; one didn't ask a busy politician to travel all the way to Norfolk for the afternoon. And one was quite relieved they didn't want to.

Sir Simon had warned her the conversation might be a difficult one. The PM had been 'thinking', apparently. There was certainly a lot to think about. It turned out that the state visit she had proposed to the new president of the USA, which had been mooted in the autumn to happen some time in the spring, was now rising rapidly up the agenda.

'The president is very keen to show his support for Britain, ma'am. As we are to him.'

'I see.'

'He'd like me to be the first foreign leader that he meets after his inauguration. He's thinking about later this month. We're working on the details.' The PM sounded delighted by this, and proud. 'As we've discussed before, I'd like to show our appreciation by offering him a state visit as soon as possible. Perhaps in the summer.'

As they had indeed discussed before, the Queen thought it a dreadful idea.

'Presidents don't usually visit until their second year of office at least,' she reminded her.

'This will show how important the special relationship is to us, ma'am.'

The relationship was special to the PM, the Queen knew, because she needed a trade deal with America to make up for the ones she would be losing with the European Union.

The Queen did not appreciate a VIP tour of her palaces being trotted out as a bonbon for foreign leaders the country desperately needed to impress. This was partly because the first time she had done it – to the magnificently ungrateful General De Gaulle – it had been an abject failure. She preferred such visits to be a mark of mutual respect. However, it was not her decision. The political atmosphere, both here and across the Atlantic, was fraught at the moment. Perhaps such a visit could help to calm choppy waters. If she could use her hospitality to contribute in any way, of course she would.

It was choppy waters closer to home that preoccupied her more now, anyway. Nearly three weeks had gone by since Ivy Raspberry made her ghastly discovery. After such a promising start, the police seemed to be back where they started. And despite all Rozie's work and Katie's help from the village, so did she. Meanwhile, newspaper speculation was rife; the *Recorder* had published every photograph it could find of royals and St Cyrs together, of which there were many. Often, the pictures were of older generations with shotguns broken over their arms, looking pleased after a game shoot. According to Rozie, who looked (the Queen didn't), the comments under the online versions of these were not favourable to the monarchy.

More to the point, Ned's body was still undiscovered. Judy Raspberry was hooked up to various machines in hospital. If Julian Cassidy and Helena Fisher had conspired to achieve this, the Queen couldn't for the life of her work out why. She refused to believe that it was because of the trampling of a lawn or, however fond she was of dogs, the death of a cockapoo.

According to Ivy, the article Judy was writing – the one that had inspired Mrs Day to wonder if the hit-and-run was organised – turned out to be prompted by a boy on the beach not much older than Ivy herself. Everywhere the Queen looked for dark conspiracies, she found commonplace events. They were sad enough for the individuals concerned, but hardly motive for murder. And certainly not the sort of murder planned as cleverly as this one, where a man had been made to disappear.

Was Ned's death entirely accidental after all? the Queen wondered. Had he walked out of his flat and fallen into a building site? Was he in the River Thames? Had he chosen to drop out of sight? And yet there was the hand. It always came back to the hand.

The Queen and Rozie had an hour planned in the diary after lunch to go through the next few weeks' events.

'Do you have any news?' she asked, without much hope.

'A little,' Rozie said. 'The police did know rumours of occasional, low-level drug dealing from Snettisham Beach. Even though it's on your doorstep, ma'am, they simply don't have the resources to investigate fully or put a stop to it. It's not that unusual. They're focused higher up the chain.'

'I see.'

'Katie's talked to her old colleagues at the Border Force. They think the bag on the beach came from a yacht travelling from Holland. They were tracking it at the time and it was heading much further up the coast. It all supports what you said Ivy told you: Judy hadn't stumbled on something big, just something that really mattered to her.'

'I'm not sure there's a difference, but I know what you mean,' the Queen said.

Rozie consulted her notes.

'The chief constable did have one update, though, entirely unrelated. Lord Mundy's son Valentine was seen having lunch with Mr St Cyr in the City of London in November.'

'Is that a problem? Ned had started to talk to the family again. They told us as much at Christmas. So did Astrid Westover.'

'It wouldn't be a problem, except Valentine lied about it. He insisted they hadn't met since his mother's funeral, until the police told him they had a sworn witness statement saying he did.'

The Queen sighed. 'Did he say what they discussed?'

'No, ma'am. Only that they were catching up on family news. There's nothing to link him to the disappearance, but his alibi is patchy. His flat in London is only a twenty-minute drive from Mr St Cyr's flat in Hampstead. He was supposed to be working from home, but he could have gone out and come back again.'

'What about his sister?' the Queen asked. She remembered Flora from the Christmas visit as the sibling with the vim. She had been the last person in the family to see him.

Rozie consulted her notes again. 'I checked the reports for all the family, ma'am. Flora and her father were at Ladybridge Hall all day on the fifteenth.'

'We know one more thing, ma'am. One of Katie's knitting friends saw Mr Cassidy at the Feathers pub a few days ago. He'd had a couple of glasses, and he was telling anyone who'd listen that he was the last person to talk to the victim, and that he'd shouted nonsense down the phone.'

'Oh?'

'Something about the scuffle, which Mr Cassidy said he'd already apologised for, and the promise that it would rain in hell. People were asking, and he said he had no idea what it was supposed to mean. If he was making it up, it was a strange thing to do. 'I mentioned it to the chief constable and asked if we should be worried about him. It seemed a reasonable enough question.'

'I agree.'

'I didn't tell him about the car because, as I say, Mr Cassidy had already reported it. Technically, they know as much as we do.'

'Exactly,' the Queen said. 'If we have something useful to add, we will, but at the moment, we seem to be going around in circles.'

Rozie looked uncomfortable. 'And unfortunately there's a problem.'

'Go on.'

'Someone in Dersingham seems to have noticed Katie's interest in Mrs Raspberry's hit-and-run.'

The Queen pursed her lips. 'Oh, dear. What happened?'

'They put a note through her letterbox late last night. It said that she'd been looking in the wrong place.'

'Ah.'

'Your name was never mentioned, though, ma'am. Hopefully, they'll assume she was doing it for her own reasons.'

'Hmm. Did they give any alternative suggestions?'

'Well, as a matter of fact they did.' Rozie took a plain envelope from her notebook. Inside was a handwritten note in a neat pencil script on plain letter paper, enclosing a folded piece of printed paper. The latter was a small article cut out of the *East Anglian Chronicle*. Rozie handed it to the Queen. It read:

TRAGIC DEATH AT BURNHAM OVERY STAITHE

On the morning of New Year's Day, the body of an elderly man, 79, was pulled from the sea near Scolt Head Island. He was identified as Chris Wallace, the long-standing member of a wild swimming group called the Dix Dunkers. He had been trying to reach the island from the beach at Burnham Overy Staithe and succumbed to hypothermia in the freezing water.

The article went on to remind readers how exceptionally attractive the area was, and how dangerous it was to swim alone, especially in winter when the water was dangerously cold.

The Queen looked up at Rozie.

'Do we know anything about the swimmer?'

'Yes, ma'am,' Rozie said. 'He came from a village south of here, called Vickery.'

'That's on the Ladybridge Estate.'

Rozie nodded. 'The thing is, Katie's a wild swimmer, too. She says that if you're very experienced, as he was, you know not to go out alone in freezing water, and not to stay out too long. She's not convinced it was an accident, and she doesn't think the person who gave her the article does, either.'

The Queen felt very bleak. New Year's Eve had been so full of happiness and hope at Sandringham, as they danced into the small hours. The following morning had been marred by Jack Lions's interview, but that had been an annoyance, really, nothing more. To think that, only a few miles away, a man's life was ending in such a tragic way.

There was a pause while she called Willow to her and stroked under the corgi's warm ears. That was the day she had found out about Judy Raspberry. She had been convinced that the hit-and-run was part of a bigger picture. Someone was covering their tracks. Yet wherever she looked for conspiracies she found coincidences. She had been too sure of herself. Even after ninety years, she needed to learn humility sometimes.

But the suspicious death of someone connected to the St Cyr family seat? That didn't smack of coincidence at all. Her moment of humility passed. She patted the dog and looked at Rozie.

'Has Katie arranged to talk to . . .' she consulted the article once more '. . . The Dix Dunkers?'

Rozie nodded. 'She's meeting one of them tomorrow, ma'am.'

PART 3

THE ENDS OF THE EARTH

Chapter 21

The little village of Vickery, much like West Newton, consisted of neat cottages lined up along well-tended roads. It looked as if it had just been swept and clipped, ready to star in the sort of Christmas movie where the heroine, home for the holidays, discovers the sexy wickedness of Hugh Grant and chooses – inexplicably – to settle down with someone safe at the end of the third reel. Rozie used to watch those kind of movies with her sister when they were both tired from studying, curled up on the duvet side by side, waiting for their mother to shout at them to turn off the light. She had always dismissed the settings as unreal, but now she knew that wasn't true: they existed, when wealthy landlords wanted them to.

It was Rozie, not Katie, who was visiting the organiser of the Dix Dunkers. Katie had called to say she'd had a bad night and could barely make it down the stairs. By coincidence, it was Rozie's morning off. She had put aside the run and the personal grooming session she had planned for herself. And here she was.

Mary Collathorn lived in 'the cottage with the two weeping pears in the front garden', as she'd explained to Rozie. 'You can't miss it.' The twin domes outside the fourth building

189

she passed looked exactly like the ones she had looked up on Google Images. She parked her Mini outside.

'So you're thinking of taking up wild swimming?'

'Mmmm.' Rozie sipped her expertly made cappuccino. It pained Rozie slightly to repay Mary's hospitality with a series of lies, but they were in a good cause. Nothing, if truth were told, would inveigle her into freezing cold water voluntarily. She wasn't *crazy*. But for the purposes of the visit, she had been recommended to the group by someone in Dersingham who had heard great things about them. She made some noises about wanting to swim in a river, rather than the sea, as that's what they seemed to do most of the time. 'I'm sorry about your recent loss, by the way,' she added. 'I read about Mr Wallace.'

'Oh, it was terrible, what happened to him,' Mary said. 'We're all reeling. He was such a fixture on the Ladybridge Estate.'

'Was he? Was he connected to the family in some way? The St Cyrs, I mean.'

'Oh! Do you know them?' Mary asked.

'I met some of them at Sandringham,' Rozie said. She usually kept very quiet about her encounters behind closed doors, but today, gossip seemed very much in order. 'Did Chris work for them?'

'Most people do, round here,' Mary said. 'Chris was a second-generation tenant, like me. His father was the mechanic for Patrick St Cyr in the early sixties. It was all very glamorous back then.'

Rozie noticed the way Mary expected her to know who everyone in the family was, and why working for someone

190

called Patrick should be glamorous. It was a bit like Sir Simon and *Debrett's* again.

'Remind me about Patrick?' Rozie said.

'He was the heir at the time – the tenth baron's son. He threw the most famous parties in East Anglia. But really, he wanted to be a racing driver. My mother remembers him dashing round the lanes in a series of blue sports cars. He used to talk about setting up his own racing team one day. Mr Wallace – senior, that is – was always working on something for him, and if he wasn't busy on the cars, there were the tractors. He made clocks, too, I remember. After the accident, he was worried he'd lose his job, but the family in those days were very loyal.'

'The accident?'

'Oh, it was awful. Patrick was racing home through the Fens in his sports car after a storm. When I say racing, they think he was doing nearly a hundred miles an hour. He hit a patch of flooding, and he didn't stand a chance. I saw the pictures of the car, upside down in a dyke. It was such a tragedy. His mother, the baroness, was a fragile woman. Her hair went white overnight, like Marie Antoinette's. She made Chris's father burn the car and dismantle the chassis and melt it down and bury what was left. She died the following year. His father hadn't been fully well since the war; he went two years later. And now there was no male heir, of course, so the title went to a different branch of the family. But you don't want to talk about them – you want to talk about swimming. You'll love it, I promise you.'

For a good ten minutes, Rozie discussed the benefits of immersing the human body in very cold water. Having tried it in the army during various exercises, she still maintained that it was a terrible idea unless absolutely necessary for the security of the nation, but she practised looking fascinated. Afterwards, it wasn't hard to veer the conversation back towards the subject of Chris, who had been such a passionate convert to wild swimming. As Katie suspected, he knew all the rules of swimming in very cold water. He simply would not have gone out alone, and stayed out for so long, by accident.

'You don't think . . .? I mean, there's no reason to suppose he wasn't alone, is there?' Rozie said.

Mary's eyes widened. 'D'you mean, did someone make him do it? Oh, goodness! What a horror! No! People aren't speculating about that in Dersingham, are they?'

'One or two were wondering . . .' Rozie said, feeling hugely disloyal to A Load of Balls and the Sweary Stitchers, even though she wasn't a member.

Mary looked militant. 'Well, you can put their minds at ease, if you can call it that. I know why he went out that day. He absolutely intended to do what he did. It was simply awful.'

Rozie said nothing. Sometimes silence and an interested expression was enough.

'He was recently widowed, you know. Laura, his wife, was the shepherdess for the farm. They'd lived in that cottage forty years. She died in the bedroom, with him beside her. The kids were born there. Laura poured her heart and soul into the place. She was diagnosed with cancer at about the same time as the baroness. The last one, I mean – Lee. They nursed each other through it. You'd think the family would have some decency. But after the baroness died . . .'

'What happened?'

Mary shook her head. 'Chris said they'd told him the cottage was wanted for a bloody Airbnb. They were giving him three months to get out. He had nowhere else to go, no idea what to do. I drank a dram of whisky with him on New Year's Eve and I could see how overwrought he was.'

'So you think he went into the sea like that deliberately?'

'Oh, I'm sure of it. I made a promise to myself that I'd go over after lunch on New Year's Day and check he was OK. But by then it was already much too late. He'd left his wallet in a bag on the beach. I was his emergency contact, so they called me.' Tears spilled silently down her cheeks. 'And I was just here, making soup.'

'It wasn't your fault,' Rozie said gently.

Mary gazed at her fiercely through the tears. 'Of course it wasn't! I know *exactly* whose fault it was.'

Chapter 22

The Sunday morning service at St Mary's in Flitcham went very well. There was a bit of a to-do beforehand when the Queen's protection team discovered a packet of drugs hidden under one of the kneelers. But the incident was over and done with before the Queen arrived.

On Monday, the outgoing US ambassador made his formal goodbye to the Marshal of the Diplomatic Corps, representing Her Majesty at Buckingham Palace. She had written the man a warm personal note for him to pass on. The ambassador had been very fond of London, and London was very fond of him. His departure marked the end of an era. The PM's formal announcement of the UK's exit from the Single Market marked another one. They were only halfway through January and what a year of change this was already turning out to be.

The annual visit to the West Newton branch of the WI on Thursday came at just the right time. Such cyclical events, like the church calendar, conferred a comforting rhythm on life which was very much needed. The Queen wasn't the only woman to feel it. Everyone seemed grateful to be there.

Of course, the talk was largely about Judy Raspberry, the much-missed treasurer. She was sitting up in bed in her ward at the Queen Elizabeth, already itching to be home, but she still couldn't remember anything about her accident. She had heard that Her Majesty herself had asked after her health, and was very touched.

Sir Simon went up to London to try and placate a disgruntled group of Scottish MPs. There were rumblings that when the UK exited the Single Market, the Scots would want to rerun their independence referendum. Ultimately, it would be up to the Scots themselves to decide, but the Queen was keen on the 'united' part of the United Kingdom. She would prefer it, to put it mildly, to stay that way.

The circumstances were not ideal, but it made it easier for the Queen and Rozie to catch up without Rozie having to lie to the private secretary about what they had discussed. And since Rozie had described her visit to Vickery, there was a lot to talk about.

'Katie managed to see Mrs Raspberry in hospital, ma'am,' Rozie said. 'She doesn't know any of the St Cyr family apart from Ned. She also doesn't know Mr Wallace. It's hard to see a connection between them.'

The Queen had learned her lesson. 'Then let's not try and make one.'

'There was one piece of good news. Katie worked out who gave her the newspaper article about Mr Wallace. It was a member of her own wild swimming group. They'd somehow found out about her Home Office background and thought she was interested in suspicious accidents because of that. They didn't connect it to Ned, or me, or you.'

'That's very reassuring,' the Queen agreed. Katie was eager to help, but she didn't have Rozie's lightness of touch when required. The Queen wasn't sure Rozie yet realised how good, and how very dependable, she was. 'What about Valentine St Cyr? Is there any news?'

'Yes, ma'am. The police are interested in the fact that Roland Peng's initials are RLP.'

'Roland Peng, his business partner?'

'In part, ma'am. I'll come to that. It turns out that Valentine had more than one meeting with Ned last year. Interestingly, they hadn't spotted them before because Ned put them in his diary as "VSC". Usually he wrote names in full and locations as acronyms. But if VSC was a name, then perhaps RIP was one, too. And perhaps he miswrote it or it was just a feature of his handwriting, but he could have meant RLP. That's what they're looking into now.'

'So Ned might have arranged to meet Roland?'

'Apparently. Roland claims to have been in business meetings both days, but there were gaps between them. He was, supposedly, with Valentine the night of the fourteenth. They are each other's alibi.'

'Are they?'

'Yes, ma'am. That's the thing. Flora told me on New Year's Eve that they're secretly engaged. She swore me to secrecy, too, but she was obviously very happy for them.'

'Valentine and Roland?'

'Yes, ma'am.'

'Engaged?'

'Yes. Roland proposed at Christmas.' Rozie smiled. The Queen thought she looked very pleased about it.

'When are they announcing it, do you know?'

Rozie noticed that the Queen was truly startled. She found the Boss generally much more open-minded than most people would suspect, but not this time. Her generation's prejudices showed through. Rozie was disappointed.

'In the summer. Flora said something about them getting used to the idea. It could be something to do with Roland's family in Singapore. The baron's been told. He took it pretty well, she said. For someone of his . . . You know, ma'am. His generation.'

'I wonder when they planned on telling me,' the Queen said, more to herself than anything. 'Do many other people know this "secret"?'

'The police don't. It's not in any of the reports. I thought they looked very happy together at the visit. I wasn't completely surprised when Flora told me.'

'Weren't you?' the Queen said, peering at Rozie through her bifocals. 'I admit, I am. And do the police have any reason to think that Roland would have wanted to kill his partner's distant cousin? He didn't park in a specific place, for example?'

'No, ma'am. It's just the initials at this stage. But they have a team working on it.'

'I'm sure they do,' the Queen agreed. 'They throw technology at problems. Think of all those phone records and traffic cameras. I'm a great believer in technology. But they haven't made the connection with Chris Wallace yet.' She was silent for a while, before adding, 'You'll like Ladybridge.'

'Ma'am?'

'I have a standing invitation. Call Lord Mundy and let him know I'd be delighted to come to lunch before I go back to London. The sooner the better. You know when the gaps in my diary are.'

After Rozie left, the Queen thought back to Valentine St Cyr and Roland Peng. They would be making history in ways that Rozie clearly didn't understand. Did their secret have something to do with what had happened to Chris Wallace? She found herself thinking about it again later, when her racing manager was helping her put the finishing touches to the jigsaw in the saloon. They completed the Constable, which was a huge satisfaction. Human puzzles, as always, were much more challenging.

Chapter 23

The turning to Ladybridge was familiar from the Queen's childhood, when she and her sister had visited with their mother. The road took them through the village of Vickery and past the long, flint-lined walls of the estate to the Ladybridge village green with its pub and the little church of St Agnes, where Georgina St Cyr was now buried in the family vault.

Today, the Queen was travelling with Lady Caroline, while Rozie and her protection officer followed behind. The Range Rovers rounded a corner near the church and drove through a wide stone archway towards the hall itself, which was tightly surrounded by its famous moat and set among orchards and meadows leading down to a little river, with fields and farmland beyond.

The picturesque view was the happy result of failure, rather than success. The St Cyrs, as any of them would tell you, had generally been on the wrong side of history: Catholic in Elizabethan times, Royalist during the Civil War, firmly agricultural during the Industrial Revolution. They had been well respected, but never rich. Poor decisions, death duties and bad luck had chipped away at the income from their land

and caused the hall itself to fall into deep disrepair at times during its five centuries of existence. But this had worked in the house's favour in the end. Limited in space by the moat that surrounded them, the motley collection of medieval and Elizabethan buildings hadn't been expanded, rebuilt or restyled by succeeding generations. Over the centuries their twisted chimneys, steep, sloping roofs and gothic crenellations had passed from unfashionable to out of date, to almost ruined, but the Tudor details of its weathered brick design had stayed intact. The last four generations had fought hard to preserve what they had, so that now the guidebooks to the county praised it as 'untouched', 'unspoilt', 'a harmonious example of Elizabethan moated architecture at its finest'. Glimpsed from a distance through Norfolk mist, it could easily be an illustration from a fairy tale.

Ladybridge was, the Queen had always thought, the perfect size for a child to grow up in – a bit like Birkhall in Scotland, where she had spent happy times with her parents on the Balmoral estate. It was not so large that you would feel endlessly intimidated by it, but big enough for hide-and-seek, for endless indoor games on rainy days and larks outside on sunny ones. Each brick and stone told the story of the generations who had lived there. The grounds beyond were ripe for childish adventures. No wonder Georgina had wanted Ned to grow up here, and what a lucky little boy he had been.

The last stretch of road had once been through a cherry orchard, which the Queen Mother had always tried to visit in spring for the joy of its endless pale pink. But now, she saw, half of it was set aside as a visitor car park. A modern carbuncle on the orchard gateway turned out to be a ticket booth advertising tours of the gardens 'Open from 1 April'. Some of the romance had been sacrificed to make what was left accessible. The Queen nodded to herself. It was a sign of survival.

The car swept across the drawbridge and into the cobbled courtyard of the main house, where three generations of St Cyrs had come out to greet them, accompanied by an assortment of spaniels, terriers and an elderly Labrador.

The baron looked as old and hunched as he had been at Christmas. He had not dressed up for her visit. Hugh's normal style, which bordered on affectation, was a patched tweed jacket, a flannel shirt and cord trousers held up with baling twine. The Queen suspected he had seen himself as a rural character from a P. G. Wodehouse novel at some point in his more sprightly middle age, and stuck with it. Several other Norfolk landowners she knew were of similar mind, but the baling twine edged it, in her opinion.

Flora stood beside him, along with her three pretty, teenage daughters, who had not accompanied their mother to Sandringham. Their father, like Ned's, was no longer in the picture. Somehow, men who were not St Cyrs by blood didn't survive Ladybridge very long. Flora wore a neat jumper over a thick skirt that suggested the heating at the hall was not up to the quality of its gardens. It was impossible to tell whether the girls had made an effort. All their clothes were ripped or half-missing or very old and creased. It might be the first thing they'd pulled out of the wardrobe, but the Queen sensed it might equally be the height of fashion for their age.

'Dad's laid on lunch,' Flora said, 'but afterwards I want to show you the gardens. I know how much your mother loved them.'

Lunch was held in the panelled dining room whose windows overlooked the moat, where four white swans floated serenely by. It wasn't *quite* as nice as the dining room at Sandringham, the Queen thought, but not far off. Conversation over coffee in the adjacent drawing room inevitably turned to Ned.

'What sort of mood was he in when you saw him?' Lady Caroline asked. 'Did you have any sense he was in trouble?'

The Queen was really very grateful for Lady Caroline.

'I thought he seemed rather grim,' Hugh said. 'But perhaps that's because he knew he'd be asking me for money over coffee.'

Flora disagreed. 'He was in full flow, most of the time. He was happy to lecture us on how to run the place, which seemed to amount to *not* running it. He wanted us to let Mundy Forest run wild, and he wanted Ladybridge to be an "inland wetland centre", whatever that is. I pointed out it's pretty wet already, what with the moat and the river. He wasn't remotely interested in what we're actually doing.' She sighed. 'I had hoped he'd come with Astrid, and we did ask if she might be around, but of course she was away in Spain. She's very good on social media. I wanted to ask her advice about Instagram. Ladybridge is so photogenic.'

'So you know her?' the Queen asked.

'I was at Pony Club with her eldest sister. I thought she was crazy to be marrying a man twice her age, until I saw them together at Abbottswood. I think it would have worked, actually.'

'I know what you mean,' the Queen agreed. 'Not that I did see them together, exactly.'

'The wedding would've been in three weeks,' Eden, the youngest girl, piped up morosely.

'Oh, dear. I suppose so,' Lady Caroline agreed.

'Ned invited us. He said now the family were back together, it was kind of important. I had this incredible Burberry dress I was going to wear . . .'

'Figgy!' her eldest sister Emerald said warningly.

'What? It was a really nice dress.'

Emerald went puce. The Queen sensed a certain tension between the siblings that wasn't entirely unfamiliar. Eden was a successful model at sixteen and a bit of a wild child. Her picture had been on the cover of a recent *Harper's Bazaar*, dressed in a scrap of green silk that left little to the imagination. Sophie Wessex had shown it to her. The Queen thought the girl looked too thin in the picture, but had refrained from saying so, because her grandmother had said the same thing about the debs after the war, and it made one sound old. Today, her chosen outfit was a slightly stained vintage coat with frogging, that looked as if it might have once belonged to a slender Cossack officer. It covered her from neck to ankle and, despite the staining, she looked very good in it.

'This was the exact last place we saw him,' Emerald said. 'In this room. He sat right where you're sitting now, ma'am.'

'Goodness,' the Queen said. 'How alarming. It must have been very awkward for you when the police came, asking questions.'

'They were here for ages,' Eden said. 'They wanted to see all the weapons in the armoury passage. They asked loads of questions. By the end I was starting to think I'd done it myself.'

'They wanted to know about our alibis the next day,' Elinor, the middle girl, explained. 'I didn't really have one. I was out on a hack on Skylark most of the day. I'm sure I'd have had time to dash up to London by train and do something terrible.'

'No, you wouldn't,' Emerald said, with a curled lip. 'That train takes forever. You couldn't even have driven it.'

'I could.'

'You can't get out of second gear.'

'I could if I had an automatic,' Elinor grumbled. She appealed to the Queen. 'They only let me drive the 2CV, which is literally fifty years old and squeaks if you go over twenty miles an hour. And it's broken right now. But I bet if I had a sports car I could have—'

'Elinor did not kill our cousin,' Flora assured the Queen briskly. 'She hardly knew the man.'

'And what about the rest of you?' the Queen asked, with a hint of a smile to suggest she was joking, which she wasn't.

'Eden had a shoot in London,' Emerald said promptly. The Queen pictured tweeds and shotguns and was surprised at the location, but quickly realised Emerald meant magazines. 'I drove her up after the lunch, because she's still a child. Yes, you are, Figgy, so shut up. I suppose we *could* have done something to him in town, but we were with the

204

magazine people all day next day. Those things go on for absolutely hours. We weren't home until teatime.'

'I still wasn't back from my ride,' Elinor said sullenly. Nobody seemed interested.

'I don't remember where I was,' Lord Mundy said.

'Yes, you do, Dad,' Flora reminded him. 'You went for tea with Mrs Capelton.'

'No, that was the day before. Ned dropped me off after lunch. She's in charge of making the new kneelers for St Agnes in memory of Lee. She's a wonderful woman but it took me two and a half hours to get away. I had to walk home in the dark.'

'Who visited you that night, Grandpa?' Elinor asked. 'I saw the taxi in the courtyard.'

'That I do remember. It was poor Mr Wallace. He was in a very fragile state. I tried to reassure him, but I'm not sure how effective I was.'

'He did look grim,' Flora agreed. 'And then you and I had a marathon session on the church refurbishment accounts with the vicar the next day.'

'Oh, yes. And an antiquarian bookseller came in the afternoon. He's interested in some of my first editions. It's a wrench to say goodbye to them, but Flora needs her cake shop.'

'I went for a ride,' Flora said. 'I'd have tried to meet up with Elinor if I'd known I was going to be quizzed about it for hours by a policeman, but sadly, I didn't. I do have a fitness tracker, though. He seemed to think that might help.'

By now the girls were getting restless and dispersed to various parts of the house. Flora invited the Queen to see the gardens, but the baron said he had something to discuss with Her Majesty, which suited her admirably. Rozie, who had agreed on the division of labour beforehand, offered to go with Flora instead.

'I'm afraid I don't know one end of a trowel from the other,' Rozie admitted, as they put on coats and wellies in the boot room of the hall. 'But I like those bushes you cut into shapes.'

'Topiary?' Flora asked. 'Sorry, we don't have much of that. It tends to be in formal gardens. Apart from the maze, ours are very . . . You'll see.'

They trudged over the drawbridge and round the gravel path that skirted the outside of the moat and led down a bank, towards a meadow fringed with willows. Rozie soon saw why Flora had insisted on wellingtons for them both: the ground was soggy and they disappeared in it up to their ankles.

'Do you do a lot of work on the estate?' Rozie asked.

Flora nodded. 'Oh, yes. It keeps me busy and we can't afford nearly enough professionals to do it all. There are the gardens and the new visitor plans. Dad manages the agricultural side of the farm, but I love the sheep. We lost our shepherdess last year. I can't do everything with them yet, but it turns out I have a knack for it.'

Rozie could see some of the sheep Flora was referring to in a distant field, beyond the line of willows. Black and white, they dotted the landscape like something out of one of those jigsaws the Queen liked to do.

They were approaching a series of ponds linked by a stream that fed into the river. She explained that it was a nineteenth-century water garden that her mother had revived. They stood on a little wooden humpback bridge and looked into the fast-flowing stream.

'I heard you had a bit of a tragedy recently,' Rozie said.

'Golly, which one?' Flora asked.

'A man called Chris Wallace.'

'Oh, him. Yes, that was absolutely shocking. How did you know?'

'It's all around Dersingham, I'm afraid.'

Flora tutted. 'Lord, the local gossips. He was devastated about his wife. Like Dad, really. I suppose that's why he went to see him.'

'I heard he'd been asked to move out.'

Flora turned to look sharply at Rozie. 'Goodness, no. Laura Wallace was one of Mum's best friends. Her children were like brothers and sisters to us when we were little. Whatever gave people that idea?'

'Sorry, Dersingham's a hotbed of gossip, as you say,' Rozie backtracked, shaking her head and grinning in a placatory way. 'The crochet group is bad, but the embroiderers . . . you have no idea.'

It seemed to work. Flora warmed up again. She showed Rozie the white gardens enclosed among lichen-covered walls and low-cut hedges, for which Georgina St Cyr had become famous. As a non-gardener, Rozie had to take Flora's word for it that the bare bushes and half-empty beds would look spectacular in spring and summer when they were full of white roses, lilies and fat hydrangeas.

'There are all sorts of rare plants here,' Flora explained. 'All my female ancestors were collectors. I fully intend to be one, too, when we can afford it. Thanks to my mother and Georgina, it was the gardens that kept Ladybridge going, not the farm. We have one of the best collections of lilies in the country, to go with the water lilies on the ponds. Mummy was passionate about water lilies. She was a real water baby. And we *did* have an exceptional poison garden, but I'm having to get rid of it because you try getting public liability insurance when your deadly nightshade collection rivals your hemlock and wolfsbane. It pains me to do it, because Georgina started that collection in the 1930s and my mother had an odd gothic streak to her, and she loved it, too. However—' she shrugged '—dead visitors are bad for business.'

Rozie stole another glance at her as they walked along the gravel path between box-edged flower beds. The dry humour of the aristocracy still caught her by surprise.

'*Has* anyone died? Of poison, I mean?' Rozie asked.

'Not that I know of,' Flora said breezily. 'Not recently, anyway. Legend has it that one of the servants was poisoned with hemlock back in Georgian times. His ghost is supposed to haunt the Long Gallery, but I've never seen it. My brother *nearly* died when he was six or seven. I think it was wolfsbane he ate. Dad was beside himself. He wanted all the wolfsbane dug up. My mother was pretty tough about it. She said he'd learned his lesson. Val didn't touch it again. Anyway, it's all gone now.'

They rounded a couple of large greenhouses and the twisted chimneys of the hall came back into view to their left, with the gatehouse further away to the right. Flora stopped and pointed.

'There,' she said, as if Rozie had asked her a question.

'I'm sorry?'

Flora was very still and thoughtful.

'That's where I saw Ned for the last time, driving away with Dad in his ridiculous pink Land Rover. He called it the Pink Panther, you know. It was painted to match his house. He waved his trilby at me.' She imitated the movement with her right hand. 'I honestly thought the next time I'd see him would be at his wedding.' She hesitated. 'Can I tell you an awful secret?'

'Go on.'

Flora smiled slightly. 'It's such a *relief* not to be hated. He pretended he didn't, but he'd resented us for so long. I used to feel his presence like an angry ghost. And now he actually *is* dead, the spirit has lifted. And I feel my mother's presence instead. Isn't that utterly bizarre?'

Rozie glanced across at the ancient bricks and stones of the hall, sitting serenely above the moat that mirrored the sky.

'I can imagine this place would encourage you to think that way.'

'It *is* ridiculous. That's what you're thinking. I'm a romantic idiot.'

Rozie had in fact been wondering if Flora – practical, competent, sharp-thinking Flora – was putting on an act. If so, it was a neat double bluff. She certainly felt as if she had been more of an audience than a confidante.

'I don't think you're an idiot at all,' she said, and wondered how the Queen was getting on.

The Queen was letting Lady Caroline do most of the talking again.

'Do you know? I haven't been here since I was eighteen. I was here with Lee. It must have been before you got married. Do you mind if we have a quick look in the Long Gallery? I remember thinking it was one of my favourite rooms in Norfolk.'

They walked down a long, panelled corridor from the hall's east wing, where the family's living accommodation was, past a series of large tapestries featuring knights and ladies in a mythical green landscape with a river running through it, whose banks were dotted with spring flowers.

'Were these here before?' the Queen asked.

'Yes,' Hugh said, 'but I had them cleaned last year, for Lee. Arthur and Guinevere. Lee always loved those landscapes. She said they reminded her of her gardens. Water and flowers and so on. I had them hung in her suite when she was bed-bound. They gave her a lot of pleasure in her final weeks.'

His grief was so different from Astrid Westover's, the Queen thought. He held it in, and held on to it. It was etched onto his face.

He guided them to the Long Gallery on the second floor of the south wing, where Elizabethans would have taken their exercise in bad weather. It was a bright, sunny space with a plaster ceiling, longer than a tennis court and lined with the family portraits Georgina St Cyr had moved to make way for her modern art collection downstairs. They stood and looked out through mullioned windows over the meadow and the riverbank beyond.

'I remember Ned bringing me up here,' Lady Caroline said. 'This was where the ghostly servant walks, isn't it? Ned tried to scare me about it. Failed miserably. I love ghosts. We rode bicycles around here like mad things. It was tremendous fun. Lee was there, too, I remember. Ned was very soppy about her. It was before you were married. Didn't he go out with her, too?'

Hugh looked acutely uncomfortable. 'They knew each other,' he acknowledged gruffly. 'Ned met her at the Agricultural College, but I knew her brother from Oxford. Once we met, we decided on marriage very quickly. I never regretted it for a day.'

How Ned must have hated you, the Queen thought. *Getting the estate and the girl.* She could almost feel the resentment sunk into the sloping floor. Not a ghost, exactly, but a malignant presence. Ned's stubborn fury made more sense now. If he had decided to kill his cousin, half a century ago, she could almost have understood. His fury had persisted for decades, but according to his fiancée he had finally moved beyond it. Was she right? Had she been telling the truth? Anyway, now the fate of Ladybridge was in Hugh's hands.

'You mentioned at Christmas,' she said, 'that Flora is inheriting, not Valentine.'

'Ah, yes, ma'am.' Hugh looked uncomfortable. 'I should have discussed it with you first. I intended to but I was somewhat distracted . . .'

211

'Does Valentine mind?' Lady Caroline asked.

'He'll get the title, of course. He's good with tenancies and financing and so on, but he's embraced city life. He doesn't want to while away his days in East Anglia worrying about milk yields and badgers and foot and mouth.'

'Most sons come round eventually.'

'Only because they have to. My father didn't want to take over Ladybridge, you know. He'd been very happy at his law firm in Ipswich. Suddenly he was lumbered with death duties and black beetle and dry rot. It would have been easier for him if Georgina had inherited from her father, but . . . male primogeniture and all that rot.'

He turned to the Queen and laughed slightly. She murmured her agreement, to an extent, although she wouldn't have gone quite as far as 'rot'. Nevertheless, she and Philip had ended the system in their own family, and not only for property but for titles, too. Little Charlotte Cambridge now held her place in the succession ahead of any younger brothers she might have.

'Valentine has other plans,' Hugh added. 'That's what I wanted to talk to you about. He and Roland are getting married. I wanted you to be among the first to know.'

'Oh, *are* they?' the Queen said, disingenuously – as if Rozie had never mentioned it. 'My congratulations, obviously. It will be a first.'

'The first man in the peerage to marry another man, you mean? Indeed. The St Cyrs are leading the way, ma'am. Another family entry in the history books.'

'It certainly will be.' The Queen was aware that her surprise at this decision made her sound stiff. It was true about the history books.

'He and Roland are planning to live in New York.'

'How *lovely*,' Lady Caroline said firmly. 'And thank goodness you have Flora to look after things here.'

'Exactly,' Hugh agreed.

They walked down a wide staircase of shallow steps and through a vaulted hallway decorated with intricate patterns of crossed swords, pikes and halberds, pistols and muskets dating back to the Civil War. Outside, in a second inner courtyard near the medieval section of the house, a wheelbarrow and two large piles of stone, wrapped in plastic, suggested the new building works were not complete.

'Is there still much to do?' Lady Caaroline asked.

'A little,' Hugh conceded. 'We're damp-proofing the rooms where Flora's new cake shop will go. Quite an undertaking with a moat, as you can imagine.'

As they stood in the courtyard, the sun, which had been hidden by a bank of cloud all day, suddenly fought its way through and bathed them in its pale gold, wintery light.

Lady Caroline beamed. 'There's nothing like a winter's afternoon when the sun finally makes an appearance.'

Hugh offered to take them on a quick tour round the moat. The clouds were rolling back rapidly now to reveal an ever-increasing patch of pale blue sky. A light breeze ruffled the grasses in the distant meadows.

'*This sceptred isle, this earth of majesty, this seat of Mars, this other Eden,*' Hugh murmured. He gave a brief, self-deprecatory laugh. 'Or so I've always thought.'

'*Richard II*!' Lady Caroline announced happily. 'We studied it at school. It's John of Gaunt, isn't it? *This blessed plot, this earth, this realm, this England* . . . I always loved that speech. It doesn't end well, though.' She shook her head and laughed, too.

They rounded the eastern side of the house and turned to the south, where the moat was bordered by a formal rose garden before a lengthy slope led down to the tree-fringed river below. There was an eerie peacefulness to the scene, pierced occasionally by stern calling and counter-calling from sheep in a distant field.

'Oh, you have sheep, too!' Lady Caroline said to Hugh. Her thoughts were on a very different track from the Queen's, and much sunnier. 'You are brave. My brother keeps them and he can't make a penny out of them. He does it for the love.'

'So do we,' Hugh agreed. 'These are Norfolk Horns. They used to be practically extinct. The fleeces are wonderful quality, but worth nothing in these days of synthetic clothes, of course. They make excellent meat, too. We were devastated to lose our poor, dear shepherdess last year.'

'Do you have much to do with the tenants?' the Queen asked.

'Socially, d'you mean? Oh, goodness, it varies. We entertain them a few times a year,' Hugh said. 'It was always more Lee's domain than mine. "Hearts and minds", she called it. Like the army, you know. Oh, look, up there.' He pointed across the meadow, above the river, where a heron was gliding silently on outstretched wings. 'Some are friends and some are absolute bastards.'

'Herons?' she asked.

'No, tenants. I'm sure you find the same thing. They all loved Lee, though,' he added softly. 'And I'm sure they'll come round to Flora, too. She only wants the best for Ladybridge.'

They kept walking around the moat until they were level with the buildings at the other end of the hall from the drawbridge, where the works on Flora's future cake shop were evident from missing window frames and loose tarpaulins at ground level, one of which flapped forlornly in the breeze.

'It's like the Forth Bridge,' Hugh commented. 'Never finished.'

'And yet always itself,' Lady Caroline said. 'I'm sure St Cyrs have been thinking it wasn't quite done from the moment they moved in, don't you?'

Hugh grinned. 'You're probably right.'

As they rounded the next corner they heard a shout and saw Flora waving to them from the far end of the path, next to Rozie. Even from a distance, the Queen thought she detected a set to Rozie's shoulders that meant her APS had something to tell her. *Good.* Meanwhile, her own thoughts were developing rapidly. They had a lot to talk about.

Chapter 24

B ack in the saloon, the family were clustered in front of the television set, watching the inauguration of the forty-fifth president. He was seventy, as commentators felt it necessary to mention – the same age as Ned, yet obviously with much life ahead of him and much to do. Not all of it popular, if the protests taking place around the world and the lack of famous faces in the crowd were anything to go by. But the Queen was taken with Senator Blunt's opening remarks about the 'commonplace and miraculous' tradition of a peaceful transfer of power.

People rather took that for granted these days, she thought. As a keen student of history, she was highly aware that transfers of power could be bloody and dangerous. Her namesake had lived in constant fear of it in the sixteenth century. Her distant cousin, Nicholas II, had lost his whole family to a revolution. The War of Independence, Partition . . . the list was brutal and long, and close to home. Philip's family in Greece had had to run for their lives. The 'commonplace miracle' of peaceful transfer was much to be treasured. If her own entry in the history books could say only one thing, it would be this: for three-score years and ten, as far as she could manage it, transfers of power to countries in her beloved Common-wealth had happened peacefully. They had not always been happy, or to governments one thoroughly approved of, but you could not have everything.

The Queen wasn't alone with Rozie for the rest of the day. Sir Simon was supposed to be bringing in the boxes the following morning, but she was relieved to see that Rozie arranged to do it herself. Rozie still had that set to her shoulders.

'Did you learn anything useful?' the Queen asked, without even making a pretence at opening the first box.

'I think so,' Rozie said. She explained how cold and evasive Flora had seemed about Chris Wallace. 'She said his wife was close to the baroness, and that their children grew up together. But nothing about him being turfed out. She absolutely denied it. Then she seemed to get distracted by the poison garden.'

'Is that still there?'

'Well, no. Flora said she had to get rid of it because of the visitors. I can see why. Her brother nearly died of wolfsbane poisoning when he was little, apparently.'

'Oh, dear.'

'The baron wanted it all dug up in a fury, even though his wife was fond of the garden.'

The Queen was surprised. 'How unlike Hugh.' She thought a bit longer. 'How very unlike Hugh. How interesting.'

'How did you get on, ma'am?' Rozie ventured.

The Queen pursed her lips, picked up the fountain pen on her desk and fiddled with the lid.

'I was reminded of just how strong Ned's childhood feelings for Ladybridge must have been. On top of that, Hugh ended up marrying Ned's girl. If it had been Ned who had killed his cousin all those years ago, it would have made sense.'

'Lord Mundy drove away with Ned. They could have argued in the car,' Rozie suggested, thinking it up as she went along. 'And then . . . Could the baron have followed him to London?'

'Only if a tenant, Flora, the vicar and an antiquarian bookseller were lying.'

'It's a very solid alibi.' Rozie grinned. 'I'm sorry, ma'am, I'm making up wild stories about people you know.'

'No, no. It's useful to think through the possibilities. However, Hugh and his son are not on good terms from what I see and hear, despite what Hugh would like me to believe.'

'He was distraught when Valentine ate the wolfsbane as a child,' Rozie pointed out.

'Yes,' the Queen agreed. 'But that was a very long time ago.'

'But Lord Mundy's been very supportive of his son. With the whole gay marriage thing. I mean, that's really something.'

The Queen noticed how Rozie was gaining confidence in the job, to the point of challenging one's assumptions, which could be very useful in this sort of situation.

'He's such a quiet, shy sort of man. It can't have been easy,' Rozie went on.

218

'Perhaps,' the Queen granted. 'I agree that it is very unusual for an old-fashioned sort of peer, shall we say, such as Hugh, to be so open to the idea. When so much is at stake.'

'At stake, ma'am?' Rozie asked.

'Ask Sir Simon,' the Queen said, cryptically. And then, more cryptically still, 'And then, there are the dogs.'

'The dogs?' Rozie echoed, feeling increasingly lost.

'Exactly,' the Queen said. 'The dogs are at the heart of everything. I'd like to know more about Valentine,' she added, thoughtfully. 'Mr Wallace's wife was close to Lee. I wonder if she knew something. Can you see if you can dig a little deeper?'

'In that case—' Rozie began.

The Queen shook her head. 'But not in the way the police imagine. I hope I'm wrong. Let me know how you get on.'

There was nothing for it. Rozie and Katie Briggs had spent the afternoon driving up the coast in Rozie's Mini, trying to work out ways of finding out more about Laura Wallace that didn't involve getting up at dawn in order to get freezing cold in an icy river with the Dix Dunkers.

Rozie thought back to hot nights in Lagos nightclubs last spring, and evenings on the sand in St Barts last summer. *They* were her happy places. However, she knew Mary Collathorn, and had an open invitation to join the group. Any other way of infiltrating the Ladybridge Estate that she and Katie could think of would seem obvious and might be reported back to Flora. They had to assume that someone would talk because, usually, someone did.

There was little Rozie wouldn't do for the Boss, but this remained in her 'not if I can possibly help it' pile.

'You'll love it,' Katie said. 'Trust me. I started wild swimming in the summer. It's changed my life. I honestly had no energy before I started. There's something about the cold water on your skin, what it does to your heart rate . . . It's the most beautiful sensation.'

'I think the active word then was "summer",' Rozie said. 'If this was July, I'd happily do it. It's January. A man literally died.'

Katie shook her head. 'He stayed out too long, deliberately. We know that. You'd only be in the water for a few seconds.'

'Why me?' Rozie asked, not unreasonably. 'You're the wild swimmer.'

'I can't.'

'You know the ins and outs of it better than I do. You've done it before. It'd probably be safer if you went.'

Katie let out an angry sigh. 'I just can't. Maybe it would go OK, maybe it wouldn't. The shock of water that freezing . . . If I overdo it, I pay the price for days. I can't risk it. Believe me, I wish I could. Pushing through only makes it worse.'

'OK,' Rozie said.

Katie squeezed her eyes shut for a moment. She was clearly still struggling with talking about whatever it was. Rozie was surprised, because she literally glowed with health.

'It's ME,' Katie said eventually. 'Myalgic encephalomyelitis. I've had it for years. I only realised while I was doing the APS job. It practically floored me. No, it totally floored me.'

'Myalgic . . .?'

'Chronic fatigue syndrome. The one where people say, "Is that a real thing?" And yeah. It's a thing. Not everyone believed me, but it is.'

'I'm sorry.'

'You don't need to be. I get extreme tiredness, like just-been-hit-by-a-truck exhaustion. I can sleep for a day and not feel better. Like I say, I'd been having symptoms for a long time, but I had these coping methods for getting through. At the palace, though . . . it's a whole new level. You can't take time off if the Queen needs you.'

'I get that.'

'You're frowning.'

Rozie shook the thought off. 'Only that Sir Simon said it was mental health problems. At least, I thought he did.'

Katie rolled her eyes. 'Yes, he would have done. He just saw someone stressed who wasn't up to the job. He tried to be sympathetic, but you could see his massive frustration. It didn't help.'

'I bet.'

'I remember, when we came here for Christmas and there were days I just couldn't move. Mrs Maddox thought I was malingering. She said her staff had better things to do than bring me breakfast in bed. In the end, Lady Caroline found a consultant for me. He'd worked with her great-niece who has it, too. Even her just believing me was such a relief, I can't tell you. Anyway, he put me in touch with this new programme.

I needed a new diet, new exercise regime, no stress, no pressure. I needed to stop, basically. You took over. I was going to move in with my mother, but she didn't know how to look after me. The Boss said I could come here.'

'But you're getting better, right?' Rozie asked.

'It's a different life,' Katie admitted. 'I'm still working it out. I miss the old me. I miss being taken seriously by people in smart offices with fancy titles. God, I sound so self-indulgent. I've got Daphne, and I can bake now. I've gone totally Marie Kondo. I can knit. I'm doing a degree in nutrition so I can get to the bottom of what works for me. Just don't make me hit the freezing water, OK? Anyway, like I say, you'll love it.'

'I can absolutely promise you,' Rozie assured her, 'I won't.'

The Queen, meanwhile, was visiting Wood Farm with Philip. They were out towards the marshes, where the Boxing Day shoot had started. This was where Philip would retire to the modest farmhouse in less than a year. He was already looking forward to a life of painting, birdwatching and visits from friends. The Queen loved the little farmhouse, too, where it was possible to relax without servants or fuss, with the rugby on the radio and an uninterrupted view of the sky towards the sea.

She would visit as often as she could, though she knew he would manage perfectly well without her, and even better without the panoply of advisers and attendants who inevitably followed in her wake. Today, meanwhile, they were outside in their coats and binoculars, walking back from the hides Philip had had built so they could watch the waterfowl side by side.

'You're looking thoughtful, Lilibet,' he said. 'Anything up?'

She was glad he'd asked. She wanted to talk to him about something. He was one of the few people who would understand her concerns without thinking them medieval – which in many ways they were.

'It's Hugh St Cyr,' she said.

'I'm not surprised. Still grieving hard for Lee, no doubt. It was good of you to visit yesterday.'

'It wasn't exactly that.' She looked across at her husband, who was as always adapting his long stride to match her much shorter one, and bending down slightly to listen. 'It was something he said about Valentine. Hugh sounded very forward-thinking. Rozie was most impressed.'

Philip glanced at her sharply. 'Forward-thinking? Hugh? Are you sure?'

'I know. I was surprised, too.'

'I always had him down as mentally stuck in the Renaissance. Solid man, very sound. But many's the time I've talked about one of my innovations on the farm and he's raised his eyebrow at me a good half-inch. I mean, the man's an expert on the Metaphysical poets, for God's sake.'

'Mmm,' the Queen agreed. 'And yet, he's leaving Lady-bridge to Flora in his will.'

'Is he?'

'And Valentine's getting married.'

'What? Really? To a girl? I thought he was with that feller who came round at Christmas. Business partner, my foot.'

'He is.'

For the first time, Philip paused in his stride. 'He's *marrying* him?'

'Yes.'

'And what does Hugh think about it all?'

'He seems pleased that it will put the St Cyrs in the history books.'

'*What?*' Philip shook his head. 'But . . . There are no other St Cyr male heirs around, are there?'

'No. Not close family. The line will die out.'

'And Hugh's *pleased*?'

The Queen nodded, to him and to herself. She wasn't being absurd to think this situation unusual.

Philip knew what she knew – and what Sir Simon would explain to Rozie, if she asked: that it was impossible in the British aristocracy for a male married couple to produce a legitimate heir. A peer of the realm could have as many children as he liked, in wedlock and out of it, adopted or whatever he chose, but only the genetic child of married parents could inherit the title. It was the law, and there were forces that wanted to change it, along with the stipulation that the child who inherited should if at all possible be male, but they weren't making much headway.

Surrogacy didn't count because the genetic parents weren't married, even if the legal parents were. Therefore, as it was impossible for two men, or two women, to produce a child that genetically belonged to both of them, gay married aristocrats could not pass their titles down. Which might perhaps explain why so far there had not been a single such couple. A man might subsequently marry his gay partner, having 'done his duty' and created an heir within a heterosexual marriage, and no doubt that would happen in time, but it hadn't yet. Anyway, Valentine wasn't doing that. This would be his first wedding. In fact, he was forty-seven and until now he seemed to have been in no rush to marry at all. And under no pressure from his father to do so. All Hugh's attention was on his daughter. This, too, was strange.

'Hugh was quite offhand when he mentioned it,' the Queen said.

Philip frowned. The thing was, he understood all the implications instantly. A nobleman who didn't care who his children slept with was not unusual, but one who didn't care about who they *married*, and the consequent loss of lands or titles, was as rare as a unicorn.

There was a pause as they stopped to admire a couple of plump partridge stalking ahead of them up the path to the farmhouse.

'Did you ever get a sense of Hugh's relationship with Valentine?' she asked. 'Hugh used to bring him shooting when Valentine was a teenager. You talked to them then, didn't you?'

'I did. The boy was a top-class shot. Very coordinated, very composed. Excellent fieldcraft – better than his father's. I always thought he'd go on to do more with it, but then he drifted off to London and never came back.'

'And were he and Hugh close?'

Philip snorted dismissively. 'Name me one teenager out of boarding school who's close to his father.'

The Queen could name several, but chose not to. 'They weren't unusually distant, though?' she asked.

Philip gazed up at the sky while he tried to remember. 'Come to think of it, they were, I suppose. Not *distant*, but disconnected. I don't remember them ever talking to each other, unless it was about one of the dogs. I put it down to Hugh being so infernally shy.'

The Queen was struck by the word 'disconnected'. That was it, absolutely. She had wondered if Hugh was acting his indifference. The man who had removed the wolfsbane from the poison garden all those years ago was anything but. However, something had changed since then. She didn't put it down to Valentine's homosexuality. Ned's uncle Patrick was homosexual, too, and the St Cyrs had treated it as just another family eccentricity – on the understanding he would go on to marry a good woman. No, there was something else. And Ned, she sensed, was at the heart of it.

Chapter 25

Was this what her world had come to?

Rozie pictured her friends in London, Lagos and New York, grabbing cappuccinos on their way into work in gleaming skyscrapers and cool workspaces, swapping stories about hot men in cocktail bars and deals they were about to do. And here she was, at the end of the world, with a group of people twice her age, about to make herself truly miserable.

It was half past seven in the morning and the sun was still rising. She stood on an old wooden jetty that stuck out into the dark green waters of the river Dix at Vickery, wearing nothing but a towel and a swimming costume, feeling the ice forming on her skin. There were four people with her, two men and two women, two string-thin and two more generously endowed, all paper-white in the unforgiving early morning light.

Katie had told her she would love it. At this moment, Katie was tucked up in bed under a nice, thick duvet. What would she know?

'Are you ready? Don't forget, two full minutes,' Mary Collathorn said. 'Thirty seconds for you, Rozie, 'cause you're a beginner. Shoulders submerged or you don't get the benefit. Ready, steady, go!'

Mary climbed carefully down the jetty steps, whooping with shock as she entered the freezing water. Her bright red swimming hat was swiftly joined by the green, blue and white hats of her companions. Rozie went last. As expected, the water stung her shins and ankles with icy fury and she had to force herself to keep descending into it. Every atom of her being told her to save herself. Her only thought was to get deep enough to cover her shoulders quickly, and to get back out as fast as she dared.

The others were swimming to the opposite bank and back, whooping and hollering their way through the shock of the cold. Rozie had let out a single loud gasp when she got in, but now she experimented with joining in with the hollering. It helped, and there was something joyful about them all expressing the craziness of this together. Even so, she wasn't sure what hurt most, her stomach, chest or shoulders. Every part of her protested at the shock. Her instinct was to leap away from it and get the hell out, but she fought it.

Mary had said thirty seconds. Rozie wasn't sure she'd last twenty – but after ten, her skin felt as if it was vibrating. It was a strange new sensation. Definitely not horrible. She remembered to breathe, and found that with each new breath the pain adjusted into something that was more of a thrill. As she slowly moved through the water, she gained new power with each stroke. The view of the bank was gorgeous from here. When Mary shouted 'Thirty seconds!' Rozie ignored her. After forty, Mary positively yelled at her and Rozie reluctantly got out.

Her heart was pumping hard. Every square inch of her skin tingled as she climbed back up the steps towards her towel. She felt vividly alive, and quite jealous of the other four, whose colourful hats bobbed on the water's surface like billiard balls as they endured and enjoyed the final minute. By the time they came back out to join her, she was wrapped up in her towel (they had told her to bring an extra large one, and she was grateful), and feeling as warm, awake and alert as she had ever been.

'What did you think?' Mary asked, slipping into her own towel, which had sleeves and became a warm, puffy coat when she put it on.

'Bloody brilliant,' Rozie yelled. 'Why doesn't everyone do this?'

'I know!' Mary agreed. 'Sometimes it takes a few more sessions but I'm glad you're a convert. Coffee? We usually go back to my place before we go our separate ways.'

Being very cold had – to Rozie's great surprise – been very good, but being warmly dressed in a cashmere sweater and jeans, drinking very good coffee around Mary's pine kitchen table was fantastic.

'Oh, yes,' Alan said with a broad smile when Rozie pointed it out. 'Everyone thinks we do it for the freezing sea, but we do it for the buzz on the jetty afterwards. And this. We're not masochists.'

'Not much,' said the woman sitting next to him at the table. Her name was Renée, aged about sixty, Rozie guessed, and a 'new girl' on the estate, meaning she had only arrived eleven years ago. She specialised in white and dove-grey furniture for

229

the recent explosion in tasteful seaside Airbnbs. 'I'm an artist, really,' she'd explained, with a certain aggressive earnestness. 'Are you into art, Rozie?' Rozie hadn't explained that she possessed her very own Cézanne. She had come by it in highly unusual circumstances, which she didn't want to talk about.

The fourth member of the original swimming group, a man called John, had already gone home, so Rozie just had Mary, Alan and Renée to talk to. She knew what would happen next, and let them ask her the inevitable questions about what the Queen was up to at Sandringham, and whether she'd recovered from her cold, and what it was like to work for her.

'An honour,' Rozie said.

'No, but, *really*,' Mary asked. 'Is she a very demanding boss? She must be.'

Rozie answered on autopilot, without giving anything away, as usual. Privately, she was asking herself if the Boss *was* very demanding? Of course she was in terms of the excellence she expected – and generally got – from everyone around her, but perhaps not in the way Mary intended. She was never rude, never unfair. Rozie had worked for officers in the army and senior managers at the bank who were more unpredictable and difficult. All her careers so far had expected her to sacrifice her time and freedom, to be available day and night to get the job done, to give up on much hope of a decent social life of her own. Maybe she chose them because that was how she was made. Did she *want* a social life? Her sister had a huge one that spanned three continents, but Rozie didn't envy it. As she pondered these things, she talked about the corgis and the Queen's recent birthday celebrations at Windsor Castle, and everyone was happy. Then, before they ran out of time, she brought the conversation around to Chris Wallace as gently as she could.

'I keep thinking about what you told me,' she said to Mary, 'about Mr Wallace worrying about losing all those memories of his wife when he lost the house. It sounds heartbreaking.'

'It was,' Mary said grimly. 'Those St Cyrs are total, stuck-up bastards, whatever anyone says. They've got the reputation for being generous and caring, with the lamb boxes at Easter and Flora going round like Lady Muck if anyone's off sick, but we know the truth now.'

'And you said the Wallaces were friends of theirs?'

'Well, Laura thought she was Lee's friend,' Mary said. 'Clearly not. But the aristocracy are another country, aren't they? They do things differently there. Without Laura, they wouldn't have kept their flock of Norfolk Horns going, and that's one of the things that makes Ladybridge special. When Lee had her breakdown, it was Laura who picked up the pieces and put her back together. Not the baron – he was useless.'

'The baroness had a breakdown?' Renée leaned forward, fascinated, and saved Rozie asking the question. 'When was that? I didn't know.'

'Mmm,' Mary said. 'It was a long time ago, when Valentine and his sister were kids. Laura lived next to the school and she had a boy the same age as Valentine, so it was easy. I always had the impression Valentine had done something.'

'Oh? How?' Rozie asked.

'Dunno,' Mary said, frowning. 'No, wait. I remember, we were outside church and I was asking Laura how Lee was – this was in the middle of the crisis – and she said nothing much, she was very discreet, but Valentine was standing about ten feet from us, just an ordinary boy about eleven or twelve, and the look Laura gave him! Of course, after that we didn't see him much. He went off to boarding school and I'll tell you one thing, before that, Lee had vowed her kids wouldn't go away. She'd always said there was a perfectly good secondary school at Swaffham they could go to. I admired her for that. But then suddenly Valentine was gone and I did ask why, but Laura simply wouldn't talk about it. She stuck by Lee to the bitter end, and look what they did to her. Turned her beloved Chris out of his house for no good reason. Rumour is, Flora wants it for her London guests, because it's warmer than the hall. I wouldn't put it past them.'

'Flora isn't popular on the estate, then?' Rozie asked.

'She was,' Alan said, hesitating a little. 'But that was before all this. You get to see a person in a new light sometimes. It's no coincidence that this all happened after her mother died in the summer. The baroness was good at holding everything together. It's falling apart now.'

They chatted on for a while about the fund that was being set up in Chris's memory to give to his favourite wildlife charities. Rozie sensed that was all she was going to learn. Laura Wallace had protected her secrets. If she had told them to anyone, it would have been to the man she shared her life with, and he was dead.

Back at Balmoral, the Queen fiddled with her spectacles. 'It's unfortunate for us that Laura was so loyal to the baroness. Lee chose her friends well. She was like that herself, you know. My mother always said that you could tell her anything and be certain it would go no further. She was enormously fond of Lee.' She frowned up at Rozie. 'You seem surprised.'

Rozie shook her head. 'Only that there must have been a big age gap between them, ma'am. Two generations. The baroness must have been about the same age as the Prince of Wales.'

'She was,' the Queen said. 'But my mother was never concerned about age. She always had great energy herself. She liked young people.'

'And I suppose they shared a great love of gardening,' Rozie said.

'Oh, yes,' the Queen said, her face lighting up at the memory. 'She visited the gardens at Ladybridge almost every summer. She thought very highly of Lee St Cyr's design skills. She was delighted when Lee offered to help with the formal gardens here. They were both avid visitors to other people's gardens. They used to share notes. When Lee went to Japan she wrote about ten pages. My mother read them out to me . . .' She trailed off, lost in thought, momentarily.

'Ma'am?' Rozie asked.

The Queen's eyes glittered with sudden intensity. 'Lee didn't confide in many people, but . . . Didn't you say that when Laura Wallace gave Valentine that odd look, it was shortly before he went to boarding school?'

'Yes.'

'And he was eleven or twelve?'

'That's right.'

'It's a bit old for a boy to go away to prep school in those days. He would normally be seven or eight. But Lee hadn't wanted him to go at all, had she?'

'No, ma'am.'

'I get the impression she needed to get him away from the hall. Away from his father. If Valentine is nearly fifty now . . .'

'He's forty-seven, ma'am,' Rozie said.

'Then whatever happened would have been around thirty-five years ago, which would make it . . .'

'Nineteen eighty-one,' Rozie added helpfully.

'Hmm.' The Queen continued to play with her spectacles for a little bit while she thought the thing through. 'My mother's correspondence is not in the most perfect state,' she admitted. Margaret had been living with their mother at the end of her life and had disposed of some of it. The Queen Mother wasn't always entirely discreet. However, she had been a prolific letter writer and there was still a lot left. 'You'll need to talk to the archivist at Windsor. You know her, don't you?'

Rozie did. She was a friendly woman and fellow owner of a Mini Cooper. They had bonded over cars when the Boss was there over Easter.

'Good,' the Queen said. 'You might ask for all the letters my mother received from anyone in Norfolk three years either side of 1980. Ask for any that she sent, too. Sometimes they end up in the collection. Do explain that time is of the essence.'

'Of course, ma'am.'

'It's a long shot,' the Queen observed grimly.

'I'll see what I can do.'

After Rozie left, the Queen turned to gaze out of the window. She didn't return to her private correspondence for quite some time.

Chapter 26

The Queen's mobile telephone wasn't working. The grandchildren had insisted she have one, and had recorded a rude message on her answering machine, which she hadn't found out about for ages. Not that it particularly mattered, because they were the only people who called her on it. She liked to use it to catch up on the news sometimes, which is what she intended to do now, while drinking her morning cup of Darjeeling in bed.

It was the twenty-first of January and, the day after the inauguration, in cities around the world, women were massing to protest the words and actions of a president who had cheerfully admitted to grabbing them in private places. What was the world coming to? The Queen had known all sorts of world leaders who almost certainly (or definitely) had done such things, but none so far who had bragged about it. She was curious, and somewhat cheered, to see women banding together for the marches. Or, she would have been, if she could have seen anything – but her phone was a blank block.

She called her dresser and pointed out the problem.

'Oh! I'm so sorry, ma'am. Someone forgot to charge it last night. I'll do that for you now.'

It took a few minutes to locate the charger and get the inert block to start up again. In that time, the Queen finished her tea and eyed up the charger thoughtfully. 'Ah,' she muttered to herself. But nobody heard.

'Do you know,' Sir Simon said to Rozie, leaning back in his office chair as he tried to remember what it was like to feel relaxed, 'this time last year the words Trump and Brexit were curiosities? We were all so sure we knew what was going to happen. We didn't question ourselves for a moment.'

'You've been teaching me history,' Rozie said. '"Events, dear boy, events."'

'Ah, yes, Macmillan. He didn't exactly say it that way, but he should have. Events, dear Rozie. I underestimated the events.'

'The Boss doesn't seem unduly worried,' Rozie pointed out.

'About the new world order? She never does. She's lived through a war that we can barely imagine. She's lost an Empire and gained a Commonwealth. She survived Lady Di.' He sat up straight. 'I must be more Queen. Less self-indulgent. How can I help you?'

'Did you see this?' she asked. She showed him a headline on her phone:

POLICE QUESTION MAN, 47, UNDER CAUTION FOR MURDER OF ARISTOCRAT WHO WAS QUEEN'S NEIGHBOUR

'Oh, that,' he said. 'Sorry, forgot to tell you. Bloomfield called last night. A fisherman's come forward. Lady Mundy

237

used to keep a clinker at King's Lynn, to sail on the Ouse. He saw Valentine St Cyr on the boat, heading out into the Wash on the twenty-first of December. That puts him in the exact place the hand probably went in. But more than that, he had consistently refused to say what he was doing that day. You'd think, if you were perfectly innocent in such suspicious circumstances, you'd let the police know before they found out for themselves and tell your side of the story, wouldn't you? Or perhaps you'd deny it entirely. Anyway, he doesn't deny it now. He claims he was scattering his mother's ashes.

'You're seeing the Boss next, aren't you? Do tell her. She'll be horrified, because she's known the man since he was a baby. But justice is justice. She'll be reconciled, eventually.'

'I see.'

The Queen seemed unsurprised when Rozie passed on the news about the ashes scattering. 'Yes, that explains everything. He probably was.'

She stared at the blotter on her desk for quite some time. 'I think I need to make a telephone call. I can't imagine Valentine would come all the way to Norfolk and take the family boat out on his own. He came as rarely as he could, from what I understand.'

'Yes, ma'am.'

'Wait there.'

Rozie stood by, while the Queen asked the palace operator to put her through to Hugh St Cyr.

But in the end, it was Flora who came on the line.

'Hello, Your Majesty. I'm afraid Dad's visiting the stables. Can I help?'

The Queen was suitably sympathetic about the arrest of her brother, but Flora sounded defiant.

'Valentine'll be out in no time. He's innocent, so they have nothing to charge him with. It's just a bore that he has to be in the news. You know how it is.'

'I do,' the Queen said. 'I'm sure the family's rallying round.'

'We absolutely are,' Flora assured her.

'Presumably you were all together when he took the boat out?'

There was a strangled cough, then silence. Poor Flora. The Queen felt her shock at being asked the question – and being asked it by her sovereign, suddenly, in conversation, and not by a police inspector, in an interview. She sounded rattled when she answered. 'Yes, we were, ma'am. Of course we were. It was a family outing – long planned.'

'Scattering Lee's ashes, I understand. Another difficult day.'

Flora rallied, gaining confidence as she went. 'Oh, it could have been worse, but I suppose it could have gone better. Mum didn't want to be in the vault, poor thing. The idea drove her crazy. She wanted to be in the sea, and in her rose garden. She was very specific about it all. We'd already scattered the rose garden half. We arranged the boat bit around Val's schedule, but I assure you it was all perfectly, *perfectly* innocent. It was a blustery day and we were quite incompetent sailors without Mum. When the wind kicked up, half the ashes ended up in our faces.'

'Oh, dear.'

'It was almost funny, really, in a horrible sort of way. We were all busy brushing her off each other. Dad had ash in his eyebrows. Of course we should have checked the wind direction, but we were idiots. Our minds were on other things.'

The Queen could picture the scene exactly. Now she was in her stride, Flora told the story with a hint of a groan and her usual panache. It sounded like exactly the sort of anecdote she *would* tell, in fact. The Queen was surprised – or rather, she would have been surprised if she didn't have her current suspicions – that the girl had waited until now to talk about it.

She felt growing certainty about how the deed was done, but as things stood, the wrong person entirely had died. And that was rather a 'deal-breaker', as Harry would say, when it came to getting to the bottom of a murder.

An hour later, Sir Simon returned to deliver his report and discuss the prime minister's upcoming trip to America. After a discussion of the special relationship, which seemed to be worryingly less special with each new US incumbent, he handed the Queen a basket of private correspondence to look through, and tapped a big, padded envelope at the top.

'It's just arrived. Rozie asked me to bring it to your attention, ma'am. Apparently, the archivist has found the letters from the Queen Mother that you asked about. One of the junior equerries was travelling from Windsor this morning and he brought them with him.'

240

'Goodness!' the Queen said. 'How quick. She must have worked through the night.'

'The archivist? She's very diligent, ma'am.'

'Thank you, Simon.'

She picked the envelope off the pile. Normally 'Thank you, Simon' was the equivalent of 'Goodbye', and he knew it, and yet when she glanced up, he was hovering. She looked at him questioningly. 'Yes?'

His own face burned with suppressed curiosity. Of course he wanted to know what was inside, and why she wanted it so badly. He couldn't ask her outright about private letters from her own family, but he was clearly hoping she'd tell him anyway. There was a brief stand-off, while neither spoke. Eventually, he gave in.

'That will be all, I take it,' he said.

'Thank you, Simon,' she repeated firmly.

He shut the door behind him and she pulled the letters out.

There were about three dozen in all. Her mother had been a prolific letter writer, with many friends in Norfolk who eagerly wrote back. It did not take long, however, to winkle out the ones from Ladybridge Hall. They were all on the same thick cream paper, embossed with the family crest and the address in blue. Georgina's had looked the same, the Queen remembered, but her signature had taken up half the page. These were all signed 'Lee', in a much smaller hand.

It was disappointing that none of her mother's letters to the baroness were in the bundle. The Queen Mother's writing style was warm and witty, very true to her character, and seemed to bring her back to life whenever one read it. However, there were seven letters from Lee to the queen, which was more than one could have hoped for. The bundle had come with a note from the archivist saying she always did her best to put the contents in chronological order, but it wasn't always possible, given that so many of them weren't dated. This proved to be true of Lee, who had a maddening habit of giving the month and day at the top of each one, but not the year.

At least her handwriting was legible. It was rounded and uneven, with curly 'y's and a long strike through the 't' that reminded the Queen of Anne's letters from school, in the same blue ink, but it was steady, with decent spacing, and not difficult to scan. The Queen was looking for the strong, confident 'V' for Valentine. Lee spoke a lot about Flora, who was learning to ride. She asked questions about the weather in Balmoral, made endless suggestions for roses and wrote several pages about a trip to the Chelsea Flower Show. She was planning a trip to America to talk to various gardening societies about her work at Ladybridge. And then, in the fifth letter, there was this:

I'm not sure Hugh will ever speak to Valentine again.

The Queen sat up straighter. She went back to the beginning. The letter began,

I write this from the priest hole. That is, my body's inside it, I can't fit my feet in. Georgina came here to write too, I gather. I pray

nobody comes to this end of the tower to find me. You wouldn't believe the bitter day I've had. I wish, wish, wish I had never heard of Ladybridge.

Maddeningly, Lee then went on to say that she couldn't bring herself to burden 'Your Majesty' with her 'disaster'. Only that she 'could hardly bear to be in her own skin', that it had all started because of 'a simple trip to hospital, a silly thing, really', and that she must 'get Valentine away from here'. At the time, she was planning to send the children to stay with a friend across the county. Another line caught the Queen's attention:

At least it's a secret between us here. One man can ruin everything. I wish him such tremendous harm I can't begin to tell you. I dream that he's dead and the nightmare is, that I wake up and he's still alive. You won't tell anyone, will you? I trust you implicitly. I think I might be going mad.

The next letter was all about Flora's first day on the jumps at Pony Club. It must have been out of sequence, because the final one in the bundle was an apology for the priest-hole letter, and was an attempt at reassurance, although the Queen wondered how reassuring her mother would have found it.

I'm not mad at all, simply wounded. V. is with the Allenbys and very happy. He'll join them at prep school next term and is very excited after all their tales of midnight feasts and camp fires. Meanwhile I feel like the fallen raven I rescued last year, battered and bruised, but slowly recovering the use of my feathers. Hugh will mend in time too. That is the most important thing.

Moira's coming next week to wrap me up in cotton wool, although knowing Moira she'll probably take me for several bracing walks and remove all fat from my diet. Perhaps that's what I need. Not the diet, but the walks. The green grass and hazy, bee-buzzed air can mend anything, can't they? Even a broken heart.

The Queen looked up. Moira had been mentioned once or twice in the other letters. She knew several Moiras, but only two who were old enough to have been confidantes to Lee St Cyr in the late 1970s, and one of them lived in the Bahamas. The other lived in a Georgian manor house, half an hour's drive due east of Sandringham. She was Moira Westover, the mother of Astrid, who had so recently got engaged to Ned St Cyr.

She picked up the phone and explained what she needed to Lady Caroline.

Chapter 27

Moira Westover stood at the doorway to her home just outside the Pensthorpe Natural Park and watched the Queen's cars draw up through narrowed eyes. This was not the reception the Queen was used to. Normally, her hosts were in their Sunday best and their faces were tight with excessive smiling. Moira wore a padded gilet over narrow jeans tucked into well-worn Dubarry boots. Her mouth was a set line, her expression wary.

But then, this visit was an unusual one. Lady Caroline had checked that Moira would be at home, but stressed that the conversation would be brief, private and informal. The Queen really didn't want to sit through a very long tea, or several earwigging friends and relations. Moira had taken her at her word, it seemed. Unlike her daughter, she had made no visible effort at all.

The two-storey house, with its elegant Georgian windows, was surrounded by a garden big enough to house a swimming pool and a grass tennis court, next to paddocks where half a dozen horses grazed. This was where Astrid had grown up, the fourth and youngest child of Moira and David who, in his lifetime, was known as one of the best shots, and most prolific alcoholics, in the county. The Queen had known an alcoholic or two in her lifetime, and knew that their loved ones had to learn to be self-reliant. They were used to being lied to by people they should trust, which perhaps explained the suspicion in Moira's eyes today. The Queen knew Moira from the Pony Club circuit, where she had ridden with Anne. As an adult, she had accompanied her husband on various Sandringham shooting parties – but it was hardly enough to explain why the reigning monarch would want to drop in on her at twenty-four hours' notice. The Queen knew she had some explaining to do.

'Is there something you need to tell me?' Moira asked urgently, as they sat awkwardly opposite each other in the pristine silk-swagged sitting room. Her taut face and ramrod spine radiated tension.

'Not exactly,' the Queen said. 'But I think there might be something you can tell me.'

Moira looked puzzled. 'I'll try.'

'What did you think I'd come to say?'

'It had to be something about Ned,' Moira responded. 'I thought that . . . After you were kind enough to talk to Astrid . . . I thought the police had told you something truly dark about Ned. What's happened to him, I mean. And you were telling me so I could tell my daughter.'

'Oh, no!' the Queen assured her. 'Nothing like that. I'm still waiting to find out as much as you are.' *Though I have my suspicions*, she thought. One day soon, she suspected, Moira would have to comfort Astrid through very difficult times. But not today.

'Oh, thank goodness.' Moira recovered herself. 'What did you want to know?'

'I was looking through some of my mother's letters recently and they mentioned that Baroness Mundy went through a particularly difficult moment. It was when the children were quite young. Valentine had just gone to hospital, I think. And you looked after Lee.'

Moira stiffened again. 'Yes, I did, briefly. Why?'

The Queen ignored the question. 'Since her death, a lot has happened. But I think it all goes back to that moment. Lee was a good friend of my mother's. Sadly, I can't ask her about it, so I'm asking you.'

Moira pursed her lips. 'I can't quite believe I'm saying this, ma'am, but I can't help you. I made a promise to Lee at that time. Her secrets were her secrets. I haven't told a soul.'

'I believe you,' the Queen said. 'I think I know what those secrets might be and I haven't heard any talk to that effect, so she protected them well. She trusted the right people.'

'I like to think so.'

'It's all very admirable, but there's a murderer at large. I believe we should all do what we can for the sake of justice. Can I tell you what I suspect?'

Moira agreed that she could.

'As far as I'm aware,' the Queen began, 'Valentine St Cyr had two hospital scares as a boy. The first time, he was about six and he accidentally ate poison. His father was beside himself. If anything, Hugh was more frightened for his son than Lee was. The second time, a few years later, Hugh was so angry at whatever had happened that Lee felt

247

she had to remove Valentine from his sight. I wonder if, that second time, the problem required some sort of blood test and the doctors discovered in the process that Hugh could *not* be Valentine's father.'

Moira gave the Queen a steady look and didn't say anything. The Queen carried on.

'I've always liked Hugh, and I'm sorry to think he was so unkind to the boy, but what if he suspected that the real father was his cousin, Ned? Valentine looks like a typical St Cyr – he has the height and hair, the distinctive profile. Who else could have given him those features? I wonder if Valentine himself saw it, too, at Lee's funeral, when Ned attended. That was the first time he had met him in person, as far as I know. There is something about meeting a relative in person that's different from seeing them in photographs. One can have an extra sense of them that can't always be explained. I've often had that feeling myself.'

Moira looked down, considering what to say. 'And Hugh suspected an affair, you mean?' she asked eventually. 'That Lee had been unfaithful with his cousin?'

'It seems an obvious conclusion,' the Queen said. 'Lee knew Ned first. I can imagine that would be very difficult for a man to come to terms with. Very difficult indeed.'

Moira tipped her head back and regarded the Queen speculatively through half-lowered lids. 'It would be, wouldn't it?' Then she got up, went to the kitchen and came back with her handbag. She took out a slim, black pen-like object and held it up. 'D'you mind if I vape?'

The Queen had grown up in a fug of her father's smoke. She still missed it sometimes. 'Please do,' she said.

Moira closed her eyes and inhaled deeply. When she opened them again, the look she gave the Queen was cool and uncompromising.

'I'll tell you the story because you've guessed half of it, and like anyone would, you've guessed it wrong. But I'll only tell you, ma'am, and if anyone in the police or anywhere else asks me, I'll deny it – under oath or whatever you like. I gave Lee a sacred promise. I think she'd make an exception for you, though.' Moira half laughed. 'And possibly the Pope.'

'Good,' the Queen said. 'I've come all this way, after all.'

Moira nodded. 'Lee met Ned through friends when he was nineteen and she was twenty,' she began. 'They often went to parties together – there were so many in those days – and she thought of him as a fun friend and useful companion because she didn't have a boyfriend. There was a bit of kissing, a bit of fumbling in the haystacks after a Young Farmers ball. Lee was a free spirit that way, she said. Ned was magnetic, hugely popular, and she loved to live in the moment. But she was incredibly innocent, too.

'And then she met Hugh, and everything changed. Her life went overnight from black and white to colour – that's how she put it. She was a guest at a hunt ball up in Yorkshire. Ned wasn't there, but her brother had brought Hugh along. At first she was intrigued by the cousins' similarities. But where Ned was shallow, Hugh was deep. Ned could be selfish and unreliable, and up to then she'd assumed all young men were, but Hugh was honest and devoted. Her still waters, she called him. She fell for him hard in the space of a weekend and never changed her mind. You know how much fun she was, how gregarious, but there was an inner quality of calm to her, too. Hugh saw it and mirrored it. As soon as you saw them together you could tell they were *right*.'

'Yes, I always thought so,' the Queen agreed.

'Ned hated it. He always just assumed Hugh had met Lee through him, because he knew her first. He had his eye on all sorts of girls in those days, but to hear him tell the tale, you'd think she was the only one. He wasn't really in his right mind at all. His uncle Patrick had died in a horrible car crash two years before. He was still coming to terms with the fact that Hugh's father Ralph was the new heir. He'd grown up always assuming he would live on the estate some-how and be a part of it. Patrick had led him to believe he could become manager in time. But overnight, Hugh, who'd always just been one of the unimportant cousins, became the heir. He'd taken Ned's birthright – as Ned saw it – and now he'd taken his girl.'

'Yes, that's what I rather imagined,' the Queen said.

'A month before her wedding to Hugh, Lee turned twenty-one. Ned offered to organise a party for her at Lady-bridge, as of course he'd often done before. He was famous for his parties.'

'Yes, I know.'

'Georgina was in the process of moving into Abbottswood, and she was very bitter about leaving Ladybridge Hall. Lee knew all this. She told me she thought Ned was very sweet and generous to come back to his old ancestral home and sprinkle his magic one last time. It seemed to be a sign that the cousins would eventually make up and get on together, which is what she wanted. Lee only ever wanted people to get on. She was very naive that way.' Moira eyed the Queen sideways through a scented haze of vape smoke.

'It's not such a bad ideal to aspire to, surely?'

'But quite impossible,' Moira said. 'She shouldn't have let Ned organise the party. She should have realised what it would put him through.'

'And what did it put him through?' the Queen asked.

'Well, according to Lee, he started drinking early that night. There was a certain wildness about him. He kept on ensuring her glass was topped up, too. Lee was terribly nervous, knowing that one day she would be chatelaine of Ladybridge, with the tenants, the farms and entertaining . . . and she found all that sort of thing quite terrifying at the time.

'He'd lit the courtyard with a thousand bulbs and installed a dance floor. She danced with Hugh there, and then again in the lush grass of the pasture, just the two of them, while music drifted across the moat. She said that was one of her fondest memories. Then they went back and joined their guests and partied until it was almost dawn.'

'It sounds delightful. But it didn't end there, I take it,' the Queen said.

'Well, no,' Moira agreed. 'Hugh "Still Waters" St Cyr went to bed. He and Lee were being very correct. She intended to be a virgin until her wedding night even though it was the late nineteen-sixties, but lots of girls were still like that. But – oh, I remember now – she told me that with

Hugh being so close, and the moon, and all that champagne, she was very tempted to say to hell with it, with only four weeks to go. She was plucking up the courage to follow him to his bedroom, when she ran into Ned in the corridor outside the billiard room where they'd been drinking, and he told her not to go. She assumed he was enforcing her original pact with Hugh, so she agreed. She was grateful, even, the silly girl. But then . . . Ned became very insistent. He was hugely charismatic, as you know. He was twenty-three and very drunk, and he went on some sort of rant about how they should make babies together, how beautiful they would be, how she had always been the only woman he had ever cared about, how their children would inherit Ladybridge following "the true line". All sorts of rot. She said she tried to talk him out of it, but . . . he was very passionate.'

'In what way?' the Queen asked sharply. '"Passionate?"'

'I don't remember exactly. She said something about him being insistent. You know how men are when they know what they want.' Moira took another drag of her metal cigarette that looked more like a lighter. 'We were talking about this ten years later, of course, she and I. I only have her side of it. I never discussed that night with Ned and I wonder if he even remembered it, given how drunk he was. I did ask Lee what she did to fend him off and she said she just went to another place. I rather idiotically asked where, assuming she'd say she ran off to her room or something, but she said she imagined she was floating over her mother's garden, paying attention to each plant. And that's all she *would* say. Whatever it was, I think it took place in the billiard room.

She very rarely entered it again, even decades later. I always saw it with its curtains closed. The next day there's a picture of her saying goodbye to some of the guests in a pretty summer dress. She looks quite carefree. Hugh's arm is around her shoulder. As if it never happened. Valentine was born nine and a half months later, on February the fourteenth. A honeymoon baby. Hugh chose the name and everyone was thrilled for them.'

'Did she know?' the Queen asked. 'Who the father was? I suppose perhaps she didn't.'

'Not then, not for certain – how could she? Valentine was either two weeks early or two weeks late, but pregnancy is such a vague science, isn't it? The doctors give you an absolute due date and you assume that's when the baby will come, but it never does. She said she *felt* it, though. She didn't know how exactly. But she said she always thought Valentine was an accident waiting to happen. I don't think she meant "accident" so much as utter, utter disaster. Not her baby boy – she loved him very much. But . . . everything else.'

'She was worried about Hugh's reaction? And Valentine's, too?'

'Well, certainly Hugh's. She had no intention of ever telling Valentine. This was long before the days of DNA, of course, but even now, if you don't take a test, how would you know? And the title and the estate were at stake. She and Hugh didn't have any other sons as time went by – only Flora. So there was the question of inheritance if it all came out and it turned out they had no legitimate male heirs.

Also, Hugh adored her, and she was very worried he might do something idiotic and go to jail if he found out, and the shame it would bring on her was unthinkable.'

'But it did come out.'

'Yes. They were very unlucky with that blood test. It was terribly simple: Valentine cut himself quite badly on some barbed wire at the farm and developed septicaemia. They thought they might need to do a transfusion and tested him . . . and I can't remember what the blood type was – O, I think – but it was about the only one that couldn't be a product of Hugh's blood type and Lee's. Hugh stupidly checked. He should have left well alone.'

'It's a natural temptation, I should imagine,' the Queen said. 'Given the consequences. I'm sure he did it to reassure himself rather than anything else.'

'Yes, I suppose so. Lee was laughing at the sheer, unlucky madness of it when she told me.'

'And what was Hugh's reaction?' the Queen pressed.

'At the time, in the hospital, almost nothing. She said he looked numb. She told him the story on the way home – because up to then they'd told each other everything. This was her one secret. She said she realised how stupid it had been to do it then, because he could have crashed into something and killed somebody. But he didn't. They got back to Ladybridge. Hugh got very drunk and raged about Ned for a night, then he went quiet. *Very* quiet. That was almost more frightening, she said. He locked himself away in his study for days, or went walking alone across the fields. That's when she called for me. Lee was beside herself. She was terrified he'd do something he'd regret. She sent the children away so they wouldn't antagonise him and begged and pleaded at his study door for him to talk to her. It was dreadful. It lasted for about a week. Then one day I was up in the Long Gallery looking out of the window and I saw Hugh go up to Lee in her rose garden and fall down on one knee, like a gentle knight from one of their tapestries. He kissed her hand. It was all over.'

'Did you believe that Lee *had* persuaded him not to do something he'd regret?' the Queen asked.

'Yes,' Moira said simply. 'Yes, I honestly did, and I still do. She made him promise to do nothing. She knew what it would cost the family if he did anything. Mind you, if it had been something done to me, David would have tracked round there and killed the man on the spot. Hugh's not like that at all. More's the pity, in my opinion. Look at him after Lee's death – he's shrivelled to practically nothing. He adored her, even in the middle of his white fugue. He'd have done anything for her. I mean, how many men, on realising their wife had a child with another man, would instantly blame the *man*?'

Moira had a point. The Queen realised she had found this story all too easy to believe, but she knew many, many men – most men, perhaps – who would have at least wondered about such a seemingly convenient explanation.

A thought occurred to her, and she had been so busy thinking of the impact on the St Cyrs all those years ago that she was surprised she hadn't thought of it before.

'And you, Moira?' she asked. 'Did you believe her?'

255

'Of course I did!' Moira said, surprised even to be asked. 'I was the only person she confided in at the time. Well, me and the shepherdess. She and Lee were close, too.'

'And yet, you wanted your daughter to marry Ned next month.'

Moira's mouth fell open and she stared back, wordlessly. It was as if the thought had only just occurred to her.

'But . . .' she said, colouring, 'it was decades ago! One time. Entirely out of character. And Ned was very drunk, Lee said so.'

'And yet . . .' the Queen persisted. She didn't want to, but she was so astonished that she was trying to make sense of the woman in front of her.

'Ned's been a model citizen for decades,' Moira declared. 'I know he hasn't been particularly fortunate with his wives, but he and Astrid were wonderful together. He got the rewilding idea from her and worked so hard on it. He made her so happy.' The Queen said nothing. 'And anyway, it can't have been *that* bad, what he did. I mean, I'm sure it was a shock, but it's not like he dragged Lee into the bushes or anything ghastly. She was right as rain the next morning and she didn't tell a soul. I'm sure she was furious with herself for letting him get away with it, but all she had to do was say no very firmly. Or put a door between them. Astrid would never . . .'

Moira stopped mid-sentence as she caught the Queen's eye.

There was a long pause. The Queen remembered a young ambassador's wife who hosted her on a tour not long into

256

her reign. On the first evening of that visit to a distant country, the Queen had caught her hostess's eye in the mirror, after the smiles and chatter of a convivial evening, while the men were drinking port and the servants were busy and the two women were replenishing their lipstick together. She wasn't sure what she saw in those eyes, but she had asked if there was something wrong and, after a silence that seemed to last a lifetime, the woman had admitted, calmly and quietly that a senior politician had raped her in that very house two nights before.

She continued to apply her lipstick while she spoke. Her hand trembled, but she was careful. The Queen listened mutely while she described in brisk, bright tones, the attack that had happened in that very room. The act had been over in less than five minutes, she said.

'I was so absolutely . . . How could he . . .? I couldn't understand it. My muscles wouldn't move. Not to speak, protest . . . anything. And so I let it happen. I thought if I didn't – I still think so – that I would die. Silly, isn't it? Surely he wouldn't have killed me here, in my house? And yet . . .' She looked into the mirror, but neither at herself nor the Queen, who was watching her reflection '. . . I watched from far, far away, as if I wasn't here at all. I thought, when he'd finished, I'd come back to myself, but . . .' She took a tissue from a box, carefully blotted her lips and fixed on a smile. 'When it was over, I adjusted my petticoat and carried on with my cocktail party, because, what else could I do?' She had since hosted a magnificent dinner party which was the talk of the town.

'Don't tell anyone, will you?' she had implored the Queen. 'I only told you because . . . I don't know why I told you. I'm so sorry. I just . . . I needed to . . . But I don't want . . . Anyway, I'm much better now.'

One minute, her hostess looked as if she would crumble at a touch, and the next, when a maid knocked on the door to see if they needed anything, she was a model of brisk efficiency. 'Keep calm and carry on!' she'd concluded, with that brittle smile. 'It's what we do, isn't it?'

From that moment, the Queen had understood the out-of-body experience of shock. She had experienced an echo of it herself, just listening to the story. Later, she had since wondered if that was what predators like that senior politician counted on. What a woman did in the moment, how a woman felt, was entirely unpredictable and personal. The horror made rational behaviour more unlikely than not. If only it was as easy as 'putting a door between them'.

Moira had called Lee naive, but the Queen couldn't help feeling that it was Moira whose naivety was showing. How fortunate she was that she didn't know what she was talking about.

Moira was still floundering. The Queen decided to move the conversation on from Astrid. 'Did Lee ever tell Valentine the story?' she asked. 'Or anyone else apart from you and Laura Wallace?'

Moira tugged on her vape again. 'I wouldn't know. She had no intention of doing so at the time. We never spoke of it again and it was because she didn't want to. It was as if she'd put it in a locked box and thrown away the key. I suppose when she was dying she might have said something to Valentine, but I can't think why she would.'

'Isn't there something important about knowing one's ancestry?' the Queen wondered. 'Not titles, I mean, but whatever runs in the blood?'

'In Valentine's case, it was vital for him *not* to know. Think what was at stake! His identity, his heredity, his trust in his mother's honour . . . everything. But he did give Ned a *very* odd look at the funeral. Something was going on between them. Ned seemed . . .' Moira paused to think. 'Amused. I remember he went over to Valentine and that boyfriend of his and was charm itself. I must say, I was very surprised when Ned got the invitation in the first place. Astrid said Ned was, too. He was very tickled about it. It made me wonder about Lee.'

'Oh? In what way?'

'Well, I'd always assumed that it was Lee who was trying to pull the St Cyr family together, but actually, given the rapprochement at her funeral, I wondered if she'd been the one keeping them apart.'

Chapter 28

The Queen had stayed longer than she intended. As the car whisked her back along the road, past old villages and modern caravan parks, she thought back to the ambassador's wife and the senior politician. He had risen further in his country's ranks and tried, more than once, to become an ambassador to the UK himself. It had even been suggested that he should be given an honorary knighthood – yet somehow, all his efforts were frustrated. Recommendations on his behalf would arrive in one of the boxes. For one reason or another, the answer was always an implacable no.

For years, the Queen had wondered why her hostess had felt able to share such private information. She certainly hadn't asked for it, but perhaps the stress of preparing for a royal visit, on top of everything else, had given the poor woman the absolute need to talk to *someone*. 'I know I can trust you,' she had said in the only reference to the desperate moment the two of them had shared – and it was true. As monarch, one was used to keeping secrets; people told you things because they knew they would go no further. What had Moira said? 'You . . . and the Pope.' Friends and acquaintances, staff, too, shared the most extraordinary information. It was as if they thought of one's private space as a confessional.

A minute later, the car drove past a square-towered gothic church, set back from the road. It soared impressively from its flat surroundings, probably built by the wealth of wool merchants in the fifteenth century, she thought. Philip would know. Once upon a time it would have been a Catholic place of worship, with elaborate stalls for formal confessions. When the Church of England took over, had it been a wrench or a relief for the local people to lose the priest as their essential connection to God's forgiveness? she wondered. In her experience, people needed *someone*. If they couldn't talk, their pain came out in other ways. She had seen so many fall apart.

And as the car drove on, she saw serried rows of wine bottles in her mind's eye.

'I'd like to visit the estate office before we go to Sandringham House,' she said to Lady Caroline. 'The car can come back for me. And can you let Mrs Maddox know I'll be a little late for tea? There's something I must do.'

The car paused outside the red-brick building while the Queen knocked on the estate office door. Once inside, passing several shocked staff, she asked Julian Cassidy if she could see him alone. Her unannounced arrival was unusual, but she sensed that he was more weary than surprised. She noticed the slackness of his tie, the saggy skin, the poorly ironed shirt, the unkempt hair that badly needed a cut, through which he was running a distracted hand. He reminded her a little of the foreign secretary on a bad day. He was a man with a lot on his mind.

Cassidy led her into his cosy office, with its old-fashioned furniture, its smell of dog, and its view of pine and birch trees.

'Can I offer you a seat, ma'am?' He indicated a sturdy Edwardian armchair, but the Queen refused. This would be a stand-up conversation.

'Mrs Raspberry was knocked over a week before Christmas,' she began. He said nothing and feigned confusion, but she saw the wariness that settled over him as he stood facing her. 'Someone was speeding through Dersingham in the dark. It was just after a bend in the road. It's not surprising, perhaps, that they didn't see her, but they would have felt something.' Cassidy was still as a statue. She wasn't sure he was even breathing. 'The impact must have caused damage to the car.' She waited.

'I imagine it must,' he said eventually.

'Whoever hit her had probably been drinking. That's why he was going too fast, why he didn't react in time, why he didn't stop.'

He swallowed. 'That may be true. I was asked about the accident because my own car was damaged two days later, actually.'

'Helena Fisher was your witness, wasn't she?'

'Yes. She happened to be passing . . .'

'Was she? And did she happen to be passing two days before, when you did indeed speed through Dersingham?'

Cassidy ran his hand through his hair again. His right eye was slightly bloodshot. She watched as he fought a look of rising panic. He reminded her of Arthur Raspberry for a moment. But she had far more sympathy for the teenager.

'I don't know what you mean, ma'am.'

'I mean that Judy Raspberry deserves better than your conspiracy with your lover. It was one of the shortest days of the year. I don't think you meant to hit her, but you were on your way home from a boozy lunch and it was already dark, you weren't concentrating on the road, and the next thing you knew—'

'I—' He stared at her. There was a long silence that filled the stuffy room. He licked his dry lips. 'I honestly thought it was a deer, escaped from the bog, or a badger. I didn't see anything, but there was suddenly just this . . . thud. And a sort of paleness against the windscreen. I panicked. I slowed down and looked behind me and I couldn't see anything in the road, and then I saw a dark shape and I thought perhaps it had been a badger after all.'

'You didn't stop,' the Queen repeated, sharply.

'I couldn't.' He flushed.

She saw how wretched he looked and added, 'I think we'd better sit down after all.'

She took the armchair he had originally offered her, and he slumped into the heavy office chair beside the desk.

'You seem to know about me and Helena,' he said dully. 'We'd arranged this night away. We tried to go somewhere nobody would see us. There's this little place near Holkham . . . We drove back separately. I'd had a couple of glasses of Shiraz at lunch and I knew if the police breathalysed me I'd lose my licence, and this brand-new job I had here, which was everything I'd worked for, and . . . Everything was so good.' He looked at the Queen with baleful, bloodhound eyes. 'It was all so good,' he repeated, 'and I didn't want to lose it all over a bloody badger.'

'A badger.' The Queen gave him an implacable stare. 'And the next day? You must have found out by then what had really happened.'

He looked down and said nothing.

'You could have gone to the police then. They were asking for witnesses.'

'Yes.' His eyes rose to meet hers eventually. 'I could. But by then . . .' He shrugged and looked defeated. 'She was in hospital. There was nothing I could do.'

'Judy Raspberry was not a badger, Mr Cassidy.'

'I know that!' His shame came out as a defensive bark. 'But I made one mistake. I tried to cover it up, but . . . It's happened and it's ruined my life anyway. I can't change anything.' He shrugged again, helplessly. 'Helena gave the witness statement. Now, she won't talk to me.'

The Queen regarded him in silence for a while.

'You seem to expect me to feel sorry for you.' He flinched. She moved towards the door and paused. 'I think you feel sorry enough for yourself. I can't make you choose what to do, but I can tell you quite categorically, Mr Cassidy, that you *can* change something. You can be honest, and you can bring some sort of understanding to Mrs Raspberry's friends and family. They may not forgive you – that's up to them – but at least they'll know what happened. They won't have that endlessly gnawing pain of uncertainty. And you'll pay a price for it, of course. The police will no doubt charge you with something. But is looking them in the eye and admitting what you've done any worse than what you're living with now?' She noticed that once again he couldn't look *her* in the eye. His own were fixed on the carpet. 'Think about it,' she went on. 'Let me know what you decide.'

He muttered something so incoherent she didn't catch it.

'What?'

'I said, I suppose you need my resignation in the morning, ma'am.'

'I need honesty, and trust, Mr Cassidy. I need a certain amount of moral courage. When you've decided what to do, we'll talk again.'

She made her own way out of the office, leaving him standing in a daze.

It had been a very difficult afternoon. She hoped there was chocolate biscuit cake for tea.

Chapter 29

The following day was Sunday, which was designated for reflection. The Bishop of Guildford, who was visiting that weekend, gave what was no doubt an excellent sermon, but the Queen's thoughts were elsewhere and she caught one sentence in ten. Fortunately, Philip would no doubt give a summary of its salient points over sherry before lunch. She would simply have to nod in agreement.

With two weeks to go until she returned to London, the Queen was keenly aware of time passing. She knew more clearly than ever what must have happened to Ned, and why. But she didn't have a scrap of hard evidence. It still wasn't enough to take to the chief constable. Or was it? As always with such cases, she was very keen to solve it, and equally keen not to be seen to do the police's job for them. It was a difficult tightrope to walk.

After lunch, she joined the small shooting party who were going out after partridge. The sky was full of thick, grey cloud, promising more snow and lending an eerie light to the afternoon. She was surrounded by friends and dogs, which was delightful, but they found her much more quiet than usual. Philip asked if she was sickening for something again, but it wasn't that. She was thinking over what she did and didn't know, and of what she was and wasn't certain – which were not exactly the same thing.

There was an edge to the house party this weekend, which included a couple of political grandees. It wasn't only the Queen who was preoccupied. The new president of the United States had decided to launch the tone of his presidency by denying media reports of the size of the crowd at his inauguration. The Queen thought of the crowds that assembled in the Mall in front of Buckingham Palace on big occasions, and was silently grateful. Sir Simon was despairing. He was not a fan of a leadership style that involved bringing basic truths into question, and the prime minister was lining up to meet him at the end of the week.

Meanwhile Philip was edgy, too. This was their last stay at Sandringham during which he was in charge of the estate, as he had been for sixty-five years. Next year, Charles would no doubt be showing off his own new leadership style. She had every confidence in their son, and so did Philip, really, but relinquishing control was not his strong suit. The mood would pass. She would weather it. She was good at weathering things.

In the morning, she was the first person to come downstairs, which was unusual. She felt a great restlessness, and knew the best way to resolve it. Willow, Candy and Vulcan were duly assembled in front of the house. Scarf on head, she took them for a walk to the church and back, echoing the one she had taken yesterday. Gradually, as she knew they would, the last few details of the St Cyr case that had been bothering her slotted into place. There was one outstanding issue, but it wasn't insurmountable. The trouble was, it was all conjecture.

Could a Sovereign of the Realm accuse a member of the nobility of murder, with no concrete evidence at all, on the basis of one passing remark made over coffee? She thought not. Mr Bloomfield and his team of twenty-first-century technicians would get there on their own, surely? With one exception as to motive, they had access to the same information she did. She just needed to be patient.

But the Queen was not patient when it came to the certain knowledge that someone in her circle was a killer who was surprisingly adept at getting away with it. In a way, it was almost admirable, but she kept thinking of the sea, and how it had claimed Chris Wallace. How long could justice wait?

The week began promisingly: DNA tests confirmed the relationship between Ned and Valentine St Cyr. Surely an arrest was imminent? Instead, Rozie reported that Valentine was free again and no further action was planned. The Queen was not a panicker, but this was alarming. If anything, they were going backwards, for goodness' sake.

On Friday, she and Philip made an official visit to the University of East Anglia. The chief constable himself was there, so she took the opportunity to ask him how they were getting on, and to her huge frustration, he seemed as stumped as he had been in December, and much less sanguine about finding a solution soon.

'Valentine St Cyr admitted he suspected Edward was his father,' Bloomfield told her, during a brief lull in the reception. 'That's what they'd been talking about in their little meetings, of course. He doesn't want it made public yet, until he's talked to Lord Mundy about it. And you, I imagine, ma'am. It's quite explosive for his family, him not being the next baron, et cetera.'

'Isn't that a motive?' the Queen asked, surprised that he seemed so phlegmatic about it.

'Absolutely, ma'am. But St Cyr has challenged us to find concrete evidence. He has a nice team of expensive lawyers. Given what happened last time . . . ahem.'

'Yes, I see what you mean.'

'His explanation about scattering his mother's ashes at sea was supported by several sources,' Bloomfield said. 'We did wonder if he was in cahoots with his sister, but if so, they managed it without leaving a trail. We've searched his flat, and that of his partner, and all vehicles they have access to. There are no signs of suspicious cleaning, and not a scrap of Edward's DNA anywhere, except on a suit jacket of Valentine's that he claimed to have been wearing when he met up with his father. Nor was any of *his* DNA at Edward's flat.' He smiled at her. 'You must be relieved, ma'am.'

'Oh?'

'Because Mr St Cyr is a friend.'

'Ah. I see what you mean.'

Philip was staring daggers at them from across the lobby of the university. She had been talking too long. 'Did you wonder about the dogs?' she asked, before saying goodbye.

'The dogs, ma'am?'

'Yes. Being left alone at Abbottswood.'

'Oh, those dogs! Yes, we did. The suspiciousness of the damage they did, you mean, left to their own devices. Don't worry, we looked into it. It was all above board.'

'And now I must go. Thank you, Chief Constable.'

She smiled and kept her frustrations to herself.

Back at Sandringham, the news bulletins featured images of the prime minister at the White House, standing next to the new president. The very first thing she mentioned was the state visit to London, 'as soon as possible'. The Queen felt once again as if she was being dangled, like a treat.

She couldn't affect what was happening in Washington at the moment, but surely she could make some progress in north Norfolk? She had ten days left and she sensed the chief constable needed as much help as she could provide, ideally without ever knowing she had given it. It was time to talk to Rozie.

They met in the Queen's office that evening, while the others dressed for dinner. Rozie was ostensibly giving the Boss a detailed debrief on the prime minister's Washington visit. It might seem unnecessarily long for something one could simply watch on the news, but a handy thing about being the monarch was that one was rarely questioned about one's need for information on international events.

'I want you to talk to the vicar of St Agnes at Ladybridge,' the Queen said instead. 'You might suggest that I have a friend who is likely to be in his congregation on Sunday and would appreciate the sermon on truth and beauty that he gave when he came to West Newton.'

'Truth and beauty, ma'am.' Rozie nodded. She got out her personal notebook, which was disguised to look like bad poetry and song lyrics, should anyone happen to pick it up. Its key pages contained the essentials from the police reports, and the additional information she, Katie and the Queen had found. She made a new note. 'I assume there's someone in particular who needs to hear it.'

'There most certainly is. There has been an inordinate amount of lying,' the Queen said. 'To one's face, by people who are dear to one, which is quite disturbing. One person has been lying consistently, although I doubt the vicar will have any effect on them. Perhaps they assumed I wouldn't notice. But as my loft manager says, "people talk". One tends to spot inconsistencies eventually. And then, there are the dogs.'

'The dogs, ma'am?'

'But first there's the question of Valentine. I wondered at first if the problem was something he'd done, but now we know it's simply who he is.'

Rozie thought at first that the Boss was referring to his sexuality. This was not a 'problem', surely? She was wondering how to disapprove respectfully when the Queen went on:

'Moira Westover suggested he first got a hint of it at Lee Mundy's funeral. It must have been quite a shock.'

'Oh, you mean his paternity. Do you think that's when Ned told him that he was his father?' Rozie asked.

'Actually I don't. I think Ned was more than happy for it to remain a secret. It suited his purposes well. But Valentine worked it out. Perhaps it was a look Ned gave him, or a gesture they had in common. Anyway, he was right.'

'You'd think, if you discovered someone was your parent, you'd want to connect, but maybe Valentine *resented* him,' Rozie said. 'It means he knows he's not the real heir to the St Cyr title. Could someone kill over *that*? A title?'

'Certainly,' the Queen agreed, without hesitation. 'There are many things men have done through history for a title. Women, too, of course.'

'So you think he's the killer?' Rozie asked.

The Queen's gaze was steady and unblinking. 'No.'

Rozie thought the Boss might be avoiding a delicate issue.

'I know it's all circumstantial evidence at the moment,' she argued. 'But the circumstances add up, ma'am. They know he had the opportunity, if he worked with his fiancé. We know he had a motive. Surely the police do, too?'

'And yet . . . there's nothing to connect him to the murder.' The Queen explained what the chief constable had told her about the lack of DNA evidence. 'DNA gives, and it takes away.'

Rozie pursed her lips and frowned.

'I know you don't *want* to believe it, ma'am.' She was hesitant. Accusing the Boss of wishful thinking was a bold move. But she felt she had to, despite the arch look the Queen was giving her. 'I realise you've known him all his life, but—'

'It isn't that,' the Queen said. 'Quite the reverse. But thank you for challenging my argument. It's what I want you to do. Sometimes I feel too close to this case. I need you to mark my homework.'

'Oh. OK,' Rozie said, unable to hide her surprise. This was a new development. Arguing with the Boss might take some getting used to. But if it helped . . .

The Queen invited Rozie to sit down with her, to facilitate conversation and avoid straining her neck. 'It starts with genetics,' she said. 'I, of all people, should understand that better than anyone. An obsession with genetics caused the original crime, but it was love that caused the next one. And carelessness that caused the third.'

'The third?' Rozie asked. 'Do you mean Mrs Raspberry?'

'No. Although you're right,' the Queen acknowledged, 'it was pure carelessness that caused poor Mrs Raspberry to be knocked over. And a cruel disregard for her life that caused her to be left there. I've spoken to Mr Cassidy about it.'

'You have?'

'We'll see what he does. It's quite obvious that he's been suffering ever since. Not enough to pay the proper price, however. Not yet, at least.' The Queen fiddled absently with the arm of her bifocals again. 'But that was an accident. Nothing surrounding Ned's death was entirely accidental, by contrast. In fact, it was all meticulously planned. The third victim I'm referring to was Mr Wallace. His death was awful and avoidable. He was only supposed to be distracted, but to drive a man to such despair . . .'

Rozie was losing track. 'Then who is the second victim, ma'am? I thought he was.'

'No. The second victim is Ned himself.'

Rozie frowned. 'Then who's the first?'

'Lady Mundy, who died in the summer. But I'm referring to long ago. You might say, Valentine, too. His life

273

was always going to be extremely complicated, through no fault of his own. And I'm sorry to say my friend Georgina was partly responsible. She bred a terrible sense of entitlement into her son. Ned took it out on Lee. I won't go into details, but Ned used Lee to try and sneak his bloodline back into the barons of Ladybridge. It was a deliberate act. The odds of it working were incredibly slim, and yet, it did. The secret was very well kept until Lee died. Then Ned met the family again and it all started to go wrong.

'And here we come to the first inconsistency. The St Cyrs told me quite clearly that Ned had offered to go to the funeral. Hugh was very gracious about it. And yet, Astrid Westover and her mother both said how surprised Ned had been to be invited. Did he offer, or was he asked?'

Rozie checked her notes. 'The police certainly thought that Ned was the first one to try and end the feud.'

'Mmm, but I disagree,' the Queen said. 'Astrid suggested that he was pleased to rebuild his relationships with his family. But, under the circumstances, I doubt very much that he would have made that offer unprompted. I think he was drawn back into Ladybridge's orbit. Somebody wanted him there. My husband was right.'

'Yes, ma'am?'

'He said from the very beginning, it's always the family.'

'So it *is* one of the St Cyrs, ma'am?'

'Of course it is. The trouble with Mr Bloomfield is that he and his investigating team have access to endless modern technology. It's all terribly impressive, but this is an old-fashioned crime of passion. It's the human element they

274

needed to focus on. And the canine element, one might say. As I say, I have no proof, and everyone has alibis, but once you think about the dogs, it's obvious how it was done.'

It wasn't obvious to Rozie. 'You mentioned the dogs, ma'am?'

The Queen looked slightly irritated. 'I'm surprised more people haven't noticed. They caused havoc at Abbottswood, because they weren't looked after properly.'

'I did wonder about the damage,' Rozie said. 'So did the police.'

'That's not what I mean. The chief constable sought to reassure me that it was all above board. I assume he meant it really was the dogs who ripped up the sitting room, not some sort of intruder. I don't disagree about that. If you leave an unhappy dog for long enough, there's no end to the damage he can do. The thing is, they hadn't been fed or exercised since the day before. *That's* what's so interesting. Ned hadn't checked the cleaning lady would be there to do it. Nobody leaves their precious dogs for such a long time without being certain they're being cared for.'

'I'm sure some people do, ma'am.'

'Not if you love them. Ned was a dog person, like Georgina. He always adored my dogs. He'd have played with them more than Charles if he'd been allowed. No, he wouldn't leave home without being confident that they would be let out and fed in the morning. If the cleaning lady wasn't coming in, he would have found someone else. I simply couldn't imagine Ned being so inconsiderate. And once you can't imagine *that* . . .'

Rozie began to enjoy this idea of disagreeing with the Boss. She could easily imagine it. 'He was under a lot of pressure, ma'am. That might have caused the lapse in concentration.'

'We don't know for certain that he was,' the Queen insisted. 'According to Astrid, Ned was very "Zen", or something of that nature. The police have assumed he was under pressure because he was acting oddly. I think the oddness of his activity is the interesting part. Take the speeding car. He conveniently broke the speed limit twice in his Maserati. It meant the speed cameras caught him. This was despite the fact that Astrid said he couldn't afford to lose his licence. It was all very theatrical. Then there was the "RIP" written in the desk diary at Abbottswood. I'm sure it was "RIP", not "RLP", by the way. It was a joke, another flourish. All it did was highlight that Ned was at home in Norfolk when he wrote it in.'

Rozie seriously wondered if the Queen was having a senior moment. 'But surely the plan was to draw attention to London, ma'am, not Norfolk?'

'Later, yes. First, there was the phone call. Julian Cassidy told you that what Ned said to him didn't make sense.'

'That's right. Something about raining in hell.'

'It's not "raining in hell", it's "reigning in hell". My sort of reigning. "Better to reign in hell than serve in heaven." It's from *Paradise Lost*. I had to study it as a girl. Anyway, here was a man calling someone he didn't know very well, talking about a fall from grace, for no obvious reason.'

Here was something Rozie could connect to. There was a lot of talk about falling from grace at church when she was growing up. With a mother called Grace, she had both taken it personally and never quite made sense of it.

'Ned doesn't strike me as the sort of man who would worry about the state of his soul,' she suggested.

The Queen nodded. 'Indeed not. I think he worried about the state of his estate. But it wasn't Ned who abandoned his dogs or drove to London, or quoted Milton at Mr Cassidy. The call was made simply to show that he was at Abbottswood, when he was not. He was already dead by then.'

'Ma'am?'

The Queen put down her glasses.

'At least, I hope he was.'

Chapter 30

Rozie rapidly reviewed what she thought she knew about Ned's last hours.

'But he was seen by witnesses in London, ma'am.'

'A tall man in a distinctive hat and scarf was seen,' The Queen corrected her. 'Haven't you noticed how the St Cyr men look alike?'

Rozie had. 'But what about the texts he sent to Astrid? She'd have known if it wasn't her fiancé sending them.'

The Queen gave her a gimlet stare.

'Would she?'

It sounded like a rhetorical question, but Rozie stood her ground. 'If it was someone else using his phone, they did a very good job, ma'am. Astrid mentioned that the texts were quite intimate.' She didn't want to embarrass the Boss, but modern sexting between couples could be pretty explicit. It was if it was any good, anyway. Although . . .

'Mmm?' the Queen murmured, seeing Rozie hesitate.

'I suppose if you had access to the text history, you could recreate the style. You'd just have to scroll up.' It might not be so hard after all. Not for one conversation, at least. Creepy, but not difficult.

'So we can't be certain it was Ned who texted Astrid that evening.'

But someone did. And they did it from Ned's phone, in his studio. Rozie consulted her notes.

'I don't see who. According to Valentine, both he and Roland Peng were in his flat at the time. Lord Mundy, Flora and her daughters were at the Hall. They're all witnesses for each other. Then Lord Mundy had the late-night meeting with Mr Wallace. Flora saw him arrive.'

The Queen nodded to herself. 'Mr Wallace is not here either to confirm or deny that story. A car arrived at the hall, certainly. It might have been a taxi from the station, however. I think where the St Cyrs are concerned, we must assume that everyone is prepared to lie for the sake of protecting the family, really. The thing is, who saw or spoke to Ned after they did?'

Rozie thought it through. It seemed unlikely, but it made sense. The problem had always been how Ned managed to disappear in London. If he never went there, a lot of questions answered themselves. And it made more sense of the location of the hand. She put her notebook down.

'There's two things I don't get.'

'Oh?'

'If it wasn't Ned, why haven't the police worked this out? Wouldn't DNA and fingerprints prove what really happened?'

'You would have thought so,' the Queen said with a brief sigh. 'It's why I've spent so long wondering if I might be wrong. If I'm right, whoever did this was very careful and very clever. I imagine they watched a lot of crime scene programmes. They're fascinating. And the police didn't think about the dogs. What was your other question?'

'How did Ned die?'

'In the most old-fashioned way possible. He was poisoned, I imagine.'

Rozie nodded. Of course. In the true St Cyr tradition.

'The thing about poison is it's difficult to use if you want it to be untraceable,' the Queen said. 'I've read enough detective novels to know that much. If you don't intend the body ever to be found intact, it's much easier. Then he was hidden away, stripped of his distinctive clothes, his phone, his keys. The killer could return later, to dispose of the body at their leisure. The important thing was to create a distraction for the next few hours.'

'So when Flora said she saw Ned drive her father away from Ladybridge . . .'

'She saw someone in Ned's car, in his distinctive coat and hat. Or else she was lying.'

Rozie tried to imagine the sheer audaciousness of it. She hadn't associated the St Cyr family with bravura. Eccentricity yes, but . . . On the other hand, was there anything you could put past the aristocracy? Even so . . .

'If you're right, ma'am, and the killer took on Mr St Cyr's identity, they could have been caught out in his Land Rover, his car, his house, his flat. The risk . . . So many things could have gone wrong.'

'It was a risk worth taking, apparently,' the Queen said. "Better to reign in hell." Perhaps things *did* go wrong. But here we are: the police still don't know where to find the body. Without it, they have nothing. And of course, if they had it, it would explain everything.'

'Do you know where it is, ma'am?'

'I think so. There's only one logical place it can be.'

'I . . . I still can't really believe it. It's hard to imagine . . .'

'That was the idea.'

'But yes, I see what you mean,' Rozie said. 'If you're right, I'd know where I'd look.'

'Good. Now I just have to persuade the chief constable to look there, too.'

Chapter 31

'Oh, for Christ's sake. They're saying we're a hotbed of drugs now.'

'Good morning.'

The Queen made herself comfortable opposite her husband in the saloon and accepted the offer of coffee from her page. Philip looked up from the *Recorder* and grunted back.

'May I see?' she asked.

He handed her the paper with a flick of the wrist. 'Bastards. Every one of 'em. The drivel they're paid to write.'

The Queen studied the article in question.

QUEEN CONCERNED ABOUT DRUG GANGS ON DOORSTEP
by Ollie Knight

The piece was surprisingly accurate. It described the money-laundering scheme, pointed out that the pigeon racing clubs in question tended to be in the west of the country, and suggested that she had expressed concern about her own doorstep, in the east. It then went on to describe the royal loft and its management in glowing terms.

Only three people that she could think of knew, or might guess, that she was personally concerned. She hadn't mentioned the issue to anyone else. Those three were Mr Day, her loft manager, his wife, and Roland Peng, who had told her about it in the first place.

Fortunately, the article didn't mention why she was interested. Her thinking had moved on now, anyway. But it did potentially solve a little problem.

Rozie was up to her neck in ice-cold water. The breath had been squeezed out of her body and everything tingled and hurt. And yet, it was life-affirming. How had she lived this long and not known how essential and fabulous wild swimming was? She was building up to a minute in the water. Around her, an assortment of swimming hats bobbed confidently in the sea.

Katie watched from the safety of the beach. She had resisted saying 'I told you so' when Rozie came back from her first wild swim, brimming with enthusiasm. Instead, she had introduced her to her own wild swimming group, based up the coast. She could see this was the start of a beautiful relationship: Captain Oshodi and cold water. On their way back, they spotted the Queen driving out to Wolferton.

'D'you know where she's going?' Katie asked.

'Wood Farm, probably,' Rozie suggested. 'She usually is.'

But she wasn't.

The Queen had a very pleasant tour of the pigeon loft from Mr Day. Afterwards, he and his wife entertained her to coffee and home-made chocolate cake. They gave her some gin to take home and try after they had all regretfully concluded that it was a bit early to crack it open now, at 10 a.m. And the Queen was driving, after all.

'Isn't it good news about Lord Mundy's son?' Mrs Day said. 'We were talking about it this morning. You must be pleased, personally, ma'am. You know him, don't you?'

'Yes, I do.' The Queen was relieved. They had indulged in several topics of conversation leading up to this one, but at last they were here.

'Did you ever think he could be a murderer?'

'No, I didn't,' the Queen said, not entirely truthfully.

'There isn't any hope that Mr St Cyr's still alive, is there?' Mr Day asked.

'None, I'm afraid.'

'I can't help picturing him in a shallow grave somewhere,' Mrs Day added solemnly.

'It's dreadful when there isn't a body, isn't it?' the Queen suggested. 'Everyone is left with so much uncertainty. The family can't move on in so many practical ways.'

'It's nasty,' Mrs Day said. 'Sadistic, I'd say. To kill someone is something, but to hide the body . . . that somehow makes it worse, don't you think?'

'I do.'

'There's no burial, no peace. It's un-Christian. I suppose if you're a murderer you don't care about things like that.'

'I suppose not,' the Queen agreed. 'Although no doubt you've heard the rumour.'

Mrs Day sat up straighter. 'What rumour's that, ma'am?'

284

'The one that says he never did go up to London.'

'No! Who said that?'

'I can't remember where I heard it.' The Queen looked vague. 'Sandringham is a fount of gossip. But someone said they knew for a fact the person who left Abbottswood that day in his car wasn't him.'

'Goodness! Who was it?'

The Queen shrugged. 'I can't imagine, can you?'

'Do the police know?'

'I'm not sure,' the Queen said, innocently.

'You know what they think of gossip, pet,' Mr Day said to his wife. 'The way they treated poor Judy.'

'True.' Mrs Day rolled her eyes. She frowned with concentration, trying to remember Ned's last movements, based on what they'd heard. 'It could've been a parcel delivery man who saw the car. Fred Sayle supplies heating oil. He could've spotted someone driving out as he was going in . . .'

'Perhaps they felt they wouldn't be believed,' the Queen said. 'Or they didn't trust their own judgement. I wish one knew more, so one could do something about it.'

'I suppose *you* could tell the police, ma'am.'

The Queen gave a perfectly honest reply. 'Without any evidence, I don't think I could help.'

'Mmm.'

Mrs Day was still thinking hard. The Queen decided that this was a good time to leave her to it. One useful thing about being the monarch – something that was often as much of a burden as a gift – was that every little thing you said was weighed and measured. She would be astonished if there were no ripples from the pebble she had cast into this particular pond.

'It's a difficult issue, isn't it? If you discuss it with anyone, please don't mention me. I don't approve of gossip.'

'Ooh, I wouldn't dream of it, ma'am,' Mrs Day said reverently.

PART 4

NOTHING GOLD CAN STAY

Chapter 32

Ollie Knight, the young stringer for the *Recorder*, sat next to a van parked on the meadow, watching as a team of police divers dressed in dry suits and yellow face masks prepared to lower themselves into the moat at Ladybridge Hall.

This ringside view was part of his reward for the tip-off of where to look for the body. Mrs Day had rung him in great anticipation three days ago.

'I'd have gone to the police straightaway, but after all the names they called Mrs Raspberry, they can sing for it, quite frankly. Somebody needs to find out if this is true. You will promise me you'll look into it, won't you?'

Ollie hadn't promised, but he'd looked into it anyway.

It took a lot to persuade a cash-strapped police force to dredge a moat. The 'how the body got there' was the relatively easy part. His first thought, like Mrs Day's, was that Ned might be buried at Abbottswood somewhere, and the police had missed it. But a bit of digging had quickly thrown up the fact that nobody who knew Ned well had seen him since he visited the hall for lunch with his much-hated family. Not only had he not left Abbottswood, there was no guarantee he'd even arrived home. Flora Osborne could easily have lied about seeing him wave goodbye. His cousin Valentine could have pretended to be him in London.

The thing was, once you started, you kept finding holes in the story the police had constructed. Ollie had spoken to the man who, according to a short interview he gave to the *Recorder*, was the last person to talk to Ned St Cyr alive. Mr Shah was the newsagent in Highgate where St Cyr had bought the items for his breakfast. He told Ollie he recognised him from his height, his clothes and the colour of his eyes. It had not occurred to him it might *not* be Mr St Cyr, who he knew vaguely. The man at the takeaway, same story. The footage from the traffic cameras wouldn't be conclusive.

The 'why' was the hard part. If Ned had died at Ladybridge, who stood to gain? After all, he was the poor relation. It had taken hours of careful research to find evidence that Ned and Valentine might be related, based on the timing of Valentine's birth. If Ned was Valentine's father . . . bombshell: no more legitimate male St Cyrs to carry on the title. If he was using this knowledge to blackmail them for money for his new project, for example, then there was your motive. One DNA test was all it would take. Maybe the police had already done it. Ollie didn't have any proof of any of this, but as a theory it held water.

He didn't know what the family alibis were, but if he was right, there would be holes. The police would already know about them, or they would find them. Ollie needed something to give them, beyond tittle-tattle, and in the end it was the age-old standby: fingerprints. He simply asked if Ned's prints were on the steering wheel of the car he'd used to drive away from the hall. Ollie's contact in the Norfolk force admitted they were heavily smudged, but this was explained by the driving gloves found in his Maserati in London. Ollie trawled through the archives of the *Recorder* and unearthed several images of St Cyr in or beside various cars through the ages. He had stopped wearing gloves in the 1980s. What about prints on the items he had bought from Mr Shah? All smudges. Nothing conclusive. Now they were starting to take him seriously. Hence this ringside view reward.

Yesterday, a police dog team had searched the hall from top to bottom, with no joy. But it didn't take a genius to see where the body would be. It turned out there were a couple of ground-floor rooms with empty windows facing the moat. Ollie was stationed opposite them now. Presumably, the body had been weighted to ensure it sank to the bottom and stayed there, so without winds or tides to shift it around, it was unlikely to have moved from the spot.

So far, the hardest part had been getting the swans out of the way. Ollie had done a bit of research on swans for the long-form magazine article he'd be writing later. According to what he'd read, they used to be a major delicacy at medieval banquets, as a result of which the Queen could claim ownership of all swans not owned by a couple of livery companies in open waters. Presumably moat-based swans didn't count. More pertinently for a day like today, they could be vicious if they felt under threat. If you weren't careful, they could break your arm.

The divers were taking forever to adjust their kit before getting into the water. Ollie trained his binoculars on the house while he waited. Was that a ghostly face at one of the windows? He sharpened the focus. He wouldn't swear to it, but it looked like Flora Osborne. What would she be thinking now?

The last guests of the season at Sandringham were finishing their stay. While Philip took them on a final shoot, the Queen was on her way to Newmarket for lunch with her racing manager and various trainers she knew and liked. Having heard about the recent police breakthrough in the St Cyr case, and their expectation of at least one imminent arrest, she could relax at last. She had been looking forward to the day tremendously. There was nothing like a good meal and an afternoon spent viewing horses and discussing the racing calendar with people who knew exactly what they were talking about.

January was drawing to a close. In a week, she would be heading back to London, and the gilded office block on the roundabout. Now that she knew the police were busy at Ladybridge, she was perfectly sanguine about this. Julian Cassidy, too, had handed himself in yesterday. She didn't know what would happen to him, but now that he had done the decent thing, she would support him as best she could. Whatever he did now, it would be better than drinking himself into an early grave. Meanwhile, despite the flu at the beginning, Norfolk had done its job and given her and Philip the dose of fresh air they needed. She felt ready to tackle whatever the new year had to throw at her.

Lady Caroline would be joining her at the racecourse, travelling from Cambridge, where her brother was master of one of the colleges. And so, once again, it was Rozie who kept the Queen company on the journey. They alternated between discussing the next few weeks' events in the royal diary and quietly waiting for news from Ladybridge. The Queen was hopeful that by the end of the day they would have a body and a murderer in custody. If they didn't, it wouldn't be for lack of trying on the royal part. She had done what she could.

'Is that it?' she asked, as the phone on the leather armrest beside Rozie lit up with an incoming message.

'No, ma'am. I'm sorry.' It was Rozie's sister, asking if she was free for cocktails in Kensington next weekend. Rozie discreetly flicked the message away.

The car had turned off the main road to avoid a traffic jam ahead. It wound its way through country lanes for a couple of miles, where the sun created jagged shafts of light through the naked branches of overhanging trees. Several fields away, the Queen caught sight of scarlet coats moving at speed in the distance. The hunt must be out. It was extraordinary, after all the controversy of recent years, that they could still do it. It had been such a common sight in her youth, but these days they chased man-made trails, not foxes. Thanks to Jack Lions and his ilk, a thousand years of tradition had been reduced to a schoolboy game.

'Ah. Trouble ahead, ma'am. Not to worry.'

The driver of the Queen's Range Rover slowed down to let two cars past. Horns blared, whistles blew and flags waved from the windows. The Queen recognised the noise: these were saboteurs, keen to find the hounds and distract them. They were convinced that the hunts still went for foxes, either deliberately or if the hounds happened to find one by accident, and did whatever they could to put them off the scent. The result was a disturbing cacophony of noise that unsettled everyone in the car. Once it had passed, the Range Rover sped up again smoothly for half a mile. Then, without warning, it braked sharply.

'I'm sorry, ma'am.'

'What is it?'

'There's someone in the road ahead.'

'Another saboteur?' she asked.

'No, ma'am. A body.'

From his vantage point in the meadow, Ollie Knight saw a hand rise out of the moat. It reminded him of a film he'd seen about King Arthur. There should be a sword somewhere. Except, this hand was inside a diving suit, and it was signalling that they had found something. It didn't take long for the divers in the moat to bring their discovery to the spot where the forensic team were waiting. It took three men to lift it. As far as Ollie could tell, it was a man-sized tube made of sacking, wrapped in a heavy chain. As it rose above the water, a human arm slipped out of the sacking, bloated and discoloured, ending at the wrist. Ollie was transfixed. When he eventually looked up to see who else was watching, the face at the upper window was gone.

A few yards ahead of the Range Rover, a girl of about sixteen or seventeen lay on her side near the verge. She was wearing riding boots and a hard hat, and a bright yellow vest over her jacket, but in the sharp light and shadows of the winter sun, she would still have been easy to miss. The driver had done well to spot her in time. The girl's limbs were akimbo and her face was very pale.

'You need to find her mount,' the Queen said. 'It must be round here somewhere.'

The driver looked round unhappily. He clearly didn't want to stay where they were, but they couldn't go on and leave the girl in place. Rozie was already leaping out of the car to see how badly hurt she was. The new protection officer, Depiscopo, had a panicked look in his eye that belied the set to his jaw. He called Rozie back, but she ignored him.

'There's a pulse,' she called. 'But she's out cold. Is someone calling an ambulance? I'm going to find the horse.'

Rozie moved the girl gently into the recovery position and ran round the bend in the road. A minute later, she was back.

'Shit. There's another one. An older woman, out cold, too. The cars must have scared their horses. I think her leg's broken and she's losing blood. We need to block the road before someone comes.'

A brief interval followed, while Depiscopo radioed for help. The trouble was, as the Queen saw instantly, that help would normally come from the south, towards Newmarket, and the main road that way was blocked with traffic. Rozie had already grabbed a medical kit from the back of the car and taken it to deal with the older casualty. Depiscopo assessed the situation and instructed the Queen's driver to get out and warn any passing traffic about the danger, while he reversed the Range Rover up a little track they had passed fifty yards earlier to get it, and Her Majesty, out of the way. The Queen knew that officially, what he should do was ignore the injured women and drive on. Jackson would have done it without a qualm; the sovereign's safety was paramount. But she took advantage of the new officer's uncertainty. Like all her staff, he would be trained in first aid. Thank goodness they were there.

He parked the car at the top of the track, on a little ridge out of sight of the road, next to an empty field. She was increasingly worried that Rozie would be busy ministering to the older rider or rounding up the horses, and might get hit by a passing car in the process.

'I'll be perfectly all right here,' she said, because she would be. 'Go and see what you can do.'

Depiscopo wavered.

'Are you sure you'll be OK, ma'am? I'll be one minute. Please stay in the car.'

The Queen assured him that she would be perfectly safe. He ran down the track.

But he was not back after one minute, or even five. Meanwhile, the Range Rover was getting cold and it was eerily quiet. On top of that, her knee was giving her gip. Outside, high above the trees, two lapwings flew in a complicated dance against the bright blue sky. She opened the door and stepped out to get a better look, and the fresh air on her face made her feel instantly better.

She couldn't see what was happening in the road below because Depiscopo had carefully chosen a parking spot masked by pines and hedges. To her left, there was a stile set into a rough stone wall, with a large paddock beyond. Her gammy knee ached for exercise. She wasn't exactly dressed for a walk in the country, but it hadn't rained for days and the path to the stile was dry. She changed out of her patent shoes into more practical boots that she always kept in the back of the car and retrieved a silk scarf that she kept in the back-seat armrest for emergencies, knotting it under her chin. Though she couldn't see the road, the view across the fields from here was delightful. There were worse places to wait.

Heading for the stile, her leg felt better with each step and when she reached the field – which turned out to be a rough paddock – she saw two ponies grazing in the middle. Depiscopo could easily find her here. He might panic for a moment when he saw the empty Range Rover, but it would be obvious where she had gone.

She had nearly reached the nearest pony, picking her way carefully across tussocks of grass and watching out for rabbit holes, when the sound of hooves grew rapidly louder and she glanced to her left to see a grey stallion sail over the hedge marking the northern boundary, before landing heavily not fifty feet from her. Its rider wore immaculate hunting pink and a hard hat. He must be part of the distant drag hunt. But they were miles away by now.

'Are you lost?' the Queen called out cheerily.

He trotted towards her without speaking. As he grew closer, her absolute astonishment was mirrored by his.

'Hugh?'

'Your Majesty?'

'But I thought—'

Lord Mundy brought his horse to a halt and dismounted, keeping the reins in one gloved hand and his riding crop in the other. His horse breathed heavily beside him. Hugh looked very different without his ancient tweed and baling twine. The smart red jacket and white stock under his chin brought back memories of younger days, when he had been a dashing huntsman. He beamed at her and bowed.

'Of all the fields in all the world, ma'am . . . What are you doing here?'

'Avoiding an accident. I might ask the same thing.'

'I took a wrong turning and lost the pack twenty minutes ago,' he said. 'Thought I heard the horn, raced over three fields and now, God knows where I am. I'm out of practice. But it's been a good morning.'

'Has it?' The Queen was starting to regret several of the decisions of the last ten minutes. There was still no sign of Rozie, the driver or her protection officer. 'Don't you have the police with you at Ladybridge?'

'Ah. You heard about that. I slipped away. No need to watch 'em spook the swans and muck up the moat.'

'Did they let you go?'

'Not specifically. But I saw no reason to watch and wait. If we don't hunt – even a drag hunt like this – we'll lose the right to do it at all.'

The Queen wondered if she had heard him right. Hugh seemed to be in an excellent mood, and more concerned about a drag hunt than a murder hunt on his own property. Once again, she had been so confident of her ideas . . . and now she was doubting them. Had she made a huge mistake? She had been so certain that by now it would all be over.

'I hope you find the others soon. I need to get back to the car,' she said, nodding and smiling at him, backing gently away, resisting the urge to run.

Hugh nodded and smiled back. But he and his horse were standing between her and the stile, and he didn't get out of the way.

'How *did* you know, ma'am?' he asked politely. 'That the police would be at Ladybridge?'

'They keep me informed of everything,' she said evenly. 'It was a courtesy. You and I are friends, Hugh, after all.'

He nodded at that, but he was giving her a very unnerving, piercing stare. This was not the grim, grey baron, knocked sideways by grief. A keen intelligence danced behind those blue eyes. She decided she had not underestimated him.

'Informed of everything . . .' he said thoughtfully.

'I hope Flora's all right. Is she dealing with the police alone? I gather they had Valentine in custody earlier. That must be—'

The baron's smile stayed fixed. 'Flora can look after herself. Valentine has done nothing wrong. Therefore, the police will find nothing. It's not my job to interfere.'

'Hugh! Really!'

'What do you mean?'

'You know what I mean.'

'If anything happened, it was warranted. It's water under the bridge.'

There was a strange serenity to him, as if what was going on had nothing to do with him. The Queen was offended by it.

'I know what happened fifty years ago. Chris Wallace died because he knew, too. That is *not* water under the bridge, Hugh.'

Hugh stiffened. 'Chris Wallace took his own life, poor bastard. That wasn't my fault. Leave him out of this.'

'But he is *in* it,' the Queen said with some passion. 'He's at the heart of it. You thought he knew what Ned had done to Lee, so you tried to upset him so much he wouldn't think straight to accuse you of revenge when Ned disappeared. But what makes it so tragic is that the police won't care about what Ned did to Lee. They'll assume his death was simple revenge for Valentine's paternity.'

'What do you mean?'

'The police have done the DNA test. They *know*, Hugh.'

He looked dismissive. 'If they find a body at Ladybridge, so what? They can't prove who put it there. For God's sake, ma'am. Ned's been missing for weeks.'

The Queen was exasperated by his stubborn refusal to face the truth. 'As soon as they start looking for evidence, they'll find it. His stomach will still contain the poison you used to knock him out. It was hemlock, wasn't it? In honour of the ghost. Lee's gardening books would have told you where to find it on the estate. It grows wild near our river-banks. It probably does near yours. You could have saved it from the summer.'

Hugh hesitated. He seemed to appreciate her acknow-ledgement of that little touch.

'If you disposed of his clothes on the estate, they'll find traces of those, too,' she persisted. 'Your alibi for the fourteenth, when you were supposed to be seeing Mrs Capelton, won't hold. It can't, because you were busy pretending to be your cousin.' She narrowed her eyes. 'I can understand your reasons,' she said, warming to her theme. 'I abhor it, but I can see your biblical sense of justice. What I really can't forgive is that you had a duty of care to Mr Wallace, and instead of protecting him you hounded him to his death, so you could get away with what you did to Ned.'

She spoke with more heat than she intended to. When she finished, a light went on in the baron's eyes. She realised she had said too much and took a step backwards. He moved towards her, still holding the reins of his horse. She glanced over the wall to her left in the fervent hope of seeing the cav-alry riding up the track, but there was only a solitary hare, who looked as nervous as she was.

'You told them all of this?'

'I did not,' she said, which was strictly true, if not entirely accurate.

'I often wondered if Lee had spoken to your mother.'

'I have no idea what—'

Hugh took another step towards her. He was taller than she remembered. Or rather, taller than he seemed at Christmas. The grief was real, but the stoop was gone. He used his height to intimidate her, and she was very aware

301

of the riding crop in his left hand. Then he seemed to change his mind and hauled himself back onto his hunter.

Rozie had finally found both horses further up the road and brought them under control. There was still no sign of police or ambulance, but both riders were breathing, the bleeding of the older woman had been staunched with a tourniquet on her leg, and a small queue of traffic at either end of the accident had been prevented from running them over. The Queen's driver was managing the flow of cars while her protection officer attended to the injured. Rozie counted them.

'Who's looking after the Boss?'

Depiscopo looked up from the teenager, whom he'd been reassuring that help was on the way.

'Shit.'

He hauled himself up and started to run, but Rozie was already ahead of him.

Hugh sat tall in the saddle and the Queen realised just how much he had been faking his recent infirmity. At full height, his St Cyr characteristics stood out more strongly. The nose, the eyes, the chin, the remnants of golden hair . . . With a trilby hat and a bright blue scarf, it would be easy to mistake him for Ned.

He was breathing more stertorously than his horse.

'Why did you have to butt in?' he bellowed. 'I told you! Chris Wallace has nothing to do with me. He was just a tenant with mental problems. What I do with my property is my affair. If you thought you knew something, you should have come to me.'

'Why?' the Queen asked, astonished.

'I could have explained. You would have understood. You say the police know Ned fathered Val, but you know me, for God's sake. I wouldn't have killed him for that. I could have told the police as much, if they'd asked me. Certainly, I'd have punched Ned's lights out, with pleasure. Any man would. No man would have judged me. But I promised Lee I wouldn't touch him.' He was agitated. The Queen sensed that the dredging of the moat was coming home to him at last. A body with poison in the stomach was something he couldn't talk his way out of.

'Then she started to die and you felt released from your vow'.

Hugh glared at her. 'You say you know what happened,' he resumed. 'You have no idea.' The horse pawed the ground and Hugh took no care to calm it, or himself. He boiled with rage. 'He held her down,' he growled, his eyes boring into hers. 'Lee was too frightened to struggle. He clamped his hand so hard over her throat while he was . . . doing it . . . that she thought she was going to die. Years later, if I put my hands tenderly anywhere near her neck, she would panic as if she was drowning. He did that to her.'

'And so you cut his hand off,' the Queen muttered, understanding at last.

Hugh glared at her. 'She deserved no less. It was over. He was dead by then anyway. No one need have known. But now . . . D'you realise what you've done?' he said. Astride his jumpy horse, he towered above her. 'It's all

303

right for you. You've got the next three generations sewn up. What about my children? My grandchildren? The police might have dredged up a skeleton in a few generations. It would have been impossible to prove how it got there. It would have been a St Cyr family mystery, that's all. I did everything to protect them.'

'You killed a man and drove another to his death, Hugh.'

He ignored her. 'Now it will be a scandal.'

'That's hardly my fault.'

'Is it mine?' He was shouting now, white with anger. 'What will Flora do? Visit her father in some common jail? How could she survive it? What about Ladybridge? Don't you care?'

The Queen felt she had already said more than enough. The skittish horse, sensing its rider's nervous energy, reared up in fear. More than ever, the Queen felt very small and very alone. How stupid she had been to let her passions get the better of her. She stretched out an authoritative arm to calm the animal, but Hugh dug in his heels and backed the horse up, as if lining up for a charge.

'You've had a good life, ma'am. But this is all your fault. You bloody interfering, old . . .'

He had lost all reason. The horse reared again, nose flared, eyes wide, panicking now under his unsteady guidance. In two seconds, it could mow her down. The look in Hugh's eyes was implacable.

'Oi!'

Tony Depiscopo charged towards the wall that led to the field. He'd spotted the horse and rider, then the telltale headscarf that meant the Boss. They'd seemed to be chatting amicably enough at first, thank God. He'd been thinking that perhaps she wouldn't notice how long they'd left her. Perhaps she wouldn't mind. Except now the horse was rearing and the Boss, who was so good with them, was stepping back. *Shit*. She was raising her arms. He reached under his jacket, where his gun was holstered.

'Stay back! Police!'

The rider turned to look at him, just as a figure streaked past him and headed for the wall.

'Stop or I'll fire!'

Depiscopo wondered if he was overreacting. He was trained for terrorists and nutters going after ministers. Nothing in his training had included a large and frightened horse in a muddy field and the Sovereign of the Realm. He aimed his weapon at the rider's head and hesitated.

Rozie, meanwhile, had vaulted the wall and now she flew across the tussocks of grass to reach the Queen. All she could think was that the Boss had to be safe. She had no weapon to make that happen, so she placed herself bodily between the Boss and those terrifying hooves.

A shot rang out.

The rider glanced back at the policeman who stood at the field's edge, weapon in hand, then at Rozie. He seemed to make a decision. His body rocked back and forward in the saddle. He lifted a hand and Depiscopo fired before he had the chance to reach whatever weapon he might be going for. But the policeman missed. In the time it took him to correct his aim, the rider wheeled the horse around, undid his chinstrap and threw off his hard hat. Depiscopo fired again and missed again as the horse moved off at speed.

The rider gave the Queen one last, brief glance over his shoulder. Then they all watched as he turned back and headed at a gallop for the furthest corner of the paddock, where the hedging was highest. There was no way he would make it over. He flicked the horse's flank twice with his crop and leaned forward in the saddle. Two paces from the hedge, he took off with all his strength, but it was an impossible task. There was a sickening scream, and then silence.

Chapter 33

'Dead, ma'am.'

Sir Simon stood respectfully to attention. The Queen, sitting at a card table in the drawing room at Sandringham, sipped at a restorative brandy. It had been impossible to continue her journey to Newmarket after what had happened. Sir Simon was merely confirming what she already knew.

'Was it instant, did they say?'

'Yes, ma'am. Massive head trauma.' Sir Simon shrugged helplessly. He was so super-smooth most of the time that it was easy to forget that his professional manner hid a sensitive soul.

'And the horse?' the Queen asked.

'The horse is fine. Uninjured, as far as I know.'

'Oh, good.' The Queen didn't want to be heartless, but the animal hadn't killed anyone – or not deliberately, anyway. She had been worried about the horse.

'What I don't understand is why Lord Mundy was there at all. Shouldn't he have been under arrest?' she asked. 'Or at least under some sort of police supervision?'

'I've spoken to the chief constable about that. They thought he *was* under supervision. He slipped away somehow, and

307

when he was challenged by a junior constable at the gatehouse, he simply said this was his land and he would do what he liked, and barged his way through.'

'But wasn't he a suspected murderer by then?'

'They didn't want to make the same mistake as they did with Jack Lions. They were waiting to see if they really would recover a body, and if they did, they weren't absolutely sure which member of the family to arrest. An excess of caution, ma'am. The chief constable is extremely apologetic.'

'He does have rather a habit of landing me in it.'

'I think he realises that. When I rang to find out what the hell had happened, he offered to resign.'

'Oh, for goodness' sake,' the Queen said, sipping her brandy, 'he's a good policeman. It's always the good ones who offer to resign and the bad ones who don't. Anyway, they have the body now. I'll expect his report when he's ready.'

Sir Simon promised she would have it. After the day he had just had, he was looking forward to a drink himself.

The following morning, the *Recorder* crowed its exclusive:

BODY FOUND IN MOAT

Missing aristocrat recovered by police after lifetime feud with family member who was friend of the Royals, killed in freak horse-riding accident

By Ollie Knight, Royal reporter

The body of Edward St Cyr, the landowner whose severed hand was sensationally recognised by the Queen, was recovered yesterday by police divers from the moat of his ancestral home. Ladybridge Hall, where the victim grew up, is owned by his cousin, Lord Mundy, who died yesterday in a riding accident. Police believe Mr St Cyr was killed as the result of a long-running family feud.

Ladybridge Hall and its estate, worth over £20 million at today's market prices, is a popular Norfolk attraction for its picturesque gardens and Elizabethan architecture. It is not far from Sandringham, where the Queen spends Christmas every year. It is believed Mr St Cyr was visiting his cousin when he disappeared. The police are not thought to be looking for anyone else in connection with the murder.

The second of February was Candlemas: halfway between the middle of winter and the spring equinox. The festival marked forty days since the birth of Jesus, when he was presented as a baby in the Temple. Nearly six weeks since Christmas, and approaching the full length of time the Queen allowed herself at Sandringham. It had been a precious, restorative time – a sort of hibernation. She always thought of these days as an opportunity to take in the things she loved, so that the next few months could be about giving what was needed. The land was the same. Bare earth was already giving way to snowdrops and Candlemas marked the day when they could be brought into the house to brighten up each room with the promise of spring. The Queen wasn't superstitious, but she found these traditions reassuring: the ebb and flow of nature, the repetition and renewal of life.

There were two large bowls of snowdrops in the Long Library when the chief constable arrived to explain the goings-on at Ladybridge. Seventy-two hours had passed since the removal of the body from the moat and the sudden death of the twelfth Baron Mundy. He wondered how Her Majesty would take what he had to say. She must still be recovering from her bruising encounter in the field. The tale he had to tell was a gruesome one and he didn't want to cause her any further distress, but these were friends of hers: she would want to know. It was why he wanted to tell her himself, so he could do it as delicately as possible.

He was shown in by one of the good-looking younger equerries, who told him the Queen had half an hour to give him before she needed to return to her guests. She swept in soon afterwards, in a tartan skirt and a cardigan, preceded by the dogs and accompanied by her APS. Her Majesty looked surprisingly chipper, he thought, for a woman who had been through such a terrifying encounter. This was encouraging. He noted the APS's studied indifference to the equerry, meanwhile, and his to her, and wondered in passing who else knew they were sleeping together.

'Chief Constable, I'm glad you're here,' the Queen said. 'Do sit down, here by the window. And what do you have to tell me?'

Bloomfield couldn't resist a little dig at a rival police force, who provided the protection officers. 'I'm very sorry about what happened to you on Friday, ma'am,' he said, settling in. 'It must have been upsetting. The Met really should have looked after you more carefully.'

'One is rarely upset, Chief Constable,' the Queen said firmly. 'I'm assured it won't happen again. I must say, I wasn't expecting to meet Hugh where I did.'

He realised he was being put in his place. 'Erm, yes. I apologise. I know you've been very gracious about it.'

'Let's move on,' she said. 'Tell me, what have you found?'

Bloomfield nodded, grateful to be on more solid ground. 'I understand Lord Mundy admitted to you that he killed his cousin. That must have been a terrible shock.'

'Oh, yes, it was.'

'The reason why is pretty obvious: Ned fathered his son.'

The Queen felt an odd duty to pass on the dead man's own rebuttal of that particular charge.

'Even so, it's hard to imagine a man like Hugh going as far as to kill Ned for it,' she suggested, curious to see his reaction.

As anticipated, Bloomfield brushed the words aside. 'It's a strong motive for murder, ma'am. Although to be fair, we don't usually expect to see it in people of his . . . er . . . age.'

'Even older people have strong feelings, Chief Constable.'

'I suppose they do. But people don't usually wait forty-eight years to act on them, ma'am. That's what threw us off the scent, even when we knew about Valentine. The baron obviously did a lot of thinking in those forty-seven years. The death was the easy part. The hard part was the alibi. He must have been working on it for months. Once Mr Knight pointed out that we had no real proof Ned ever left the hall, everything else fell into place. With the exception of one stubborn witness. But that was quickly resolved.'

'Oh?'

'Mrs Capelton was the woman in question, ma'am. She's the sort of person you can generally absolutely rely on. Churchwarden, stalwart of the WI. She was adamant Mundy had been with her all afternoon. But she rang us yesterday. We were already wondering about her by then. She'd had a crisis of conscience – something the vicar had said in church, apparently. Mundy had spun her a clever line.'

'Really?'

'He'd appealed to her humanity. He popped round on Boxing Day and said he was in a spot of bother with his daughter. On the fourteenth of December he'd gone into Ely to "satisfy his manly urges", he told her. I think that's the way she put it. He was a widower, and he said he knew she would be sympathetic, which she was, but he didn't think his family would understand. He swore her to secrecy and she felt she was doing the right thing by not betraying his trust. It never occurred to her that he might actually be the person we were looking for.'

'I see. I didn't know Ely was a hotspot for such activities,' the Queen noted.

'It isn't, any more than anywhere else, ma'am. But she was hardly going to check that out. Meanwhile, he was letting himself into St Cyr's house with the man's own keys, using his phone and his computer to create the sense that St Cyr had been there, and packing a bag. We haven't found much DNA at Abbottswood – not more than could be accounted for by a casual visit, which Mundy admitted to. But Mundy had ordered hairnets, plastic caps, surgical gloves, the works, on his computer. He had planned this, ma'am. Planned it down to the last detail. It's the only way he could have done it. And he didn't slip up once.'

'Well, there were always the—' The Queen stopped herself and smiled. 'Didn't he? Not once?'

'No. He gave the impression of bumbling – that was the clever thing – but in fact there was a sharp mind and endless research and preparation. He made sure he picked a day when Abbottswood would otherwise be empty, and the fiancée was abroad. He even took a broken phone charger up to London with him, so it would look natural that St Cyr's phone had run out of power. Otherwise, it would have looked strange that he wasn't using it at this mysterious meeting of his the next day. In fact, Mundy must have ditched it as soon as he'd used it to text Miss Westover. After that, he raced for home. We've checked the train times. It was just doable. We'd always suspected someone else might have been at the flat. The issue that bothered us was how the killer got St Cyr out of it and what they did with the body. But Mundy didn't have to worry about that. The body was already where he needed it to be.'

'And where was that?' the Queen asked, though having seen a flapping tarpaulin at the hall, she thought she knew.

'In one of the medieval rooms that was undergoing building work at Ladybridge Hall, ma'am. The windows were partially open to the elements. The perfect place to store a body in winter: cool and ventilated, like birds in a game larder. Forensics suggest it was wrapped in plastic and hidden behind some building equipment. Mundy complained of a

313

head cold on the seventeenth, so he didn't join his family when they went to the ballet. The servants were at the other end of the house. Nobody usually enters that older part of the house. Mundy had plenty of time for what he needed to do. He wrapped it in chains so it would sink and lowered it through an open window. All the evidence adds up.'

'Do you know if Ned died quickly?' the Queen asked. It was possible to imagine various scenarios. She had tried hard not to picture some of them.

'There was poison in the stomach, ma'am. But also, his neck was snapped. He may have been hit on the head as well at that time. We think he was dead before Mundy left him. Later, his skull was caved in with a blunt instrument. A cricket bat, we're pretty certain. The divers found one of those in the moat, too.'

The Queen patted her knee and Willow the corgi came over to sit on her lap. 'Go on,' she said.

'It's the cutting off of the hand that makes no sense to me,' Bloomfield said. 'It was the only body part that was missing. Mundy had smashed the skull, but the right hand was intact. He hadn't tried hard to make the body unidentifiable – and of course there was no point, given where we found it. It must have been something to do with the ring, but I doubt we'll ever know exactly.'

'No, I suppose not,' the Queen agreed. She didn't discuss her conversation with Hugh. Instead, she mentioned something else, which she suspected might also have contributed to the act. 'I've been thinking. Ned was about to end up in the moat. The ring was a symbol of family belonging. I suppose Hugh had to put the body in the moat because it was the easiest place to hide it . . .'

'But he didn't want Ned to belong. Is that it, ma'am?' Bloomfield nodded soberly. 'And I suppose it would have given him an excuse to mutilate the body. It reminds me, the choice of the plastic bag . . . I always found that intriguing. Something cheap and throwaway. It was an odd thing to take on that journey to scatter his wife's ashes, don't you think? Perhaps he chose it subconsciously—'

'To grant Ned the least honour,' the Queen finished for him, nodding to herself. 'That could well be it.'

'"The least honour", ma'am. Exactly.'

'But it had the effect of preserving the hand in the storm, didn't it? I wonder if he meant to take it out, but was almost caught in the act by one of his children. I can picture him panicking and throwing the whole thing in.'

Bloomfield nodded. '"This my hand will rather the multitudinous seas incarnadine",' he quoted.

The Queen looked at him politely. 'Shakespeare? *Macbeth*, I assume, if it's about hands.'

'Spot on, ma'am. I did it at school. I was Duncan, but I never forgot the boy who played Macbeth talking about washing his hands of blood. It was chilling, even in a sixth-form production. As you mention, Hugh must have disposed of the bag under the noses of his children. I think Flora might have suspected something.'

'Oh, really?'

'She was always keen, in interviews, to support whatever alibi her father or brother gave. She was out in the boat with them that day, so when the hand washed up she could have put two and two together and realised one of them was probably guilty. Presumably she thought it was Valentine, who was younger and fitter, and in London.'

'And yet, she knew both of them very well,' the Queen said. 'She might equally have suspected her father's hidden depths.'

'I'm not going to pursue it. She has enough to deal with now. She said she thinks her father was thinking of her when he headed for that high fence. He knew what we'd find. He wanted to spare her a trial and all the scandal. That must be very difficult to live with.'

'I wonder,' the Queen said. Sitting on his high horse, however much he ranted and raved about his children, Hugh had still been thinking of himself. His lust for vengeance had been as strong as ever. She had always thought of him as the mature cousin of the two, but it was really Ned who was more settled in the end. Hugh was stuck in the past and Ned was thinking of the future. Now Flora had to live with the consequences. She must see how the poor girl was getting on.

She thanked Bloomfield and his expansive team for all their work on the case.

'We got there in the end, ma'am,' he said happily. 'I'm not sure we'd have looked in the moat without the help of the industrious Mr Knight. Thank goodness for the hard work of the British media, eh, ma'am?'

'Absolutely,' the Queen agreed. 'What would we do without them?'

Chapter 34

'What will you do?' the Queen asked.

Flora shoved her hands in her pockets and looked towards the statue of Estimate. It was another blue winter's day, cloudless, with a low sun that cast long shadows.

'Carry on,' she said. 'I don't really have much of a choice. And I don't want one.' She squinted up at the sky. 'The girls will do brilliant things with Ladybridge one day. I can see them making something extraordinary out of it for the twenty-second century. It's got this far – I just need to keep it going.'

The Queen knew exactly what she meant. They headed round the side of the house, towards the north garden, overlooked by the Queen's bedroom, whose box-edged rose beds Flora's mother had helped design. The dogs ran ahead, paws crunching on the gravel path.

'Will Valentine help you?'

Flora smiled. 'He will, actually. Ladybridge is in his . . . Ha! I was going to say *blood*.'

'I gather things weren't always easy between him and Hugh,' the Queen said gently.

'No. But he didn't know why. He was hardly short of friends who had stuffed-up relations with their parents, though. It seemed normal. He didn't think about it much until Mummy's funeral. He's suspected since then that he wasn't Dad's child. Some look of Ned's. He said he just knew. He didn't know what to think of Mummy, though. And he couldn't ask Dad, for obvious reasons. That's what he was trying to find out from Ned – how it all happened. He couldn't imagine Mummy being unfaithful. It was just too weird. But I suppose . . .' Flora shrugged. 'You think you know someone. Even your own mother. And maybe you don't, completely. They were happy for fifty years. I suppose that's all you can ask.'

The Queen could have explained, but chose not to. It wouldn't help.

'Did Ned explain anything to him about his birth? How it came about?'

'No, he wouldn't talk about it. He wouldn't even admit it. He said Valentine was going to make a great thirteenth baron. Val got the impression he didn't want to get in the way of that, but he was pretty disgusted. Just between the two of them, he could have embraced his own child. Mummy was gone by then: it wouldn't have hurt her to explain the truth.'

'Perhaps Ned was trying not to break family bonds, after all this time,' the Queen said diplomatically.

Flora was dismissive. 'If he cared about Val, he had an odd way of showing it. He said he'd heard about Val and Roland and he hoped Val was going to do the decent thing and find "a nice young filly", like he had himself, and settle down before it was too late. Val was crushed. He felt like he'd lost two fathers.'

'He has you,' the Queen said.

Flora paused on the path and gave the Queen a warm, frank smile and a quick, not unwelcome hug. 'Thank you,' she said. 'He does, doesn't he? And he has Roland. He can make his own family. We keep being told we have a lot to live up to and a lot to live down. We're just going to hold our heads high, and live.'

'You will survive,' the Queen told her. 'Your father knew Ladybridge would be in safe hands. Now, let's find your mother's rose beds. There isn't much to see at the moment, but in summer they'll be quite splendid.'

When she returned to the house, Julian Cassidy was waiting to see her, as arranged. She received him in the small drawing room. It was a stand-up meeting.

'I gather you're leaving us.' she said.

'Yes, ma'am.' The bean counter looked defeated.

'Well done for making the right decision.'

He had handed himself in two days ago. There would be a hefty fine, and a possible prison sentence for "failure to stop and report an accident." His belated confession made jail unlikely, but his job was untenable.

'I'm sorry for letting you down', he said.

'It's Mrs Raspberry's forgiveness you need, I hope you earn it.' She wondered if this would be the end or the making of the man. Either was possible.

'Good luck' she said, and meant it. He had a long road ahead of him.

Chapter 35

On Sunday, Rozie watched the Queen hand out prizes to local schoolchildren after church at West Newton. Back at Sandringham House, the maids and dressers were busy packing for tomorrow's return to London. Massed clumps of snowdrops fringed the paths through the tree canopy on the estate. Spring was, if not quite here, then certainly announcing its intentions.

Tomorrow was the 6th of February, when the Queen would mark her sapphire jubilee: the sixty-fifth anniversary of her accession. Her ministers and the press always seemed to find it a cause for congratulations, but to the Boss, Rozie knew, it was, more than anything, the day her father died. She would mark it privately here, before travelling by train to London and a crowded calendar in another busy year.

After the visit, the Queen was, as usual, hosting a lunch. Rozie wasn't needed, so she called at Katie Briggs's cottage and drove north-east with her to Burnham Overy Staithe beach, for one last blitz of sea air, sweeping views and vast Norfolk skies. They walked the mile from the car park, along the track that skirted the salt marshes to the gap at Gun Hill, and sat on the sand near the grassy dunes, wrapped in their coats, while Daphne ran joyful rings around them. Ahead, the sea stretched north to Greenland, with little in between. Low waves crashed onto the shore with seductive regularity. Rozie savoured the moment to hold on to when she was back in town, between the frenetic politics of Whitehall and the traffic din of Hyde Park Corner.

'OK, so tell me,' Katie said, having checked that there were no dog walkers within listening distance. 'Truthfully. Did he nearly kill her? That's the gossip I heard.'

Rozie pictured the scene on the way to Newmarket: the rearing horse, the running police officer, herself running faster, how terrified she had been.

'I don't know,' she said honestly. 'I thought so at the time. But the way the Boss was looking at that horse – I don't think it would have dared.'

'I assume Depiscopo's on guard duty at some depot in the Outer Hebrides.'

'I don't think he's going to be on royal duty in a hurry,' Rozie agreed.

'What was he thinking?'

'He wasn't. He was focused on the women in the road. He assumed the Boss would do what she was told. He hadn't worked for her long, unlike Rick Jackson, who'd known her for fifteen years.'

'It worries me,' Katie said, 'this new policy of sharing the protection officers around.'

'It worries everyone. But the Boss can look after herself. I've seen her do it.'

There was something else, though Rozie didn't say it. *She* would look after the Boss. She had been there when it mattered. She had put herself in harm's way – of course she had – and it had felt entirely natural. The Boss needed her, and she was up to the challenge. This business about feeling on the edge of things was all in her head. Edges were good, anyway. Edges were sharp.

That moment facing down the stallion had given her the same sort of buzz she got from swimming in open water. You couldn't rescue a queen from a murderous madman every day, but you *could* swim. The water reconnected her with her sense of self and purpose. If she had brought her kit, she'd be in it now.

Along to their left was the low, grassy mass of Scolt Head Island, from where they could hear the hoots and honks of nesting birds. This was where Chris Wallace had walked into the sea. How could he have said goodbye to the world in such a lovely place? Rozie wrapped her arms around herself, resting her chin against her knees and gazing out across the water.

Katie put an arm on Rozie's shoulder.

'I know what you mean.'

'What?' Rozie asked, surprised. But Katie's expression showed she understood.

They sat in silence for a while, until the puppy's need to play roused Rozie from her funk and got her running along the beach, filling her lungs with air, grateful to have this moment.

It wasn't St Barts, and she'd never imagined that somewhere so biting cold and far from a cocktail bar could

322

become one of her happy places, but between this sea and sky, north Norfolk took a lot of beating.

The Queen had a very pleasant tea with Judy Raspberry, who was convalescing at home. Half the contents of the Sandringham shop seemed to have been put in a hamper for her. As well as a mug about pigeons. Judy was delighted with the mug most of all.

Supper that night was not in the candlelit dining room, but at Wood Farm, where Philip was already making himself at home, in anticipation of his retirement. He cooked them both steak, supplemented by a selection of vegetables prepared by one of the chefs. The wine was, as always, excellent. Dessert was chocolate mousse, which he avoided and she devoured. Afterwards they washed up together, before settling down in front of the television to watch a comedy show.

'What would your father have made of this?' Philip wondered aloud, looking round the rather ordinary room with a fond, proprietorial eye.

'I think he'd have found it very comfortable.'

'Good enough for his daughter?'

'Well, I do have the house down the road.'

'Bought and paid for.' Philip smiled.

It was true: Sandringham was her own, and not the Crown's. Her father had had to buy it from his brother when he became king, because as private property it was naturally inherited by the older son, and David – or Edward VIII as he briefly titled himself – had insisted on being paid for it, even though he loathed the place as much as his younger brother loved it. Without the abdication, what would have become of it, and her?

She had so very nearly lived a very different life. One's destiny hinged on such small accidents of fate: a meeting with a glamorous American divorcée, in this case. A man who gave up his throne for her. A brother who reluctantly took his place. A little girl – herself – who would have been very happy living out of the spotlight. Instead, what a whirlwind it had been. And it had lasted for nearly a century.

She marvelled briefly on how hard humans tried to shape the future, herself included, and how much it was really in the lap of the gods. But she wasn't excessively given to introspection: that way, madness lay. She allowed Philip to pour her a glass of whisky and determined to enjoy these last few hours quietly, before she headed back to the city, and her other life.

Acknowledgements

I owe eternal thanks, once again, to Queen Elizabeth II. I'm so glad she got to see the crowds that massed in front of Buckingham Palace for her Platinum Jubilee celebrations while I was finishing this book.

The news of her death came the day I handed in the proofs, so I'm rewriting this page in a state of shock, despite knowing full well this day must come. Much of what I want to say about her character, her role in our lives and her impact on our world is here in these stories. I intend to write more of them as there is still so much of her life to explore. Readers will know how fond of the Queen I am. She was human and humble, but also undeniably great. We know her dedication to her life of public service, so I hope her real Christmas holidays were more restful than I made this one.

A huge thank you to all my editors, translators and marketing teams in the UK and around the world. Your support for this series is fabulous and I'm so grateful for everything you do. Particular thanks go to Ben Willis and his team at Zaffre, and David Highfill and Julia Elliott at William Morrow for your infinite patience with me this time. We got there in the end.

To Charlie Campbell at Greyhound Literary, the best agent in the business, and Sam Edenborough, who turns out to be not only brilliant at selling the rights abroad, but at giving great editorial insights too. I remain eternally grateful to Grainne Fox and the team at Fletcher & Company, Nicki Kennedy, and the team at ILA.

Thanks to the team at Sandringham House who made researching this book a real pleasure, and to the rewilders and conservationists at Knepp and Holkham, whose work I was privileged to experience. To the people of North Norfolk, who made me feel so welcome. I'm so glad to have discovered this special spot. I will be back.

Thank you to all my readers, and especially those of you who have contacted me via my newsletter and shared some of your own stories and gardening tips with me. Please keep them coming!

Thanks to the girls who keep me going with your friendship and inspiration: the Place, the Sisterhood, the Masterminds, and the Book Club, and especially to Caroline Lawrence and Sarah Wooley for the walks.

To Emily, Sophie, Freddie and Tom, who put up with me not always being around when my head is in a book. (Thank goodness you can cook.) And to Alex. On this book in particular, you held me up. Thank goodness for you.

You can contact me via my website, at sjbennettbooks.com and sign up for my newsletter. It's always lovely to hear from you.

If you enjoyed *Murder Most Royal*
why not join the
S. J. BENNETT READERS' CLUB?

When you sign up you'll receive an exclusive short story
featuring the Queen, THE MYSTERY OF THE
FABERGÉ EGG – plus Royal Correspondence about the
series and access to exclusive material. To join, simply visit
bit.ly/SJBennett

Keep reading for a letter from the author . . .

Hello!

Thank you for picking up *Murder Most Royal*.

This book is the latest in the *Her Majesty the Queen Investigates* series. I'm pleased to say we have reached the trilogy stage! There will be more books to come, when I intend to go back in time, to insert more mysteries into the Queen's long and fascinating life. Meanwhile, if you haven't yet read *The Windsor Knot* and *A Three Dog Problem*, now is your chance to catch up on the Queen's sleuthing adventures so far. Rozie gets up to some pretty interesting things too. I promise you won't be disappointed.

Having set the first book at Windsor Castle, and then one at Buckingham Palace, I decided to travel to Sandringham this time, for a traditional royal family Christmas. To start with, I knew that Sandringham was a big house in East Anglia where the royal family liked to go shooting, but that was about it. I hadn't realised it was near the sea, or that there was a wildlife sanctuary on its borders, or that its estate contains several farms, where the Queen and Prince Philip enjoyed experimenting with sustainable farming methods and which Prince Charles is now turning organic as fast as he can. I didn't know this was where Prince Philip intended to retire, or why he would want to spend the last years of his life in North Norfolk. Now I know all those things, and having spent some very, very enjoyable weeks there doing my research, I quite understand the royal couple's love of the place. The area is in fact sprinkled with celebrities who are quietly living their best life.

North Norfolk is rural, traditional and coastal. Don't go there if your ideal holiday is the nightclubs of Mykonos. Do go there if your idea of the perfect beach is something vast and windswept and almost empty, until visited by a thousand wading birds. The county is also home to lots of fictional detectives – some of which may already be favourites of yours – and I hope my royal sleuth fits right in.*

My interest was piqued by the question of who owns our countryside, who else loves it and how do they get along? When I started researching, rewilding was a niche topic that few people I spoke to knew about. Now it's everywhere, and I challenge you to find a British aristocrat who isn't trying it out. I was also fascinated by the country's houses great and small. I have invented Abbotswood and Ladybridge Hall, and had a lot of fun doing so, but Sandringham House is available to visit. You can even stay in the old head gardener's cottage or an old water tower on its grounds.

If you would like to know more about the real-life inspirations for *Murder Most Royal*, along with snippets from my research about the Royal Family, then visit bit.ly/SJBennett where you can sign up to receive Royal Correspondence about the series. It only takes a few moments to sign up, there are no catches or costs.

*(My own favourite Norfolk-related detectives include Lord Peter Wimsey, as written by Dorothy L Sayers, whose ancestral seat of Bredon Hall was in Norfolk, and Ruth Galloway, the archaeologist from the fabulous modern series by Elly Griffiths. I highly recommend both.)

Bonnier Zaffre will keep your data private and confidential, and it will never be passed on to a third party. We won't spam you with loads of emails, just get in touch now and again with news about my books, and you can unsubscribe any time you want.

And if you would like to get involved in a wider conversation about my books, please review *Murder Most Royal* on Amazon, on Goodreads, or wherever else you share your thoughts online, or talk about it in real life with friends, family or reader groups!

Thank you again for reading this book, and I hope you enjoy the rest of the series.

With best wishes,

S. J. Bennett

Keep reading for an exclusive extract from the next
mystery in the Her Majesty The Queen
Investigates series . . .

A Death in Diamonds

Coming February 2024

A Death in Diamonds

Paris, May 1957

The Queen knew instantly that she had made a fatal mistake, figuratively speaking.

'Mais bien sur, madame. Ca arrive.'

During the candlelit dinner at the Louvre to celebrate her second night in France on this, her first state visit, she had merely mentioned, perhaps a shade too wistfully, that she had never seen the Mona Lisa. The Salle des Caryatides was packed with *le tout Paris*. Every minister, grand hostess and eminent dignitary was here, it seemed, sitting elbow to elbow, dressed in their finery, watching her closely. However, beyond the odd statue and ceiling, she had yet to see any art.

Now, after a brief consultation among the luminaries of the museum, two porters were carrying the Leonardo into the room, resplendent in its ornate gilt frame. They leaned it against a chair for her to look at, and it was the most extraordinary moment: those two famous eyes, staring impenetrably back at her from under their heavy lids. One knew the image so well as an illustration that it was astonishing to come face to face with the real thing. The Queen felt for an instant how so many people must feel, perhaps, coming face to face with *her*.

The portrait carried a huge weight of expectation, but was remarkably human in scale, close to, in the flickering light. Behind the eyes, the Queen saw a young woman, beautifully composed and a little bit self-conscious in the act being scrutinised. *I know how you feel*, she thought. The artistry was wonderful, of course, but it was hard to concentrate while everyone was leaning forward to see her reaction.

'*C'est merveilleux, n'est-ce pas?*' she said, fully aware that this might well be the understatement of her visit.

Shortly afterwards, when they were joined by yet more of the great and good in the lavish summer apartment of Anne of Austria, the spotlight on the Queen herself was even more intense. Hundreds of people jostled together, eager to greet her, and not a few sharp elbows dug into elegantly-attired waists as they jockeyed for a better view. As the crowd surged forward in a wave, the Queen felt the press of the throng and for a moment she was almost frightened. She was quite hemmed in and there was no room to breathe. It was gratifying to be so popular, but right now, she would be grateful to get out of the evening with her clothes and person intact.

She steadied herself and put on a brave face. Her grandmother, Queen Mary, had taught her well. But as she looked out over the sea of eager faces, two stood out. One was not looking in her direction exactly, but at someone in the crowd to her left. His face was briefly twisted into an unguarded scowl and there was a look of savage hatred in his eyes. The Queen had seen that look only a few times before, as a teenager at Windsor, when officers or their families had described some of the worst atrocities of the war. She knew who he was, understood his history, and guessed who he might be staring at. The other face was scanning the room with undisguised disdain, the mouth crimped in frustration. At last, the eyes found hers, and instantly the face went blank. But the Queen had seen enough. This was someone she knew very well. It explained a lot. She had work to do when she got home, because it was clear that someone from inside her closest circle had been trying to sabotage this visit. Her response would be delicate and difficult, and she wasn't sure who she could trust.

H   l
w   er
ear.

ink, Lizzie. Here we are. The stars are
nkling up above.' Those strong arms slowly
ked around her waist and pulled her closer.
ou gaze up at me with convincing longing,
ld fool will assume we are having a tryst.'

ing against his logic was prevented by the
ously close sound of another call from
her unwelcome beau. 'Lady Elizabeth! Is that

With the most limpid expression she could
manage, in a blind panic Lizzie stared
ingly up at Hal. He winked encouragingly
then, to her complete shock, dipped his head
ressed his lips to hers.

The sky tilted. Or perhaps it was the floor.
Either way, the experience knocked her off-

Unconsciously her own lips began to respond,
her eyelids fluttered closed and she found
herself rising on tiptoe to press her body
against his. More worryingly, she was reluctant
to prise herself away. Later, she knew, she
would claim this was all part of her act, but for
now she was prepared to acknowledge it for
what it was.

A revelation.

Hal quickly closed the distance and whispered ag... ...close to her

Author Note

After I wrote *Her Enemy at the Altar*, a few people suggested there should be a sequel. Like me, those people had fallen in love with Aaron and Connie, and wanted the opportunity to see them again. They were such adorable characters—the feisty yet self-conscious heroine and the dashing yet tortured hero—and so perfect for each other. When I was offered the chance to write a Christmas story I decided to treat myself to that sequel and see how they were getting along.

But, as so often happens, I also fell in love with my new characters, and my sequel rapidly became their story first. Connie's brother Hal is a notorious rake, with no desire to settle down. Lizzie has been badly let down by a man and never wants another one. However, both feel that life is missing something— which is obviously each other, but they were both very troublesome as I got them to realise it.

At times, although they instantly became the very best of friends, the pair of them were so stubbornly resistant to romance that I found myself shouting at my keyboard. Fortunately the story takes place over Christmas. Which means there is always mistletoe…